Mohr: a novel

●

Frederick Reuss

Unbridled Books

All photographs and postcards used in the creation of this book are from the collection of Nicolas Humbert and are used here by permission. All rights to these photographs are reserved.

The Morgenstern poem that appears on pages 57–58, "Sieh Nicht, Was Andre Tun," is by Christian Morgenstern, translated by Eileen Hutchins and Ursula Grahl. Reprinted from *Anthology of German Poetry from Hölderlin to Rilke* (New York: Doubleday, 1960), ed. Angel Flores.

Unbridled Books
Denver, Colorado

Library of Congress Cataloging-in-Publication Data

Reuss, Frederick, 1960–
Mohr : a novel / Frederick Reuss.
p. cm.
ISBN 1-932961-17-8 (alk. paper)
1. Mohr, Max, b. 1891—Fiction. 2. Authors, German—Fiction. 3. Jewish authors—
Germany—Fiction. 4. Physicians—China—Shanghai—Fiction. 5. Germany—Fiction.
6. Shanghai (China)—Fiction I. Title.
PS3568.E7818M64 2006
813'.54—dc22
2005037958

1 3 5 7 9 10 8 6 4 2

Book design by Claire Vaccaro

First Printing

To my mother

Schwer zu entdecken sind nämlich
die zwischen den Schiefertafeln
eingelagerten geflügelten Wirbeltiere
der Vorzeit. Seh ich aber die Nervatur
des vergangenen Lebens vor mir
in einem Bild, dann denk ich immer,
es hätte dies etwas mit der Wahrheit zu tun.

For it is hard to discover
the winged vertebrates of prehistory
embedded in tablets of slate.
But if I see before me
the nervature of past life
in one image, I always think
that this has something to do
with truth.

– W.G. Sebald

Part One

In early morning, when the house is silent and the sun has not yet risen above the eastern ridges of the Tegernsee valley, it is tempting to think that the heartache that once filled these rooms is gone, vanished with another era. Open the front door, step outside into the morning air—crisp and frosty in winter, moist with dew and the smell of cows at pasture in summertime, walk the gravel path around to the side of the house, sit down on the bench, and watch the shifting hues of dawn on the steep slopes of the Wallberg. The cross on top of the mountain, like the one on the peak of the old farmhouse, has been there for so long that nobody notices it. This morning, you want to take in every detail: the crow calling from a tree at the forest edge, the vapor rising from the sun-warmed treetops, leaning fence posts, peeling paint on the shutters and condensation on the windowpanes, the distant ringing of a bell. The morning gradually brightens and with it a sense that each of these details is crucial; none is more crucial than the simple fact of your presence here. You grip the edge of the wooden bench with your hands, breathe in and out. Your breath condenses and the billowing steam makes you want to go inside and get your cigarettes, but, no, you also want to savor the first tobacco-free moment of the day, so you remain.

Feeling slightly absurd for all this heightened self-consciousness, you smile to yourself; then your smile fades because, no, there is nothing funny or false about this feeling of connection. There is nothing wrong with it, just as there is nothing wrong with supposing you belong to a continuum of human events that links you to a vanished past, part of which you may come to know, and all of which you are free to imagine.

I say *you*, but I also mean *me.* In novels, personal pronouns can be misleading. This is not an easy idea to express, and some will call the notion absurd. But why not? Why can't I be you? Or him or her? At least here, for now, sitting on a bench outside this old Bavarian farmhouse called Wolfsgrub early one October morning in 1934? And if I can be Max Mohr, I can be his wife, Käthe, too—whom he has left sleeping to come downstairs and light the stove.

Picture it. There are, after all, photographs. A great many photographs, piles of evidence that stand for something a little different with each viewing: so lovely, and not at all out of date.

Last night, you went up to the attic to sit for a time at his writing table. On it was a note from Käthe written on an old scrap of saved stationery. The desk is set between two narrow windows and faces the wall. He always wrote at night, so there was no need for a view. You sat down, adjusted yourself on the wooden chair. Once upon a time he kept his empty ink bottles lined up like little soldiers at the edge of the desk. One day, he gave them all to Eva to play with. You held Käthe's note to your nose. It was not scented, which caused a twinge of regret. It would have been just the perfect gesture. Like you, he was here and not here. He was going away and not going anywhere. She was sad—but also, perhaps, happier than you have ever been.

Liebster. Please know how much I love you. There is nothing more to say. Think how happy we were here together. Try to remember what a lovely place this was. K.

4

Mohr folded the note and slipped it into his pocket. Käthe must have put it there sometime during the afternoon—when he and Eva were bringing Minna in from the field. His fingers felt thick, his hands large and clumsy. He wanted to go downstairs right away, to be with her until the very last minute. But something kept him. He had passed so many hours at this little desk under the eaves. The larchwood paneling was dark with time. Late at night when the house fell silent, he listened to the creaking rafters, could hear the woodworms boring their tiny holes in the old beams.

TUCK YOUR HANDS, palms flat, underneath your thighs. A shiver of cold concentrates your thoughts of what might have been.

Glance up.

THE PATH LEADING up into the forest stands out clearly in the early morning light. It cuts through frosted grass and disappears into the trees. How much wider might it have become with Mohr tromping up it to work every day? A little cabin to write in. Would he have been thrilled, gone happily off to work deep in the rustling forest? An image flashes, of smoke curling from the cabin chimney, and Käthe down at the house, seeing it rise up through the treetops, and sending Eva up with a freshly baked loaf, some apples, and a piece of cheese to tide him over.

No. That would never be. On his last day in Wolfsgrub, Mohr doesn't want to think of what will never be, however lovely. He can't hold on hold on hold on; never give anything up. That would be fatal. Knowing when to let go is more important than fretting about what's been left behind.

Impatient, you jiggle your legs, shake your head once again at the idea of him scribbling away in a little cabin deep in the forest. You recall Lawrence's description of the crucifix-studded Bavarian uplands, the wooden Christs presiding over the whole countryside. When Lawrence spoke about Germany and Germans, Mohr always had the feeling he was addressing his Jewish nature, as if he knew what it was better than Mohr did; some secret voluptuousness he engaged in. The trouble with their friendship was not that Lawrence asserted so deep an understanding of Mohr but that he asserted it to everyone except Mohr himself. If he were an anti-Semite—and there were times when he seemed so—he never forswore any friendships because of it. It didn't seem to matter to him that his opinions could inflict pain. Remember how you felt when you read his first impression of Mohr? *A last man, who has arrived at the last end of the road, who can no longer go ahead in the wilderness nor take a step into the unknown.*

If only he'd lived to see the unknown that Mohr would come to face.

And not just Max, but Käthe, too.

WHEN SHE CAME downstairs and saw his packed bags neatly stacked in the hall, and the front door slightly ajar, she stepped outside, walked around to the side of the house, and sat down next to him.

"Let's not be glum," he said and put an arm across her shoulders, drew her closer. "I will always remember what a lovely place this is." He smiled and patted his breast pocket, where he was keeping the note she'd written yesterday. "Thank you," he said and kissed her forehead.

Now they are sitting at breakfast, trying to put the best face they can on the day.

"Can I take a picture?" Eva points to the camera on the table.

"If you promise me one thing." Mohr draws her onto his lap, whispers into her ear. Eva slides off his lap and picks up the camera again.

"Promise," she says.

"Promise what?"

Eva glances at her father. "Can I tell?"

"Of course," he says emphatically.

"That we will come to China soon."

"Sooner than soon," Mohr corrects.

"Of course we will." Käthe's voice sounds weary. How many times can she repeat such a promise? It isn't empty, just hopelessly abstract and distant, like China itself.

They sit for Eva's photograph. Mohr makes a funny face, which causes Eva to laugh. She takes a second one, and this time nobody laughs. Käthe has felt observed by Mohr all morning, lost in her own quiet nowhere, counting down the hours until Zibert comes to drive them all to the train station. The breakfast plates on the table are empty; a few cold sips of coffee remain at the bottom of each cup. They are waiting, but the wait is already over.

All this determined cheerfulness isn't easy. Eva had come downstairs crying. Mohr swept her up in his arms and they went to the henhouse to fetch some eggs; then he took her upstairs and drew his bath. Käthe watched as Eva stood over him in the bathtub. He sank slowly under the surface of the water, wetted his hair. Then he resurfaced, brandishing an egg. "Voilà, Mademoiselle! *Bitte schön!*" He handed the egg to Eva with a grin and bowed, offering the crown of his head. Tap tap tap, the egg was broken, and Eva stepped back giggling while he massaged the gooey mess into his scalp, singing, "Eeenie beenie suplameenie deevi dahvi domineenie."

As the shampoo was concluding, Nanni's voice rang from downstairs to say that she was leaving the butter inside the door.

"Tell her to wait!" Mohr sputtered from the tub.

Käthe ran downstairs and called to Nanni, "Dr. Mohr is leaving today! He wants to say good-bye!"

Nanni hung her woolen cardigan on the hook inside the door and waited in the kitchen. She was the eldest of the Berghammer girls, simpleminded, good-hearted, and she adored Mohr.

"Is that Nanni I hear?" Mohr called down the stairs. "You were going to let me go without saying good-bye?" He came into the kitchen, hair tousled, still shiny and wet. He put a hand on Nanni's shoulder and gave her a friendly shake, then hugged her. Nanni blushed, and when he released her she drew back and punched him with her fist.

"Ouch!" Mohr gripped his arm. Nanni was momentarily uncertain; then Mohr laughed, snatched her back, and hugged her tightly once again.

"Papa is going to China," Eva announced from the doorway.

Nanni glanced about. "Why?" she asked.

"Because it's there," Mohr said.

"Where?" Nanni inquired after a short pause.

Mohr reached into his trousers pocket and took out an imaginary compass, held it in the flat of his hand. "Well, let's see." He turned and pointed. "It's over there."

"That's the stove!" Nanni objected.

"He means that's the way you have to go," Eva said.

"If my compass is correct," Mohr said, slipping the imaginary instrument into his pocket.

KÄTHE SLICES THE bread, and begins to set the table as Mohr entertains Nanni and Eva with one of his nonsense stories. His manner is a little forced, but only Käthe would notice. She passes in and out of the kitchen three times with the breakfast tray, pausing to listen. Mohr leans against the stove, fills the room with his presence. He cleans his glasses on his shirt, twists them back onto his ears, combs his wet hair with his fingers, all the while expanding on a complicated tale of a lost school of Mexican dancing fish and a band of robbers.

She can't listen, nor can she bring herself to interrupt. She goes into the next room to wait at the breakfast table. Through the closed door she can hear Mohr's voice, the giggles of Eva and Nanni. Is this last little burst of storytelling meant to be remembered? One final thing left behind?

She pours herself a cup of coffee and stares through the windows at the frost-covered meadow that slopes up steeply behind the house, every blade of grass stiff and glistening with ice. Yesterday it was still warm, and they were all outside in shirtsleeves. The temperature dropped sharply overnight. Several times she was awakened by gusts of wind rattling the windows.

After Nanni leaves—with tearful promises of letters, though she can neither read nor write—they come in and sit down to breakfast. Mohr's spark fades, a silence falls. Butter and marmalade, coffee and milk, eggs in little cups, late-October air, woolen sweaters, the crackle and pop of wood in the stove. All at once, he puts down his knife, looks up, and says, "I won't be pushed out. I'd rather just leave."

Käthe puts her hands in her lap and waits for him to continue. Eva meticulously dips little pieces of bread into her egg, licks off the yolk. Mohr cleans his glasses once again.

"Can I sit in the front of the taxi?" Eva asks.

"You can sit on the roof if you like." Mohr pinches her cheek. The resemblance between father and daughter is remarkable. Dark hair, light hazel eyes, sharp, square jawline, and an impatient, impulsive nature prone to veer in all directions at once. Eva has grown several centimeters in just the last few months. Käthe can see the lineaments of the future woman emerging, not in fragments but whole, and not a Westphal but a Mohr.

The telephone rings. Mohr rises to answer but changes his mind and sits down again.

"Aren't you going to answer, Papa?"

Mohr shakes his head. "I don't want to talk."

The bell clangs several more times and then falls silent. For the past week, calls have been coming in from friends and acquaintances. His story, *The Diamond Heart,* had been serialized a year ago in a Hamburg daily. The editor, Jahn, had telephoned the other day to say good-bye and they had talked for over an hour. The last call, and the one he had least wanted to take, had come from his sister, Hedwig. A letter had preceded it in which she tried to argue that he should allow himself to be baptized, as she and her husband had done—many years ago. After handing it to Käthe to read, he tore the letter to pieces.

"A little severe, don't you think?" she said.

"Not nearly as severe as her stupidity." He glanced at the strewn bits of paper and flushed. She waited for him to continue, but he didn't. The redness in his face dissolved. When she began to gather up the scraps from the floor, he made as if to help, then stopped himself and left the room.

That Mohr was a Jew had never been an issue of any significance between them until these last few years; no more than her Hamburg Protestant origins. If anything, they both considered themselves refugees of the horrible and confining *Bürgertum* they had both been brought up in—of which Hedwig's letter was such an unwelcome reminder.

Yesterday, up on the roof, she'd tried one last time to engage him. He was replacing some broken tiles and she climbed up to take in the view and keep him company. It was a sunny day and the slopes of the Wallberg stood out clearly and in full autumn color. As she made her way gingerly across the gently pitched rooftop, it felt as though they'd always been together here, and would always remain so. She sat next to him on the roof ridge, tucked her skirt up. It was pleasantly warm. He slid a new tile into place and hit it with the hammer. It broke. He turned to her with a strange smile and said, "Voilà! The world resolves itself in twos." After a short pause he said, "We should keep that in mind."

"Keep what in mind?"

"That we can be apart and not apart. Together and not together."

"You think that sort of talk makes things any easier? Why don't you try to see things a little more simply?"

He shook his head. "There's nothing simple about anything."

She watched as he fitted in the next tile. It was not a job he was familiar with. The last time the roof had needed repairing, they'd hired somebody; but Mohr had insisted on doing this job by himself, and worked as if he knew just what he was doing. "Why China, Max?"

He didn't answer, and continued working.

"Why not someplace closer? Like Prague? Or Vienna?"

Mohr stopped and leaned back on his haunches. She knew he understood what she meant. He tapped the edge of the tile into place with the rubber hammer. There was nothing she could think of to say, so she kept him company up there until he was finished. Strangely, she wasn't frustrated or impatient. Not at all. It was nice to sit quietly together. Theo Seethaler appeared in the yard below.

"What are you doing back here?" Mohr called.

"I came to say good-bye."

Mohr tossed his tools down into the yard. Käthe sensed that there was something he still wanted to tell her, and also that he was glad for this sudden distraction. Seethaler held the base of the ladder as she descended, talking the whole time about having had to leave school to come home and help his father, who had fallen ill. The boy—no longer a boy, but already twenty—made no attempt to hide his disappointment. Mohr came down right behind her, jumped from the ladder several rungs before the bottom. He marched into the middle of the yard to survey his work. "Perfect!" He lit a cigarette, and pointed to the roof. "You can't even tell they're new."

Seethaler helped Mohr carry the ladder and tools to the barn. Käthe went inside to take down the wash from the upstairs balcony. The low slant of the sun cast everything in a golden light. They returned from the barn, and Mohr invited Seethaler to sit with him on the bench. She folded clothes and listened as they talked. There was something sweet in the trust the local boys placed in Mohr, the way they telegraphed so much of themselves in conversations about ski bindings or bicycle racing. Seethaler was clearly upset about having to help in the family plumbing business.

"So, you prefer life in the big city," Mohr said.

"Don't you?"

Mohr didn't answer right away, then he said, "If being comfortable means having your fat behind padded, then I guess the city's the place. But upholstery costs money."

Seethaler laughed. "It's better than being stuck out here."

"What is it that you like better in the city?" Mohr asked.

"Everything."

"Go back, then. People who want money should stay in the city. It's the people who want to get *away* from money who should come here."

She heard him stand up and go around to the side of the house. A moment later he walked out into the yard carrying a wooden chair. He set the chair down on the grass, flashed a grin, then took a few steps back, rubbing his palms together—one, two, three—and with a loud yell leaped over the chair and landed on his feet on the other side.

Eva appeared at the top of the meadow where she and Lisa had been playing, and the two of them ran down to join the game. Mohr beckoned to Seethaler and stood aside, hands on hips, beaming. "Come on down," he shouted up to the balcony.

"I can see just fine from here," Käthe called back.

Seethaler failed to clear the chair and fell in a heap. He insisted on a second try, and when he failed, Mohr urged him to take his time and try again. When he failed a third time, Mohr lifted him up from the ground and took him inside for a farewell schnaps.

In those last autumn days and weeks, they were conscious of marking time. It grew cooler; the trees blazed with colors and dropped their leaves. They slept late, took their time around the house, went on longer and longer afternoon walks. They prepared the house for winter, split and stacked wood, filled the cellar with beets and onions and potatoes. At night, after Eva went to sleep and Mohr went upstairs to his attic room to work, Käthe would read or knit by the stove. If the calm that had settled on her was comforting, the clarity of it was frightening. She would look up from her knitting or her book, acutely conscious of the passing moment.

On one of their last walks together, Mohr told her how anxious he was to get going. It was painful to hear. "How can you say that?"

"I'm going to start a new life for us in China."

"But everything's being uprooted, torn apart."

Mohr shook his head. "Plants have roots. The world is big and we're still young and life is long."

Did he really think he could escape the problems of the day just like that?

They were on the footpath that led across the valley toward Kaffee Angermaier, the inn where the Lawrences had stayed when they'd come to visit just a few years earlier. Lorenzo's death had contributed much to Mohr's crisis. It wasn't merely the loss of a friend but a feeling of irrelevance, of time wasted. The famous Englishman had cut a wide and deep swath in the short period of their friendship. He had always been harsh in his judgment of Mohr's work. A strong and mutual affection compensated for the harshness, but even that became complicated as Lawrence's health deteriorated. Mohr saw his friend's long, drawn-out illness and death as a sign. He said he needed to find a new direction. Käthe watched the change come over him gradually, and for a time felt a tinge of resentment toward Lawrence. There is something awful in making a legacy of a friendship, but that was what Lawrence had left Mohr with in the end.

They stopped walking. "What do you call this?" Käthe asked, trembling. "What is this, if it isn't home? Our home?"

Mohr dug his hands into his pockets and looked at her with a slightly shamed look. "I don't know what to call it anymore. I don't think I even recognize it." He turned slowly, hands in his pockets, as if taking in the entire panorama of the valley, hatless, hair tousled in the breeze. The fields were plowed up on all sides and smelled strongly of newly spread manure. She tried to imagine what lay ahead in the years to come—when they were reunited in China. Would they live in a big, modern apartment? Go riding in the countryside, learn Chinese and

English, and be healthy? Eva could take singing lessons. They would go to concerts.

But China was so far away, another world entirely.

EVA IS WATCHING her mother. Käthe bites into a slice of buttered bread and chews with a soft click click in the left side of her jaw. Mohr is all bunched up in his tweed traveling jacket and bow tie. He seems physically altered, as if the changes that will come over him in time are already rising to the surface. He has been smoking heavily, and his pallor is not healthy in spite of six weeks of fresh air and outdoor work. The flab he put on in Berlin is gone. In the last month they plowed and prepared a whole new field for planting. Käthe now has nearly half a hectare of delphinium under cultivation, and enough hay cut to last the animals well into the winter.

"Are there elephants in China?" Eva asks.

Mohr puts down his cup. "A very good question. If I find any, I promise to send you one."

"An elephant? How?"

"By post, of course. Trans-Siberian."

"You can't send an elephant by post."

"Why not?"

Eva stands up. "They're too big."

"Have you ever seen a Chinese elephant?"

Eva shakes her head.

"Indian elephants, African elephants, they're big. Maybe Chinese elephants are small—the size of a little dog."

Käthe gets up to put another log into the stove. The speculation about Chinese elephants continues. "In China there are dragons, and monkeys, and silkworms, and giant panda bears that live in bamboo forests."

"There are dragons?"

"That's what I hear. So why not miniature elephants?"

"Tiny ones?" Eva cups her hands. "Like this?"

Mohr begins to clear the table. "Yes, little tiny ones." Eva follows him into the kitchen, and afterward they all go outside together to say good-bye to Minna. The cow comes loping over to the fence. Mohr strokes and pats her nose. "Good old Minna von Barnhelm. I remember the day we first saw you." He turns to Käthe. "Remember how skinny she was? We thought she'd never produce a single drop of milk." He cups Minna's wet nose in his hand, then turns and gazes down toward the house. He fishes a cigarette from the pocket of his shirt, lights it, and they stand there quietly for a time. It is just after nine o'clock. The whole day lies ahead: the taxi, the train to Munich, the final good-bye.

Back inside, Mohr sits beside Käthe on the old green sofa. She puts her head on his shoulder. Eva looks on, uncertain. The room has never seemed so small, the ceiling so low, the stove so warm, the floor planks so creaky, the windows so narrow, the sofa so musty, their fourteen years together in this three-hundred-year-old farm house so quickly vanished. It can't be recaptured, only evoked . . .

. . . IN PHOTOGRAPH after photograph as you review them late one night, one by one. There are moments when you can imagine them suddenly appearing beside you, breathing the same air. Max and Käthe Mohr, little flecks of captured light. What is it that moves you so? Why do they seem so familiar? Their gaze is all that remains—looking out, far beyond the frame of each photograph, straight into your heart.

Return it.

He detects a faint whiff of perfume. A singsong girl from a nearby bordello, perhaps? Gently, she lays the baby on the examination table. He feels the infant's hot little feet and arms.

"*Hou tung?* How long sick?"

The mother doesn't answer. He touches the baby's swollen throat, holds the stethoscope against the tiny chest and listens to the infant's heartbeat, glancing up at the nervous mother with the preoccupied doctor's mien that hints at consolation without actually offering it. Since returning to medicine, he's had to retrain himself not to feel, to keep his eyes fixed on the frail human surface of things. It goes against his nature to do so, but that he has finally succeeded is oddly comforting.

"*Sheeay bing?* Diarrhea?" He squeezes the baby's belly gently, and knows the answer even before the mother can shake her head.

"*Sin kau tung?*" He draws his thumb from abdomen to esophagus. "Vomiting?"

The mother shakes her head again and says something he doesn't understand. He can't distinguish much between Wu, the Shanghainese language, and the other Chinese dialects that swirl around him every day. He has trouble enough understanding the local pidgin, his own attempts at which usually go uncomprehended. "Four day," she murmurs, holding up four fingers.

He finishes the examination and gestures for her to take the baby from the exam table and sit down. She presses the infant to her breast. "Four day no chow," she says, tears rolling down her cheeks.

"Please, wait," he tells her, and leaves the room to think.

In the bedroom he fills Zappe's dish with seed. The mynah was a gift from an elderly Chinese patient he had treated last year for opium addiction. A caged bird? The poor creature's wings had been clipped. He called it Zappe after the character from his play *Improvisations in June.* And the little black bird speaks—pidgin! *No can do, no can do.* He's taught it some German, too—*Brüderlein fein, Brüderlein fein.*

It is getting hot, the air damp and heavy. It rained all June, but nothing compared to the heavy floods of two summers ago, when 200,000 bodies floated down the Yangsee. He puts Zappe's cage on the windowsill. The bird bobs its head, ruffles its feathers. He lights his first cigarette of the day. Three Castles, usually. Chesterfields "when there is company"—as the enormous new billboard across the road proclaims. A row of idle rickshaws stands against the curb, the pullers gathered around a steaming tea cart. Yesterday he had photographed a young mother on the sidewalk feeding her child from a dirty bowl, shoveling scraps of food into the little mouth with chopsticks. He'd treated the child some weeks earlier for scarlet fever and was pleased to see it so well recovered. The rickshaw pullers laughed as he took the pictures. He clowned for them a little, dropping to one knee, then standing up; backing away, then coming forward to snap a quick set of pictures. There is something comforting about the mask a camera provides: the photographer's intentions so plain to see, yet also inscrutable. Standing at the window now, he can hear the voices of the rickshaw coolies blending in with the steady roar of traffic. Vogel is always urging him to move, find someplace quieter. He has offered to lend whatever money it will take; an old China hand, as the British say. But Vogel isn't British. He's a Jew from Berlin, and displays all the affectations of having lived in Shanghai for too long, most notably a big Packard, an armed driver, and a mysterious web of connections reaching like tentacles up and down the social ladder.

Mohr glances at his watch. He's due at the Country Hospital on Great Western Road at eight o'clock. Finishing there, he'll go straight to Lester Hospital on Shantung Road and work there until two. The hospital work is an important supplement to his income from the practice. Shanghai is crowded with doctors of every nationality, but the Germans all want Aryan doctors. "A Jewish doctor getting started has only so many options in this city," Vogel explained to him the very day he arrived. "In Shanghai it's scrape scrape scrape, friend."

And that is what Mohr does. He scrapes and supplements and spends half of what he needs on the practice and loses half of what he manages to send back to Käthe through transaction fees, inflation, and other rogue factors. It's ridiculous—both what he needs and what he's able to send. He needs clean towels and linen and medicine and cotton bandages, too. But how to explain to Käthe, to whom he managed to send only two hundred dollars last month, that he now has a car? Does he really need it? Bussing and rickshawing to and from the hospital was exhausting. He hates to complain and accounts for every last dollar in letter after letter.

He finishes the cigarette and returns to the woman, whose baby is probably going to die. She is sitting where he left her. He squats down, holding on to one arm of the chair for support, and looks directly at her. "Diphtheria." He pronounces the word slowly, as best he can in English. He doesn't know the Chinese word for the disease but assumes it's more descriptive than *Corynebacterium diphtheriae* or *Klebs-Löffler*. The ethereal vocabulary of medicine has always been difficult.

The woman stares back, uncomprehending.

"Wong!" he calls, and stands back up.

Wong appears almost instantly.

"Catchee car, Wong."

"Car bottom-side, Master."

He slips the stethoscope from his neck, goes to the sink, and begins to scrub. Speechless and cold, the woman holds her baby in her lap. He glances at her, then down at his stained white coat, his cracked and spotted brown leather shoes. The pipes chatter when he shuts off the water. He wrings his hands—once, twice—over the basin, dries them with a clean towel. The woman is watching. Without really looking, she is watching; in watching, she is telling him she knows there is nothing he can do. Nothing. He drops the towel into the laundry bin. It isn't the small, measured movement of the herbalists he has observed in the old Chinese City, rich with age and patience, but just the crumple, crumple, snip, snip of modern medical practice, so big and power-less it makes him want to whistle.

THE COUNTRY HOSPITAL is for foreigners only, but 1937 has been a good year for epidemics and overcrowding is forcing an uneasy egali-tarianism on all Shanghai hospitals. In early June, the Country Hospital began admitting Chinese cases of scarlatina, meningitis, and diphthe-ria. Seventy-six at last count. As of a day ago, seventeen have died. Over at the Chinese-only Shantung Road hospital, 2,412 cholera cases have been admitted since the first of the month. As of yesterday, 735 have died. Mohr can't help taking note of these numbers. Statistics have never interested him much, but life in the International Settle-ment is nothing but numbers: commerce, nationalities, frightened people.

The car makes its way through morning traffic. Mother holds her baby tightly, pressing herself into the farthest corner of the backseat. Mohr sits silently, taking in the view. Rickshaw traffic, roadside com-merce. Tea, rice, sugarcane, watermelon and sunflower seeds, candy, fruits, vegetables, full-course meals bubbling on kerosene stoves, ear cleaners (who keep him supplied with a steady stream of patients with infections), astrologers, letter writers, tailors, beggars, monks, crip-ples. Red silk banners hang from every shop front, billboards and neon lights in every direction. The war in the north has not altered the pace of the city. Every morning he scans the headlines in the *North China Daily News.* He would like to meet the mordant White Russian car-toonist who signs his name "Sapajou."

Cigarette smoke curls up between his fingers. He glances again at the young mother and her baby and suddenly recalls a dream he had had the night before about Wolfsgrub. Very detailed. He flew over Ti-bet, swooped down over the forest edge, and landed. Everything was very still. He stood on the hill looking down at the house. The meadow

was plowed. Everything as it always was—and very, very distinct. Eva wasn't there. She was in school. The sofa stood before the front door, the old green one. Käthe had just finished cleaning. She was wearing a kerchief, and the dog was lazing on the ground. Sunshine, plowed earth on the high, steep fields, and blue delphinium, row upon row of them, top-heavy, in full bloom. His shoes grew heavier and heavier as he walked downhill. Käthe was dusting the sofa and looked up but didn't see him. His guilt became overwhelming as he drew closer. He told himself that now everything would be good again. He'd come from Tibet, run back home. Wutzi growled. As he took Käthe in his arms and saw her blue eyes shining, he woke up. Wong was standing there with the morning paper and tea and warm milk. His clothes were laid out; the bath water was running. Outside, the sound of an argument on the street, some rickshaw pullers from Yates Road, moving in on the ones who are regularly encamped here . . .

WONG OPENS THE car door. The mother glances nervously across the vast plateau of backseat, unsure, then steps from the car, clutching her bundle. Mohr leads her past the two Sikh policemen standing guard at the front entrance to the nursing station on the first floor. After a brief flurry over what to do, he watches as the young woman and her baby are taken through the doors and into the isolation ward. She glances over her shoulder just as the doors begin to close. He smiles, offers a halfhearted wave, feeling that, perhaps, his skills of dissociation have been developed a little too far.

Then upstairs to Nagy's office. The Hungarian pediatrician manages the staff of part-time doctors who work at the hospital. It has been two weeks since Mohr has received any salary. Nagy is in his office. "Good morning," he says without looking up. A compact man in his midfifties, bureaucratic in the old-school manner. His upper lip, though always clean-shaven, seems to bear the shadow of a large Balkan mustache. If he has never worn one, perhaps he should start. As Mohr waits for Nagy to finish writing, his eyes wander to the wall of photographs that have interested him from the first day he called here. They are arranged in four rows of five, in identical black-lacquer frames. Dead trees. Nothing else. Just dead, leafless trees. As Nagy finishes the note, he begins talking about a refrigeration crisis and the problem of evaporating ether. Then, suddenly, he breaks off, opens a drawer in his desk, and takes out a book. "Your novel," he beams. "*Die Freundschaft von Ladiz*. Would you do me the honor of signing it?"

Mohr is too surprised to answer.

"I got it at Kelly and Walsh. They ordered it directly from Zurich." Nagy smiles, offers the book.

Mohr flushes, red heat in his cheeks, his ears. He turns the book over, reads the description on the back cover: *A mountain-climbing adventure, a story of heroism and friendship.* Then he shakes his head and places the book facedown on the edge of the table. "No." He shakes his head again. "Thank you, but no."

Nagy is taken aback. "But I thought you would be pleased to know that your books are still available." A nervous smile. "Personally, I would find it an honor to have my work banned by the Nazis."

Mohr glances at the book once again, then at Nagy. "I don't know," he stammers. A rising anger, a familiar and unwelcome lack of clarity. He fingers the handle of his medical bag, feeling unsteady and somehow trapped, regards Nagy for a moment longer. Then, with sinking calm, he mutters, "I'm sorry," and strides out of the office without another word—down the corridor, down the crowded, narrow staircase, through the front doors, and out into the full heat of day. "Shantung Road hospital," he tells Wong as he climbs into the backseat.

Driving through the crowded city, the big Ford V8 feels excessive, big enough to house an entire Chinese family. He has always felt conscious of taking up too much space here, rushing about, tactless and not quite welcome. It is hot. He lowers the window, takes the little

ivory fan from the side pocket of his medical bag, begins to fan himself. Beautiful little objects, fans. In one of his first letters home he drew a picture of one for Eva, with pagodas and dragons and promises to take her out to find one for herself the moment she arrived—of paper or bamboo or ivory, painted and carved and decorated and hanging in roadside stalls all over the city. And moonstones—because anything that falls to earth from the moon brings good luck, little Eva. And noodles. And bean sprouts. He smiles at the thought of Eva using chopsticks. It is something he still can't do himself, in spite of several attempts, and Wong eager to demonstrate. "No b'long plopper, Doctor. No can do." Food dribbling down his chin, he persisted until the front of his shirt was completely ruined. Wong laughed and shook his head. "Doctor no b'long Shanghai side."

He is right. *Doctor no b'long Shanghai side.* Mohr's temper subsides as he flicks the little fan back and forth near his cheek, takes in the tree-lined elegance of Avenue Foch. *Dr. Mohr no b'long.*

The Lester Hospital for Chinese, generally referred to as the Shantung Road hospital, is one of the oldest in Shanghai. Twice a week, Mohr treats a steady flow of outpatients in the "chit clinic," where, upon presentation of a signed note, free treatment is given to the Chinese employees of foreign-owned firms whose contributions support the hospital. "The coolie hospital" is the other name, and an accurate description of the medical work he does here, setting fractured limbs, suturing the wounds of godown porters, dock workers, and other manual laborers.

He heads straight to the second-floor ward, taking the stairs two at a time and hoping, as he does every day, not to run into Timperly, the hospital superintendent. The corridors of the old building are narrower and dingier than those at the Country Hospital. The way the light filters in through the tall, north-facing windows, and these furtive daily arrivals, reminds him of school, the old Königliches Gymnasium in Würzburg.

"Dr. Mohr!" Timperly calls up the stairwell. The black bag feels like a dead weight as Mohr turns and waits on the second-floor landing. "You're here early," Timperly says. Mohr is about to offer an explanation, but Timperly cuts him off. "We're closing the pediatric ward."

"Closing?"

"We've taken in forty diphtheria cases since yesterday. There are no more beds and we're out of antitoxin."

"I saw one this morning. Mother and child."

Timperly takes this in. "It doesn't look like we'll be getting any more antitoxin until tomorrow." He looks at his watch. "If you don't mind a little change, I'd like you downstairs in the emergency room. Nurse Simson will assist you for the day."

"If that's where I'm needed."

"That's where you're needed," Timperly quips back. His manner has always been distant, professional, which is either a general antipathy toward Germans or latent anti-Semitism. Or, maybe, both. Timperly's manner hasn't changed since the day he had walked into Mohr's practice and announced he wanted to hire him.

"What brings you here, to me?"

"We're always on the lookout," Timperly had explained. "Anyone willing to treat poor Chinese. I've heard your clinic spoken of. You treat for free."

"That's not exactly correct."

"Excuse me. According to ability, of course."

"According to willingness would be more accurate."

"I can offer you a small salary. Not much, you understand. But at least it's something."

"I will do it," Mohr said straight out.

"If you need some time to consider."

"Not necessary. I will do it."

Timperly didn't hide his surprise. "I appreciate a man who can decide things quickly," he said. "I don't think you will regret it."

Mohr lit a cigarette and smiled from behind the curtain of smoke. "Purple plums, yellow melons, the village roads smell sweet," he said.

"Excuse me?"

"From Su Tung Po." He gestured to the window, still smiling. "I am always surprised by all this city offers, the sights and the smells."

"Ah, I see. You are a student of Chinese poetry."

"Not really," Mohr said, enjoying the difficulty the Englishman was having in taking his measure.

In eighteen months the measure-taking has not ceased. Mohr follows Timperly to the emergency ward. His scruffy red hair is uncombed, and in his wake Mohr detects a faint odor of unmetabolized gin and tonic, that drink the British here are so fond of. In the emergency ward, Timperly introduces Mohr to nurse Agnes Simson, then excuses himself and hurries off.

Mohr stands aside as the nurse finishes removing the bandage from a man with a deep gash in his leg. "He was run over by a truck unloading cargo," she says over her shoulder, then steps aside, invites him to examine the wound.

"His son was hit, too," she explains. "They were carrying a large crate and didn't see the truck coming." She is in her midthirties, with black hair and dark eyes that seem on the verge of cheer, but somehow only on the verge. She talks as Mohr examines the leg. "Disgraceful conditions. Landing piers, godowns. Nothing but death traps."

Mohr nods agreement. She is Anglo-Chinese, and he immediately feels they have something in common. He can't say exactly what it is, beyond the assumption that she must also feel herself to be something of an outsider.

"How long ago was he injured?"

"He came in this morning."

"The leg is already becoming infected. It must have happened some time ago."

He stands aside as she prepares a new bandage. When it is ready, they work together, cleansing the wound with carbolic acid. The man lets out strangled gasps and sucks air between rotting teeth. Although he can't be more than forty, his face is dark and leathery, deeply lined. When he tries to sit up, Nurse Simson pushes him gently back down onto the cot.

As Mohr finishes cleaning out the wound, another nurse appears. Her name is Chen Siu-fang and he has noticed that she comes and goes from the hospital by car and driver. She is young and pretty. Her bearing suggests a class element that Mohr can only guess at.

"Excuse me," she says politely, then whispers something quietly to Nurse Simson, who winces and shakes her head.

"Is something wrong?"

"His son has just died."

Chen Siu-fang excuses herself and hurries off. Mohr glances up the row of cots as Nurse Simson pats the man's brow with a damp cloth, carefully refolds and places it on his forehead, then resumes bandaging. He notices the finely articulated bones of her hands, how she concentrates on her work as if attending to some inherited custom. By her hands he can see that she is older than she looks. She finishes wrapping the leg, then turns and asks, "Will you tell him, Doctor?"

"Me? But I don't speak Chinese."

"Tell him in English. Or German, if you like. I'll translate." She begins clearing away the blood-soaked cotton.

"May I ask why?"

She stuffs a bundle of dirty bandages into the metal pail underneath the rickety instrument cart and turns to Mohr with a careworn look. "A few minutes ago I said his son would be fine. It was the only way I could get him to calm down and let me look at his leg."

The man senses something as Mohr steps up to his side, touches his forearm lightly. *"Es tut mir sehr, sehr leid,"* he begins, then switches to English. "I'm very sorry, but your son has passed away."

The man stares, uncomprehending, then looks to Nurse Simson, who speaks to him softly in Chinese. He regards her for a moment, then turns away. Tears well up; he shakes his head from side to side. Mohr touches the man's forearm again, lingers for a moment, and steps away from the cot. Nurse Simson remains with the man while Mohr moves to the next patient, trying to collect himself.

"Thank you, Doctor," she says, catching up some moments later. Mohr glances at the man, who has covered his eyes and is weeping into the crook of his arm. It isn't the first time he has had to break such news, but every time feels like the first time. He is about to say this to the nurse, then realizes by her look that he has just done so.

"How old was he?"

"Eleven or twelve."

"My daughter is twelve," Mohr says all at once, then stops short. Nurse Simson acknowledges his sudden embarrassment with a smile, and sets straight to work on the next patient.

For the rest of the morning he follows her ward to ward, cot to cot, patient to patient. A thirty-minute rest at midday, then they resume work in the afternoon. Very little passes between them, but he observes her closely. The way she tilts back the head of a semiconscious man by pressing the heel of one hand against his forehead, then pinching open an eyelid with her thumb; the way she unwinds a bandage with rapid circular twists of the wrist. By late afternoon the air on every floor of the old building is stifling. He pats his forehead and neck with his handkerchief, pauses here and there, embarrassed to be slowing down. In spite of open windows and ceiling fans slowly turning overhead, his shirt has become damp with perspiration and clings to his back.

The nurse shows no sign of being uncomfortable, even seems privately amused to see him flagging. In response, Mohr begins speaking to her in the clipped manner that he has always found so offensive in other doctors. *Scissors. Tape. Hypodermic.* Then, as they are examining a young boy with an inner-ear infection, he is suddenly nauseated. Short of breath.

"I need to sit down."

"Oh my, Doctor. You are pale." She guides him to a small chair at the end of the ward and sends for water.

"Do you have any aspirin?"

She rummages through the pockets of her smock, produces a small packet.

"For him." Mohr points to the boy, leans his head back against the wall, and loosens his collar. Ears ring. Darkness closes in from the periphery. A metal cup is placed in his hand. He lifts it to his lips. How wonderfully cool and good it tastes.

"Would you like to lie down?"

Eyes closed, overwhelmed, a feeling of things incomplete.

"Doctor? Are you all right? Would you like to lie down?"

He shakes his head.

She tries to take his pulse, but he pulls away, then swoons trying to stand up too quickly. She helps him back down onto the chair. "I'll get a doctor to come look at you."

"No, no. Please. Not necessary."

"But a doctor . . ."

"I am a doctor!" He has felt this nausea and shortness of breath once or twice before, but each time it has passed quickly and been forgotten. There's no reason to think this time will be any different. Already, he feels himself returning to normal. "I'll just go home and rest." He stands, without difficulty this time. "Would you mind telling Dr. Timperly?"

She nods.

"I can't bear to," he adds wryly.

"Let me help you to your car." She takes his arm and they make their way through the ward together, ignoring the curious glances of staff as she guides him down the stairs and out the main entrance. With collar unbuttoned and bow tie hanging untied from his neck, he feels like one of those senile old men always getting lost in the corridors. There is something grimly amusing in being escorted out of the building like this. He is pleased by the way she has taken his arm. The way she is holding it. Holding him. Would it be pathetic to make another joke? The aged cavalier?

It's humid outside, and the smell of car exhaust is thick in the air. The sky is overcast. The rain, when it comes, will be heavy. "Are you sure you are all right, Dr. Mohr?"

"Yes, I'm sure. Thank you." He can feel his strength returning.

"Where do you have your car?"

He points across the street. The car is parked virtually on top of a small sidewalk fruit stand. Still holding his elbow, she walks with him to the curb. As they wait to cross the busy street, he asks how long she has worked at the hospital. She seems surprised by the question. "Ten years," she says.

"How is it that you came to work here?"

She looks at him as if the answer should be obvious. "I had no choice."

Mohr works to interpret the remark, then grins and says, "Me neither."

When they arrive at the car, Wong begins to argue with the fruit seller over who will have to move. Mohr is in no hurry, and eases himself slowly into the rear seat. She hands him his medical bag, which he hadn't realized she has been carrying all along. He accepts it with a sheepish smile, puts it on the seat next to him. Wong closes the door. Mohr fumbles slightly as he slips a damp card from his pocket and passes it through the window. "If you would like to visit sometime. To see my clinic."

She inspects the card, one side printed in English, the other in Chinese. "Thank you. I would very much like to see your clinic, Dr. Mohr."

"Low shun low shun." Mohr smiles, deploying his best phrasebook pronunciation.

"Bitte schön, Herr Doktor. I hope you feel better." She smiles and waves as the big black car merges into the throng of traffic flowing out of the old Chinese part of the city.

Avenue Edouard VII, Avenue Foch, Thibet Road. The crowded streets shimmer in the late-afternoon heat. The tightening in his chest has eased. He is tired and needs to sleep. Should he have let her fetch a doctor, let himself be looked at? Dozing in the back of the car, Mohr recalls a day eight years ago when the Lawrences were visiting. An urgent note came from Frieda: *Lorenzo is going to die. Come immediately!* Mohr followed Hartl, the little boy whom Frieda had sent to fetch him. It was a crisp autumn morning. They marched along the dirt path that cut across the valley. The sun had just broken over the eastern ridges, casting long shadows in the damp grass. Kaffee Angermaier was directly across the valley from Wolfsgrub. The sunny southern side, a very pleasant spot, fifteen minutes away. Mohr had been so happy when Lawrence said he was coming to visit that autumn. "I'll tell you when to tune up the accordion," he wrote.

Hartl skipped ahead, swatting fence posts with a stick. Mohr tried to send him home, but the boy was determined to deliver his charge in person. Frieda was waiting for them. She hurried out the door in a breathless panic. "He is going to die," she gasped. "I was just in his room."

They ran up the narrow staircase and paused just outside the bedroom door. Then entered quietly.

The room was filled with morning sunlight, curtains and window wide open. Frieda hurried to the side of the bed and beckoned to Mohr. Lawrence was lying under a thick pile of down. Mohr squatted beside the wooden-frame bed. Suddenly Lawrence's eyes sprang wide open. He turned his head. "Ha!" he chortled. "I know just what you have all been thinking!"

Ha ha ha. A short while later they were sitting downstairs in the dining room, eating breakfast.

"When are you going back to Berlin?" Lawrence wanted to know.

Mohr shrugged and rubbed the stubble on his face. "I don't know. I was thinking I'd stay here a little longer."

"So you are *enjoying* yourself, then! That's very good. The man who likes to buzz around." He fixed a look on Mohr, a look that had come to be a trademark of their friendship—a murky imputation of unhappiness. "Come with us to France. I know a wonderful place near Marseille. We were there last winter. Good, and cheap." He slapped the table with the flat of his hand. "You don't have to be in Berlin to buzz, Mohr. You should know that."

Mohr returned Lawrence's look. "For your information, I've been buzzing all night. If it wasn't for your emergency, I would be home sleeping right now."

Lawrence laughed. "I can't help it if Frieda gets a shock every time she looks in on me. It was she who sent for you. And *you* who were out carousing."

"I was not carousing. I was delivering a baby. The woman's husband was the one carousing. I sent for him four times!"

"He never came?"

Mohr shook his head. "He staggered in drunk just as I was leaving."

Lawrence broke into a hearty laugh and quickly dissolved into a fit of coughing and gasps of "Marvelous! Marvelous!"

Later that same day, they were sitting outside at Wolfsgrub. Eva bounded around in the grass with the dog. A warm afternoon, basking in the sunshine. Frieda and Käthe were discussing the water in the moss-covered rain barrels in front of the house. Käthe said it tasted better than spring water because it came from the sky. Frieda said it should be used only for washing and the garden. Lawrence reached into his pocket and handed Mohr a piece of paper. "Apropos of the new father this morning," he said, smiling.

Good husbands make unhappy wives:
so do bad husbands, just as often;
but the unhappiness of a wife with a good husband is much
more devastating
than the unhappiness of a wife with a bad husband.

Just as Mohr had finished reading, Eva came racing toward them, leaped into Lawrence's lap, nearly sending him over backward.

"Eva!" Käthe reprimanded in a stern voice.

Eva held up a fistful of wildflowers, gentians. Lawrence accepted them with a smile, then stood up. "You must show me where you found these," he said, and they toddled off into the meadow together.

"Do you think it's all right?" Frieda asked when they were out of earshot.

"Is what all right?"

"Should I tell him to keep his distance? He's infectious."

Käthe looked to Mohr. He folded the paper and slipped it into his pocket. "No harm can come from Lorenzo," he said and went inside, knowing it was not true and wanting, suddenly, to be alone.

BEING ILL DOESN'T suit Mohr. On the other hand, it suits him just fine. Strange how the same verb applies to infirmity and desire: a passing illness, a passing fancy. When transitory states become permanent, do they also become malignant? Is being in love different from being sick? Or being in exile? Cliché questions.

He should ask Käthe.

No, he shouldn't.

Is something wrong with his heart?

Mohr manages to remain in bed reading until just after nine o'clock, when Wong announces the first patient. After Mohr sees the man—a Russian with advanced cirrhosis—the *Clinic Closed* sign is put out and he returns to bed. By midday he is restless and uneasy. He feels wide awake, just fine. There's nothing wrong, no need for prolonged idleness, so he reports for his regular shift at Lester Hospital—only to discover it is Nurse Simson's day off.

The rounds go smoothly enough. Nevertheless, he can't help feeling a mild disappointment. He tries his best to ignore it, but it's not easy, and by the end of the afternoon Nurse Simson is still very near the center of his thoughts. No, she is not a thought, but a well-veiled feeling. How strange to want to fend it off, like trying to hide from oneself. Somehow, he feels compromised. Yet what has he done?

On returning home, he is surprised to find Nagy waiting outside the apartment building. He steps from the shadow of the front entrance. "Good evening, Dr. Mohr!"

"Good evening," Mohr stutters, glancing at his watch. Embarrassed, he grips his medical bag tightly.

"I owe you an apology."

"And I as well."

"No, no," Nagy insists. "You have every right to be angry for not having been paid. Checks were supposed to have been delivered by now. It was thoughtless of me to ask for a personal favor under the circumstances."

Nagy's apology comes as a surprise. "I hope I haven't given you a shock," he says and delivers a gregarious pat to Mohr's shoulder.

Mohr loosens his grip on the bag. "I don't get many visitors."

"I came to invite you to tiffin."

"Tiffin?" An odd gesture. Mohr glances up at the windows of his flat. Accepting invitations is awkward. He doesn't go out to eat very often. It isn't just a question of expense. Mainly, he prefers his modest diet and Wong's cooking. He's never been an adventurous eater and lately has been putting on weight, has had to let his trousers out twice in the past year. Bread, cheese, a cutlet. For salad, a tomato and cucumber, lightly peppered. He's also come to enjoy Wong's preparations of rice and vegetables, sprinkled with soya. Wurst from the German butcher on Hankow Road is one of his guiltiest pleasures. It is stupidly expensive, but their bratwurst is almost better than back home.

Nagy produces an envelope from his pocket and offers it. Mohr accepts with a nod of thanks, slips it directly into his pocket.

"I took the liberty of advancing you next month's salary. There is so much uncertainty these days."

It takes a moment to register. A month, plus the two weeks he is owed, comes to nearly seven hundred Shanghai dollars. Not counting the diamond in Vogel's safe, this is more wealth than he's had on hand since his arrival. "Come upstairs with me," he says. "I must first see if any patients are waiting."

He leads the way up the dark staircase. The sign on the door reads: *Dr. Max Mohr, M.D. General Practitioner, Specialist in Nervous and Mental Diseases, Homeopathy.* Fumbling with keys, he describes the overflowing wards at the Shantung Road hospital. "The situation is severe. No medicine. Not even ether."

An agitated Wong pulls open the door—*"Cheu kan kan! Cheu kan kan!"*—and points to the open examination room.

A man is lying doubled up on the floor. Mohr kneels to examine him and immediately recognizes his neighbor from downstairs. He has been badly beaten, is bleeding. There is no odor of alcohol on his breath, nor does he seem under the influence of opium. He is young and Jewish—from Frankfurt, Mohr guesses. To call him shy would be an understatement. Mohr has spoken to him only in passing on the stairs.

"What happened?"

The man groans. His nose lies flat across his face, eyes badly swollen. Nagy rolls up his shirtsleeves, helps the man onto the examination table, then holds him down firmly as Mohr cleans the blood from his face, sets the broken nose. "You may have a fractured skull," Mohr tells the man in English when he is done. "You should go to hospital for observation."

The man shakes his head. "No. No hospital," he sputters back in English.

Mohr switches to German. "You could have a concussion," he says. "Let me take you to hospital."

The man shakes his head, gets down from the table. He is unsteady on his feet. His face is raw and badly swollen. Mohr feels a sharp pang of recognition and regards him carefully, knowing all he cares to know. He's had enough of this story and that story, his story and her story, the whole seasick world floating in an ocean of hate. His skin has grown thicker here, and he admits to being used to it, used to the way life here rubs up against life, a blur of struggle. Sometimes he wishes he'd accepted the offer to work in the mission hospital at the Tibetan frontier station. High up in the mountains. But is there any place beyond trouble? The rickshaw coolies here drop dead of heat prostration in summer and freeze to death on the streets in winter while he tries to keep his shirts clean, gives injections, sets limbs, pumps stomachs, and writes letters home to Käthe.

"Do you know what happened to you?"

"Bandits," the man says somewhat unconvincingly.

"Then we must call the police."

"No!" The man shakes his head, touches his bandaged nose.

Nagy turns away with an exasperated shrug.

"Can we at least help you down to your flat?"

The man refuses.

"Do you know him?" Nagy asks when the man has left.

"Only in passing. He came in January." Mohr remembers seeing him in the Chocolate Shop down the street, and was a little surprised to see him sitting at the counter, calmly reading a book in the midst of a throng of noisy English children. A birthday party was under way with cake and candles. For a moment, he felt the strongest urge to join it.

. . .

A SHORT WHILE later, Nagy and Mohr are sitting in the Wing-On rooftop garden restaurant, at a table with a view up Nanking Road toward the Bund. It is cooler up here than down at street level. The red-tiled floor glistens with water, sprinkled by little boys who pass between the tables carrying brass pails. Wet tiles, a cool breeze. The lighted tower clock of the Customs House—Big Chin—dominates the nightscape. Nagy orders tea and some rice and dumpling dishes. "Have you been up here before?" he asks.

"Never."

"It was the first modern department store in Shanghai. Built just after the war."

"Like KaDeWe in Berlin."

"Exactly," says Nagy. He becomes serious. "I would like to apologize again for yesterday. I feel absolutely foolish."

Mohr sips his tea, finding the lacquered splendor of the bustling rooftop restaurant a pleasant diversion. The waiter places some dishes on the table.

"They are pork dumplings. A little like *Leberknödel.*" Nagy picks one up with his fingers, pops it into his mouth. Mohr follows his example, and chews slowly, nodding approval. Delicious.

Atop the Customs House, Big Chin's six-ton chime erupts. The bell tolls, the city blazes. Off the Bund, the river is littered with ships and junks and sampans of all sizes. On Soochow Creek, boat traffic is at a standstill. Mohr begins to relax in a way he hasn't been able to for a very long time. He imagines bringing Käthe and Eva up here and ordering these same dumplings and tea, showing them how to enjoy this big, exotic Oriental city. Nagy summons the waiter for more food and starts to talk about the recent visit to Shanghai of the German minister to China, Trautmann. "Just horrible," he says. "Hitler Jugend and Bund Deutsche Mädel marching through the streets."

Mohr had seen the pictures in the newspaper. "I thank god every morning that I don't have to worry about the Roman Empire." He smiles wryly, helps himself to another dumpling.

"That martinet! Did you see how he looked? Hair dangling in his eyes. Like he shares Hitler's barber!"

Yes, he's seen all the photos, and ignores them the way he ignores all the other things he struggles daily to put out of mind. A fresh breeze blows across the rooftop, on it a profusion of fragrances—food, tobacco, eau de cologne. He is only half-listening to Nagy, and sips his tea, letting his eyes wander to the other tables scattered among the inlaid lacquer screens and potted plants. The lushness is a little too metropolitan for his comfort, but he enjoys it all the same, and feels no compunction to talk. Why should he? It feels good not to be a talker, for a change. One of the unique aspects of life in the International Settlement is the way people make themselves over from the very moment of arrival. A curious and very rapid process.

Nagy is still talking, his mouth full, eating and talking. The incident that morning seems distant. So does the bout of nausea at the hospital yesterday. "Vacation," Nagy is saying as Mohr's eyes fall back into place.

"Excuse me? I didn't catch the last part."

"A vacation," Nagy repeats.

Slightly addled by the strong tea, the buzz of talk, Mohr reaches for his cigarettes. A stylish couple at a nearby table has attracted his attention. The woman looks very familiar, but he can't place her. A movie actress? Perhaps. Broad-shouldered, with hat fashionably cocked on her head, confident of her effect on the room. The man is older, slightly paunchy and gray. Mohr feels oddly displaced by their presence. "Vacation?"

A smile crests at the corners of Nagy's mouth. "When did you last have a rest?"

Mohr eases back in his seat. "I can tell you exactly. It was between October and December, 1934. Aboard the *Saarbrücken*. Seven weeks on the open sea."

"And since then nothing?" Nagy calls the waiter. "I'm having a whiskey soda. Will you join me?"

He glances again at the movie couple, feeling suddenly impelled to alcohol. He hardly ever drinks anymore. "Why not?" He lights a cigarette with a nightlife flourish, inhales deeply. "May I confide something?"

"Of course."

"I came here to begin a new life."

Nagy smiles. "Like everyone, I assure you."

"I also came here to earn a living. As a doctor." He puffs on the cigarette, taps the ash into the little porcelain dish at his elbow.

"Don't tell me you've stopped writing!"

The formulation is slightly irritating. He doesn't quite know how to respond, except with a shrug. "It's more basic than that; something more fundamental."

"I'm afraid I don't follow."

"Imagine this." Mohr rocks back on his chair as the waiter sets the drinks down. "You are trying to escape. From what, exactly, you don't know. You lack words to describe it, are totally bewildered. You come down from your mountain and see a huge, modern city in front of you, which you recognize as the place where all your contemporaries live. You realize that you no longer belong to a natural world. But you also don't belong to the mass of humanity that lies before you, the big, noisy city. You stop and sit down to rest, pluck a handful of thyme from the ground, rub the leaves between your fingers, sniff. You can still smell the delicate aroma. But is it the same aroma that your ancestors, or even your parents, smelled? No. It isn't. Something has disrupted a once clear relationship. You glance back at your mountain. Should you return? Give up on this expedition to the city? You can't. A dark, heavy Nothing lies between you and all the things of nature. You can't escape it, and there is no turning back."

Nagy leans forward, taking in this flight of fancy. "Go on, go on."

"So, you head down to the city to see what's going on. You decide you would rather give yourself over completely to that dark, heavy

Nothing, would rather experience complete, total alienation, than deceive yourself with false connections. So, forward march!"

"Into the city?"

"Into today! The middle of the century!" Mohr stops and glances around, aware that his voice is carrying, but also enjoying himself.

"So you're saying this is a bad time for writers everywhere, not just in Germany."

"Who's talking about writers? I'm talking about all of us. You, me, those people over there."

"But you have to admit, for writers times are especially bad," Nagy persists. "Especially Jewish writers."

Mohr turns his glass in his fist. "Times are bad for everybody. What matters is whether connections still exist between people, if there is anything left linking people at all."

"I hope you don't mind me asking you these personal questions."

"Personal?" Mohr smiles, shakes his head. "My dear Dr. Nagy, what you're asking is far beyond personal. You're asking me to speak to my *condition*. I'm not sure I can even comprehend it, much less speak to it."

Nagy considers this for a moment. "I don't think you give yourself enough credit."

Mohr looks down into his glass. "I feel foolish talking about it."

"I see nothing foolish in what you are saying," Nagy objects.

Mohr shrugs, slips another cigarette from the pack lying on the table. "A person like me must live without the will and the shall and the future. It's the only way."

"What about your work?"

"The same thing. Without the will and the shall and the future."

The waiter stops by the table.

"Another?" Nagy asks.

"Why not?" The idea of becoming drunk has taken on a certain appeal. He stares for a moment at the glowing end of his cigarette. "I am a dilettante, Dr. Nagy."

"You are too hard on yourself."

Mohr shrugs, removes his eyeglasses and cleans them with an edge of tablecloth. "And I never could keep my mouth shut," he says at last, taking in the fuzzy lights of the hanging lanterns strung underneath the roof awning, the laughter from the surrounding tables. "Never mind. Plenty of poets have worked for the water bureau." He smiles, puts his glasses back on. "Let's not take ourselves too seriously."

A short time later they are walking together up Nanking Road, very pleasantly drunk, ambling along in crumpled, sweat-stained linen. Mohr's stride is a challenge for the shorter man, who skips alongside, equally drunk and singing with a strained British accent: *On the way to old Nanking! Tibet and far Yunan . . .*

A jai alai game is under way at the racetrack. They weave through the evening bustle. Nagy has just told him that he came here in 1927 from Szged, and claims to be a misfit and an outsider. "Like you, Mohr. Just like you."

"Like me? What do you mean like me?"

"A Jew. Just like you."

Mohr stops short, inspects his hands, palms up, palms down, in mock panic. "Really? Just like me?"

Nagy laughs, a nasal honk that draws glances. Mohr keeps the pantomime up, light-headed, wisps of the schoolyard. Funny, how he finds himself recalling so much of innocent, cabbage-white boyhood lately. He is dizzy, disoriented, still thinking about the young man downstairs, how he refused help and staggered off like a beaten dog. He's seen it so often, beaten Jews staggering off, refusing help. Suddenly he feels ashamed, and stops again. A streetcar clangs past.

"What's the matter?" Nagy asks.

"I don't much care for all this Jewish talk. Never have. The world would be so much better off if people just stopped it. All this preoccupation with identity."

"You may be right. But it's hard to ignore something when it is foisted on you."

Mohr takes out his handkerchief, pats the perspiration from his forehead, his neck. "Do you know what it is to feel a connection? I can close my eyes and feel a connection. A real connection to everybody whom I have known and even those I never knew—whole families dead and gone. I can see their faces, as if I were looking at their photographs. When I open my eyes again they are gone, and I am all alone. I wish I could be among them always—the living as well as the dead. A true connection. It's beautiful and horrible at the same time. I don't know where it comes from." He stops, wondering if what he is saying makes any sense at all. Is it the alcohol? Nagy is looking at him with baffled admiration.

Mohr tucks the handkerchief away. "I will sign the book, Dr. Nagy. I don't know what it means, but I will sign it."

Nagy nods his thanks, slightly embarrassed. They continue walking.

"August would be a good time," Nagy is saying as they finally arrive back at the Yates Apartments. Mohr fishes the keys from his dampened trousers pocket, feels the whiskey evaporating from his skin, smells it percolating on his breath. "There is an American doctor coming from Canton," Nagy says. "You are free to go as soon as he gets here."

"Go? Go where?"

Nagy shrugs. "Anyplace you like! To Ching-tao. To the seashore. It's where everybody goes in summer."

The idea of going where everybody goes is not at all appealing. Mohr offers his hand. "Thank you. I enjoyed the evening."

Nagy clasps Mohr's hand tightly. "You're no dilettante," he says, leveling. "I will remember our conversation tonight."

A gracious nod. Nagy's sincerity makes Mohr feel foolish. He knows better. The smell of food cooking wafts from the building as he approaches the front door. Before going in, he turns to watch Nagy settle back on the upholstered seat of a rickshaw, then disappear with a wave into the melee of Bubbling Well Road.

Wolfsgrub

he drain in the kitchen isn't working properly and Seethaler won't be free to come until the end of the week. Käthe lifts a large pot onto the stove and lights the burner. The drainpipe collapsed yesterday. Fixing it isn't beyond her. She's done many and far dirtier repairs on the house by herself, but digging up a dirty old drainpipe isn't worth the risk of a back injury—even if it means having to haul dishwater outside for a week.

The kitchen windows are open to let in the morning air. Berghammer is cleaning the stalls next door. His cows have been grazing in the upper meadow for two days now. In another day, he'll bring them down. She scrapes the breakfast crumbs from the kitchen table with the edge of her hand, tosses them outside for the birds. It's Eva's last day of school, a beautiful summer day. Hiasl came by earlier, his cart loaded with fresh plums. She bought an entire basket from him, and has just taken the cake she made from them out of the oven and set it to cool in the next room. Of course, Eva will be too excited to eat when she sees the present from Papa. It arrived just two days ago. The enclosed letter contained another surprise. Japan? A vacation? She looked in the atlas to see how far from Shanghai it was. Just a finger-width on the map. Even so, she can't help feeling that it is too far away. Anything that increases the distance between them is too far away.

She pins up her hair and sets to work on the dishes, listening to Berghammer's shovel scraping next door. Her apron is smeared with plum juice and dusted with flour. Eva teases, calls her a messy cook. Amusing that a child would notice such things. Where does she get it from? Frau Daibler? There's a woman who keeps things tidy. Sometimes Käthe slops around the kitchen on purpose just to make the point that she's a woman with her own way of doing things. No *typische Hausfrau*.

She is repairing the fence around the vegetable garden when Eva finally gets home. The heavy bicycle is maneuvered through the gate— battered old wicker basket hanging precariously low from the handlebars. She leans the bicycle against the fence, and races up the hill waving something over her head. Final grades. Käthe holds out her arms for a congratulatory hug, but Eva stops short and thrusts an envelope at her. "Is it true, Mama? Is the school closing?"

Käthe reads the notice twice, tucks it into her apron pocket, and nods.

"But why?"

"They're closing all the private schools."

"Who is?"

"The government."

"Why?"

"I don't know."

"Is there something wrong with my school?"

"There is nothing wrong. Your school is a fine school."

"Then why should they close it?"

Käthe sits down in the grass. Eva drops down beside her and pulls up a fistful of soft turf. "Why should they close it, Mama?"

"Because they want to control everything."

"Frau Waldheimer said we'll all go to school in Bad Tölz."

She shakes her head. "I don't think so."

"No?"

"It's not for Frau Waldheimer to decide where everybody goes to school."

A smile plays at the corner of Eva's mouth. She knows her mother's feelings about the woman all too well. "We'll find you a tutor," Käthe says.

"To come to our house?"

"Maybe."

Eva jumps up. "You mean I won't have to go to school anymore?"

"Why not?"

Eva is beaming with puzzlement. Käthe smiles, gets to her feet. What a surprise. No more school! Perhaps circumstances have actually improved for a change. "We'll see what we can do."

The table outside is set for lunch. As always, Käthe sits facing out into the garden. A man and woman have just emerged from the woods and are coming down the path that runs along the edge of the cow pasture. There seem to be more tourists around than usual this year. Mostly they keep to the lakeshore, but lately more and more of them have been striking out for this quiet corner of the valley. The dirt tracks that wind between the fields are busier than she can ever remember. The other day a large group of men tramped by as she was leading Minna back to the barn. She watched as they stomped by noisily and disappeared into the woods. It was a very large group, close to a hundred—and they weren't boys but men with red faces and sagging bellies out on their *Kraft durch Freude* walking tour of the Tegernsee valley.

Eva rushes through her meal. Käthe sits back to watch, astonished by her daughter's growing appetite. "Would you like more soup?"

"No, thank you."

Käthe stacks the empty bowls on a wooden tray, and slides across the bench. "Wait here. I have a surprise for you."

"It's not a surprise, Mama. I saw it already. It's right inside on the table."

"I'm not talking about the cake," Käthe teases, and hurries inside. When she returns, Eva has cleared a space on the table, is squirming with delight. "Oh. I knew it, Mama. It came last week, didn't it? On Thursday. Am I right?"

Käthe places a small box on the table. It is wrapped in very thin red tissue that has left a slight stain on her fingers. The little box absorbs all of Eva's attention, as does every gift that comes from China. They come in a variety of ways—Trans-Siberian Railroad, steamship though the Suez Canal. The most surprising and extravagant are always the packages that come from Captain Brehm. They are the ones that contain the real treasures of the Orient: a mahogany side table richly carved and inlaid with ivory, porcelain, silk robes and slippers, puppets, tasseled lanterns, carved figurines and fans—many, many painted fans. When Käthe objected to such extravagance, Mohr wrote back that he was wasn't wasting money but only sending things every tourist in China buys; to make the point, he enclosed receipts.

Eva removes the wrapping paper carefully to reveal a small black-lacquer box. She turns the dainty object over. "I think I know what it is." She lifts the top to find a very tiny scrap of stationery atop a wad of cotton. She unfolds the note with ceremonious deliberation. "Papa can write like a flea!" she giggles, and reads out loud:

Sieh nicht, was andre tun
der andern sind so viel
du kommst nur in ein spiel
das nimmermehr wird ruhn.
Geh einfach Gottes pfad
lass nichts sonst Führer sein
So gehst du rect und grad
und gingst du ganz allein.

Look not what others do
too many throng around
they draw thee in their game
where peace is never found.
But go the path of God
where none may guide but he
for straight and true it leads
however lone thou be.

She glances at her mother with a flush of uncertainty.

"Let me see." Käthe takes the note and reads it out loud once again. "I think it's quite nice," she says afterward, hiding her irritation. What could he have been thinking? Telling a twelve-year-old girl to go her way alone. She is alone! Has no idea how alone she is. Käthe brushes back a flying strand of hair and puts the note on the table. "Papa is just trying to say that you should always do what is best for you. Not follow behind others."

But Eva has already forgotten the note. "Look, Mama! A diamond!" She holds the box for Käthe to see.

"It's a moonstone." Käthe plucks the little gem from the box. "Very lovely."

"Does it really come from the moon?"

"No. But sometimes I think your papa does. They're his favorite. I have some from him, too." She drops the stone into Eva's outstretched palm, noting the child's slightly muddled pride, and gets up to go into the house.

"What should I do with it?"

"I have been saving mine and one day I'll have a necklace made."

"That's what I want to do, too." Eva rolls the stone in the palm of her hand, then returns it to the box, pressing it firmly into the cotton. "But not until we're with Papa. When are we going to China, Mama?" she asks.

It's a question Käthe doesn't have an answer to; she goes inside without offering one.

THEY PARK THEIR bicycles and follow the footpath down to the lakeshore. It's a crowded, hot afternoon. Eva races ahead to find a spot as close to the water's edge as possible. There are long lines at the changing cabins, women tucking their hair up in rubber caps. Marie Berghammer recently told Käthe about an FKK club someplace along the lake, and they'd had a good laugh together at the idea of local farmers doffing their clothes for a rollick in the nude.

Käthe settles down on a relatively open patch of grass and helps Eva into her swimsuit. A breeze is blowing across the lake, and though the sky is blue and clear, a front is moving in slowly over the mountains. There will be rain, possibly before nightfall. Eva squirms into her suit and races off to the water. Käthe takes her sewing from the basket, removes her shoes. The blue-green water is slightly choppy today. The little boats that ferry tourists across the lake have a hard time of it when the water is rough. Burbling, straining motors. She drops her sewing as the bells of Saint Laurentius begin to chime the hour. Their sound always brings back memories. This little beach at the southern tip of the lake was one of Mohr's favorite spots. She thinks of him often here, remembers the old swimming pier (now gone), and Mohr with his blue-striped trunks pulled high on his waist, wet hair combed straight back, smoking his customary "*après*-swim" cigarette. A quick glance around at the men out here today—not one of them comes close. What secret pride she used to feel when they came down here together. His gregarious physicality was even slightly embarrassing to her, being out here with the famous doctor and writer—handsome, athletic Max Mohr.

When Eva finally leaves the water, her lips are blue and she is shivering. Käthe wraps her tightly in a towel. "How can you stay in the water for so long? You're frozen through." Eva drops onto the blanket, scoots up next to her mother, teeth clattering in merry little bursts. Käthe returns to her sewing, pulling each stitch carefully and deliberately, amused by Eva's happy shivering, and the way she gazes contentedly across the lake with glazed eyes, a little joy released into the world. Every so often she finds herself remembering little phrases Mohr would come up with on the spur of the moment, a way of fixing it like a photograph. All she wants is to talk with him again. Face to face. But all she has are hundreds of letters, all bundled up and tucked away, and his impulsive and urgent little telegrams:

The old tabby cat in the Café Dobrin has become a good friend. MM.
The pralines are delicious. Eat them all yourself. MM.
Letter abandoned. I love you. MM.
Advertisements radio a thousand wild proposals. MM.

He always signed them MM, like a quiet, self-deprecating hum. To have so many words and yet also to have nothing but words.

MARIE BERGHAMMER is outside in her garden as they arrive back at Wolfsgrub. She is tending a stand of hollyhocks planted along the side of the house. "A beautiful afternoon," she says, crossing the yard. Marie is sturdy, a cheerful, sober woman. She and her husband manage a little dairy of fifteen cows. Although Käthe and Marie have always been friendly, there is still a vestige of reserve on Marie's part. Käthe gave up trying to break it down years ago, realizing how her egalitarian urbanity only stiffened Frau Berghammer's more formal country manners.

"We were down at the lake," she says, pulling to a stop.

"A perfect day for it." Marie brushes the dirt from her apron.

"Marie, they've closed the school." Käthe steps off the bicycle, leans it against the fence.

"Summer vacation."

"No! For good!"

Marie squints back, something she often does in place of asking questions.

"They sent a letter. The such-and-such regulation of the such-and-such administrative reorganization of the so-and-so. Anyway, the school is now officially closed. Finished."

"Forever?"

Käthe nods.

Marie brushes the front of her apron again. "What about the children?"

"They will all be sent to Tölz."

She feels her pulse quicken, an urge to explain, to take Marie into a deeper confidence. They are friends, after all. There can be nothing wrong between them. "I am thinking of hiring a tutor." She stops there, wondering if Marie will read anything into it. There is a canny streak in the woman that Käthe regards highly, if a little grudgingly. It came into full relief over the parcel of Berghammer's land they bought after Mohr's play, *Ramper,* was turned into a film. It wasn't anything to do with the actual deal. It was what Marie had said shortly afterward—that it was a sign of trouble when a man who is so often away from home buys land for his wife.

"It's how things used to be," Marie says thoughtfully. "Lessons in the morning, work in the afternoon." She bends to pluck a weed from the upturned dirt along the fence and chuckles. "Herr Lickleder. We drove him mad. Always skin and bones, poor man; came here to write—like your husband—except he wasn't a doctor, so he had to give lessons."

Käthe knew old Lickleder well, the first of the local eccentrics Mohr had ferreted out when they first moved here. He died a few years ago.

"Ach! He drove us crazy with his poems. *'Wenn der Morgen trunken heraufgeht.'"* Marie laughs, shakes her head. "You were baking this morning. I could smell it."

"For Eva's last day of school."

Käthe waves good-bye and pushes the bicycle the short distance home. Back inside the house, Eva is sitting at the kitchen table, feeding Wutzi the last crumbs of cake from the palm of her hand. She glances up as her mother enters. "Why do we have to go to China? Why doesn't Papa just come back here?"

Käthe regards the pile of dirty dishes stacked on the counter, decides to wash them before preparing supper. "I've told you. It's complicated. Papa is in China now so that he can earn money. When the proper time comes he will send for us."

"Why don't we just go now?"

"Is something wrong? Are you feeling sad?"

Eva shrugs, pats Wutzi. "You never talk about Papa anymore."

"That's not true. We talk about Papa all the time."

"Not about the old days. You never talk about the old days anymore."

She is about to protest but stops herself. Eva is growing up, isn't satisfied with promises of good things to come. She needs more than promises. Käthe thinks back to the poem Mohr sent. Perhaps she had it all wrong; perhaps some fatherly intuition gave him just the right sense of what Eva needs to know now. There are bonds and there are bonds; those that connect and those that strangle. Time spent together in the kitchen is a bond. Suddenly Käthe realizes her daughter is asking for something only she can give her. A sudden twinge in her stomach. How could she not have noticed? Hasn't she been paying attention?

She takes a large pot from under the sink and begins filling it with water, glances over her shoulder and sees that Eva is waiting "What would you like to talk about?"

"I don't know." Eva picks up a knife and begins drumming idly on the tabletop, then suddenly perks up. "Tell me the mountain-climbing story."

"Again? You've heard it so many times."

"You haven't told it in a long time, Mama. Please?"

The dog gets up, lopes out of the room. Käthe lifts the pot onto the stove and lights the burner, then sits down beside Eva. The kitchen ceiling is lower than any other room in the house. A beam running down the middle makes it necessary to duck going from the stove to the sink. Another time marker, when Eva begins to duck. Käthe takes the knife Eva has been drumming the table with. "We'd been married just two years." She wipes the blade clean on her apron, then sets it aside. There's a difference between what once happened and what once was. She would like to explain this to Eva, but stops herself. Maybe when Eva starts bumping her head on the ceiling.

"Go on, Mama," Eva says impatiently.

"It was 1922, a terribly cold winter. Just going outside for more than a few minutes at a time was difficult. One day, your father announced that he wanted to climb the Gross-Venediger."

"Where's that again?"

"In Tirol, near Kitzbühl, over three thousand five hundred meters high. I didn't want him to go."

"But he had done it before, right? He was a good climber."

"Yes. He'd climbed it once before the war, so I knew I had to let him go. Not that I could have stopped him."

She glances at the pot on the stove. Eva is right. She doesn't tell stories of the old days anymore. It feels strange, but she's confirming something—the way a person is reminded of the moon on a moonless night.

"I watched him get packed and ready. 'Don't worry,' he said. 'Nothing's going to happen.' The morning he set off—it was very early, four o'clock—I went upstairs, got back into bed, and watched from the window as he skied off in the dark."

"He skied there?"

"No. He skied to the station in Tegernsee and took the train from there. Six days later a telegram came. *Arrive tomorrow 11 A.M. Bring sleigh. Max Mohr.* At first I was relieved. But 'bring a sleigh'? And

signed 'Max Mohr'? He never signed his telegrams with his full name. What was going on? Oh, God.

"It was early morning when the telegram came. I was all alone. I ordered a sleigh. And waited all day and prayed and prayed. I couldn't sleep. Finally the time came to go. The sleigh took me to the station and the train arrived and everyone got off. But no Papa. I waited and waited—old people, stragglers, and still no Papa. Then I saw the conductor get out carrying Papa's rucksack and skis.

" 'Where is he? What's happened?' "

" 'Back there,' the conductor said. 'The last car.'

"I ran down the platform, scrambled onto the train. Papa was lying there with both his feet bandaged and raised up, tears streaming down his face. Out of happiness, he said. His whole body was shivering. Both feet were frozen up to the ankles. Third-degree frostbite."

"Is that the worst?"

Käthe nods, glances again at the pot of water on the stove. "An infantry doctor in Rosenheim saved him; worked on him all night. Gave him tetanus injections. Without that doctor Papa would never have made it. If he hadn't suddenly turned up Papa might have been stranded in Tirol. The doctor in Mittersill had wanted to send him to Salzburg to take off both his legs! But Papa wouldn't allow it, wouldn't let anybody into his room. For two days he lay in a little guesthouse in Mittersill. Finally an ambulance came. He had to change trains seven times to get back here, but, finally, he did."

Eva puts her head down on the table.

"Are you tired?"

Eva shakes her head vigorously. "Go on, go on," she insists.

Käthe takes a moment to check the pot on the stove, thinking, for some reason, of Mohr's letter—the dream he wrote about, of walking down to the house from the upper meadow, and her outside, beating the dust from the old green sofa. Is that really his vision of home sweet home? With her playing the good little *Hausfrau?*

Gross-Venediger. Kürsingerhütte (2558 m.) u. Gr. Geiger (3365 m.)

"Go on, Mama," Eva says, growing impatient. "I'm listening."

Käthe sits back down. "Remembering is hard work." She strokes Eva's hair. Swimming has made the child tired, though she denies it. "Where was I?"

"At the train station. He had to change seven times."

"Right. At the train station I rounded up some men to carry him to the sleigh. When we arrived home, Kerbel, the coachman, and Hiasl got him into the house."

"Old Hiasl carried Papa?" Eva laughs.

"Fifteen years ago he was one of the strongest woodcutters anywhere. Anyway, as soon as Papa was inside the house, he began feeling better. He played his accordion."

"What did he play?"

"I don't remember, exactly. Some old song."

"I bet it was '*Wenn die Hähne kräh'n.*'"

Käthe laughs, remembering Eva's little-girl look of nervous anticipation as she waited for Mohr's window-rattling cock-a-doodle-doo at the end of the song. "Yes. That could very well have been it. Anyway, it didn't last long. The pain started to get worse again. And worse and worse. We just sat there, completely helpless. We had no clue how dangerous it was. Papa couldn't walk, not one single step. Hiasl had to carry him upstairs to the bedroom. It was cold up there. And the bed was too short. His feet had to be kept raised. I lit the stove, set a little table at the foot end of the bed, and piled pillows on it. Then I wrapped his legs in blankets. No! No! Too heavy. For God's sake, take them off. So I took them off, and he began to shiver with cold. I shoveled more wood into the stove, but then it got too hot. Air! For God's sake! Back and forth, back and forth. There was no way to make him comfortable. Night came. I sent Hiasl home. We began to get scared."

"What about a doctor?"

"I had called the doctor in Tegernsee, but he couldn't come until the next morning. Back then you could only telephone during the day, so there was nothing we could do but wait. And so, that evening, between bouts of pain and talk about how we would handle the situation, Papa told me the entire story of what had happened."

The water is now too hot to wash with. She turns off the burner, adds some cold water, and puts on her apron. Eva begins tapping with the knife on the tabletop again. "So tell me, Mama. What happened up on the mountain?"

"He arrived in Mittersill on the first day and stayed overnight at the Deutsch-Österreicher Alpenverein. He was a member, and was given keys to the group's climbing shelter up on the mountain. The next morning he packed some firewood and headed out. The route up the lower glacier to the shelter wasn't particularly difficult. Papa had done the tour before the war and knew the route well. But it had been a long time and the glacier had changed quite a bit. On top of that, the whole place had been more or less deserted since the war. Right away, he knew things were not going to go the way he had thought. He had to cut steps into the ice. All day long he worked hard with the pick, but it was January and the days were short. He wasn't getting far enough. The damn ice. To lighten his pack and make better time, he threw away the wood he was carrying. He worked and worked, step by step. Twilight fell. Still no sign of the shelter. Finally night fell. A frigid night. Bitter cold. Papa said the stars seemed too close and too bright. He stopped for a rest and thought, Oh God. It's all over. And then he drifted off."

"On the ice?"

Käthe laughs. "No, in bed, as he was telling me the story." She is enjoying Eva's suspense. "The story didn't come out all at once," she teases. "He told it to me very slowly and quietly, as if in a trance. It was as if he kept having to remind himself of how it felt to be all alone out there, how it had taken every last bit of his strength."

She hoists the heavy pot and tips the water into the metal basin in the sink. She will have to use the basin until the drain can be fixed.

"Then what happened?"

"Help me and I'll tell you." She turns on the ceiling light. Right away, a moth flutters and buzzes around the bulb. Eva heaves herself up. Käthe hands her a towel for drying, pins her hair back with an extra pin. The warm water feels nice as she begin washing. The sharp soap smell tickles her nose. She rubs it with the back of her hand, passes the first clean dish for Eva to dry, and resumes the story.

"He finally reached the shelter at about two o'clock. But the door was completely blocked and he had to clear the snow away. He dug and dug and at last he got it open. He had thrown away his wood, so as soon as he was inside the shelter, he had to chop up a chair to make a fire."

"That was bad, throwing the wood away."

"He needed to go faster and to save his strength. There wasn't anything else he could have done. Anyway, that's when he began to notice that his feet felt strange. But it was too dark to see very much, and he was dead tired. He pulled his boots off and fell straight to sleep. When he woke up it was morning, and very cold inside the shelter."

"And his feet?"

"They were frozen, swollen thick, completely numb. He went outside and tried to warm them in the sun. But that only made it worse. He had to turn back right away. But he couldn't get his boots on! The situation was desperate. He knew it would take everything he had, every ounce of strength, right up to the end. I have to go back, he said to himself. I have to make it. Calm down, try to stay calm. Have a cigarette. Concentrate."

"What about his shoes? Did he get them back on?"

"No. But luckily, he had a pair of soft leather house slippers, which he had brought to wear inside the shelter. He was able to get them on. He took the straps from his rucksack, somehow fastened the house slippers to the bindings of his skis. Everything else he left behind. And off he went."

"How could he ski with frozen feet?"

Käthe shakes her head. "God knows. But Papa is an expert skier. Somehow, he managed. Sometime around midnight, a group of drunk men were leaving the village tavern, singing, playing the accordion. Papa yelled to them from where he was lying beside the road. They brought him into the tavern, laid him next to the stove. It was two days before the ambulance came to take him."

She hands over the last dish, and dries her hands. The moth continues to flutter and buzz around the light. She pauses for a moment to watch it. Telling stories often brings on a curious feeling. She belongs and lives here with all her being, but something happens whenever she begins to tell Eva of the past. For a moment, rather than filling the house with her presence, she feels like a mouse running along the floorboards. It's not so terrible. She hoists the heavy basin from the sink and carries it outside to the vegetable garden, watches the water course through the little runnels between the beds until all is absorbed into the soil.

They are eating dinner when Berghammer and his cows finally come down from the meadow. They pass directly in front of the house, fifteen in all, mooing as they approach the barn. Suddenly the lights flicker and go out. They wait for a moment in the dark, and when the lights fail to go back on again, Käthe goes outside for a look. The lights are out at Berghammers' as well.

Eva has already lit the kerosene lamp and is collecting the plates to take back to the kitchen when Käthe returns. "Let's continue with the story, Mama," she says. "It will be fun in the dark." She finishes clearing the table as Käthe lights the lamps in the hallway and in the kitchen, pours a second cup of tea, and goes outside to sit on the bench by the front door. The moon is rising over the mountains. Eva comes out and sits beside her. Sipping tea, Käthe resumes the story.

"We were all alone. Just like the two of us are now. I don't remember how the rest of that first night went. The doctor from Tegernsee came in the morning and wanted to cut off Papa's toes. Papa sent him away, even though they hurt terribly."

"How could they hurt if they were frozen?" Eva interrupts.

"I don't know."

"Sometimes when I wake up at night and my arm is asleep, it feels dead. It doesn't hurt, it just feels funny."

Käthe shrugs. "I can't explain it. All I know is Papa didn't have a moment without pain. Somehow we made it through the next few days. Papa was so exhausted that he couldn't eat. And he reacted badly to the medicine, which he gave himself. Nothing could take away the pain. Not even morphine. We didn't sleep. There were brief moments of hope, but then the pain would return worse than before. Early on Sunday morning I heard someone downstairs. It was Krecke."

"Who?"

"Krecke. A surgeon from Munich. He used to come down here on Sundays to ski. We had met by chance a few weeks earlier, up on the Wallberg, as a matter of fact. Papa had given him some skiing pointers, told him about his plan to climb the Gross-Venediger. And now here he was at Papa's bedside! He had heard about the accident from somebody in town and said he had treated lots of bad frostbite cases in the war. So, suddenly, there was hope. Krecke said he'd seen some amazing cases during the war. Do nothing except have patience and try to withstand the pain. As soon as he left, everything changed. We had a goal. We had hope. We knew the way, had a purpose. We began to arrange things right away. The feeling of despair lifted—when you're young you can do almost anything. I got up early every morning, tended the goats and the chickens—we didn't have Minna back then. There were ration cards in those days just after the war, but nothing to buy in the stores. Then breakfast. No, first I would light the fire upstairs, then we would have breakfast together, just like you and I do now."

Eva is sitting at the end of the bench, sleepily hugging her knees. There are so many details to recall, an enormous number of things to remember. One day she will write them down. But how to record time spent waiting? Waiting is what she recalls above all else. Like some slow-circling bird overhead, waiting, waiting for others who seemed to have never had to wait for anyone or for anything, ever. Why does she wait? Is it possible not to wait? To stop waiting? What is there to look forward to when the waiting is over? When night falls, waiting becomes something she does with her whole body. She looks up into the sky, the mountain peaks rise up, black tatters blotting the stars. There is no place she'd rather wait than right here, outside, on a summer night. What an unquiet thing she is; she has rehearsed all the words she plans to greet Mohr with when she sees him again. But now tomorrow seems too distant to think about. Does it come too late or too soon? She can't decide. It doesn't matter; she is still waiting. She nudges Eva, who rubs her eyes sleepily, and leads her upstairs to bed.

Alone now in her own bed with the windows open to the night air, she tries to imagine life in Shanghai. Servants, skyscrapers, fishy smells from the river—crowded, muddy, and endless. Remember his little joke up on the roof? She must tell him he is wrong. The world does not resolve itself in twos, but in a lingering loneliness. She is waiting for it to end.

Shanghai

Wong announces a lady visitor.

"Nah ee go lie dee?" Mohr asks, though he knows the answer. It's early evening and he has just finished a telephone consultation, a young American journalist with stomach flu. Did he say he was from San Francisco? Lately Mohr has been daydreaming about America, thinking about Frieda Lawrence. Her last letter had come from Kiowa Ranch. *So gross tut die Natur hier alles,* she'd written. Nature does everything so BIG here! Their correspondence had resumed just two years ago, when he wrote asking for her consent to publish a selection of his letters from Lorenzo in a Shanghai literary journal. When they were printed he felt a twinge of regret. Lawrence had always disparaged literary magazines, said he had no use for semi-intimate backchat.

Wong stands inside the door in a new tunic, all white, with a low collar. The sleeves are too short. His hands hang at his sides, overly large. He hasn't been his cheerful self lately. *"Ching tah dzin li,"* Mohr tells him. "Show her in."

He lights a cigarette and looks in Zappe's cage. The bird has been strangely quiet for the past day or so. He opens the door and the bird hops onto his index finger. His hands tremble as he lifts it to his shoulder, feels the sudden grip of little feet through his light summer shirt. A woman has come to see him. It isn't something that happens often. He glances down at himself. White trousers, clean but rumpled. Shoes in need of polish. White shirt. Bow tie—the symbol of his Shanghai-side *vita nuova.*

Why the sudden self-consciousness? What happened to the franker, simpler tramp? The spontaneous young man sitting atop the wood-pile outside the house, wearing cavalry boots and playing the accordion with Käthe beside him? He had worn those boots for years after the war. They were the best boots he ever had. Somehow he'd managed to hold onto them as a prisoner of war in England. At first Käthe had seemed intimidated by the old farmhouse, and spent the first days there scrubbing the floor planks and taking down all the curtains, rotted and stinking. A city girl from Hamburg, she said she was tired of curtains, told him she wanted to see the slopes rising up behind the house, the cows grazing, the play of sunlight on the treetops. He'd lain half-awake all night, listening to the animals in their stalls. "Do you think they can get into the house?" she asked.

"If we leave the doors open," he teased.

"I noticed hoof marks in the corridor," Käthe said as he rolled onto her, lips sealing lips.

Next morning he was outside, sitting on top of the woodpile, playing his new accordion and tapping his heels against well-seasoned oak and birch and ash. The war was over. By a miracle of good luck, they owned an old farmhouse, were alive, in love. He wanted to meet every farmer in the valley.

When Käthe came outside, he showed her the notice he'd written.

"What is it?"

"An announcement."

She went back into the house. A few minutes later she was tramp-

ing toward him through the wet grass, carrying a loaf of bread, two apples, and a piece of cheese in the folds of her apron. She passed it all up and he handed her the notice to read. "We'll print it up and send it out this week."

Zur Wolfsgrub, Post Rottach
Am Tegernsee
Dear friends and family
We live in the Wolfsgrub, near Rottach, on the Tegernsee.
We wish you all the best on all your coming birthdays, and every new year. Since we are unsure whether we will be able to make our wishes clear in advance of our departure, we would ask that you refrain from sending flowers to our funeral.
Greetings always,
Dr. Max Mohr
Käthe Mohr, nee Westphal.

"You can't send this!" Käthe laughed.

"Why not?" To live in an old farmhouse. To be alive. It was all so much more *enchanting* than he could ever have dreamed. "Europe is dead!" he shouted. "Long live the Europeans!" Then he jumped down, gave Käthe his hand, and they went back to bed for the rest of the morning.

NURSE SIMSON APPEARS in the doorway. "Excuse me for not telephoning first," she says.

With the bird perched on his shoulder, Mohr invites her in, offers his hand. Wong is standing behind her. "Nice of you to come."

"What a pretty little bird," she says, reaching up to stroke it. She is wearing a yellow cotton and silk dress, short-sleeved and slit up the sides. Her hair is bobbed short. She strikes him as a completely different person without her nurse's uniform—a fashionable Shanghainese woman. "How are you feeling?" she asks.

"Much better, thank you." He returns Zappe to the cage and closes the door, reminded suddenly of the old folk song about the cuckoo bird who tries to persuade the cowherd that its life is so much finer than a man's.

She smiles, glances around the cluttered room. Mohr takes his accordion from the bookshelf.

"Are you going to play, Dr. Mohr?"

"Don't call me doctor," he says, slipping his arms through the straps.

"What should I call you?"

"Mohr. Just call me Mohr."

"And please, you must call me Agnes."

Mohr nods, puts his fingers on the keys, tests the action. "I haven't played in a long time." He unfastens the brass hooks. The bellows expand with a gasp. "I was just remembering an old song. It's about a cuckoo and a cowherd. I used to sing it to my daughter." He clears his throat, once, twice, and begins. Music fills the room. He is badly out of practice, but somehow his fingers manage to find the keys. He learned how to play from his father, who also taught him this song. He begins to sing as Wong enters carrying a tray with tea and biscuits and sets it down, beaming. Mohr has played for Wong once or twice, but has never sung. He finishes, bows to polite applause.

"I wish I understood the words," Agnes says.

"It's about a cuckoo bird who claims to enjoy life better than the cowherd. It's supposed to be funny."

Wong fills their teacups and then retreats.

"Is the joke on the cowherd or the cuckoo?" Agnes asks.

Mohr looks over at the birdcage. "What do you think, Zappe? Which of us enjoys life better?"

Agnes glances at the cage and smiles. "It's not such a silly question."

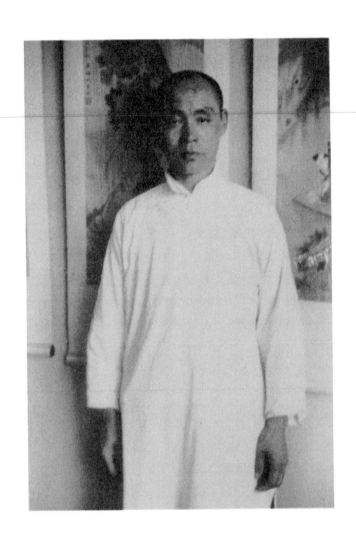

A sharp observation. Mohr is very happy to push beyond small talk. "I once had a good friend," he begins after a brief silence. "We spent a lot of time together, first at my house in Bavaria and then in the south of France in the last months of his life." He pauses to sip his tea. Agnes is sitting very properly, straight, legs crossed European fashion. Mohr puts down his cup and offers a cigarette. She nods politely as he lights it. "He would often say to me, 'We don't know one another.' The closer we became as friends, the more he would insist on it. It was very strange. 'I don't know you and you don't know me,' he would say. 'Let's not pretend.' I didn't understand what he meant."

Slightly preoccupied, Mohr tilts his head, exhales a thick, pleasant stream. He leans forward, taps the ash into the ashtray.

"That is very Chinese," she says.

"I knew nothing of China back then." He smiles. "I know even less of China now."

Agnes smiles back. "That means you're learning."

He holds the accordion in his lap, fingers the keys, cigarette dangling from his lips. Somewhat impertinently, he asks, "Which is your Chinese side? Mother or father?"

She sips her tea before answering. "My mother. My father was English."

Mohr squeezes a few chords from the instrument. She seems disinclined to elaborate. "Two very different worlds," he offers.

"Yes, that's true." She hesitates and adds, "But in this city, one learns to overlook the differences."

"Do you ever feel caught? Between the differences, I mean?"

She considers the question for a moment, then shakes her head. "No. I don't feel caught. Do you?"

Mohr laughs. "Me? I always feel caught." He glances at Zappe's cage, and squeezes another chord out of the instrument. The bird cocks its head. Mohr sets the accordion aside and falls quiet for a moment. Lawrence would have twisted the question in precisely that way—and not sweetly, but with a chiseled glare and a challenge to answer. "My friend used to say that he was a giraffe. And his fellow Englishmen, they were all well-behaved dogs. They were different animals." He tamps his cigarette out in the ashtray. "In Germany today, people like me are the giraffes, and the well-behaved German dogs are all being told to chase giraffes."

Agnes puts out her cigarette as well, then stands up and smooths her dress. "You said you would show me your clinic."

"Yes. I did."

He leads her down the short corridor, gestures to the door on the left. "The waiting room. Wong sleeps there at night." He produces a key, and stops short at the sound of a woman's voice coming from behind the waiting-room door. Mohr shrugs and pushes open another door. "My examination room," he announces, flipping on the light switch.

Agnes steps to the center of the room, crosses her arms, nods approvingly. Mohr points out all the features of his modest little practice—the examination table, the glass instrument cabinet, the metal washbasin. The paint on the ceiling is chalking and beginning to flake in areas. On the wall hangs a silk scroll reproduction of Su Tung Po's famous bamboo painting. He had bought it the very week he arrived. A Chinese lamp sits atop the instrument cabinet.

"Very nice," Agnes pronounces.

They stand in the center of the room together, silently appraising. "The low-budget doctor of Shanghai," Mohr jokes. "But look! A refrigerator. American."

"And medicine?"

"Well, that's another matter." He glances at his watch in a sudden burst of inspiration. "Do you have time for a little outing?" Before she can respond, Mohr is moving toward the door. "Wait here. I'll be right back."

"But—"

"I'll only be a minute."

Half an hour later they are sitting in the eighth-floor lounge of the Cathay Hotel. Mohr is dressed in a tuxedo, the one he bought for his forty-fifth birthday last year. He sat for an entire evening all alone in this brass-and-marble lounge, drinking champagne and reading *The Sun Also Rises*—also purchased as a birthday present for himself. "Have you read any Hemingway?" he asks, remembering the spell the book cast on him, and how, as he sat here reading it by Lalique chandelier-light with Mister Nelson's Hot Shanghai Jazz Band playing in the background, he tried to imagine himself as one of those spoiled Americans, drinking and roaming the globe.

Agnes shakes her head. "I have only heard of him. Is he good?"

A waiter sets down two whiskey sodas with a lingering glance of disapproval at Agnes, who ignores him. They are sitting in large leather chairs, separated by a small table. "Yes. He is very good."

"My father loved Thomas Hardy. Do you know Thomas Hardy?"

"The Mayor of Casterbridge. The Return of the Native." Mohr recites the titles. By her smile he guesses that she has just telegraphed something about herself. He remembers Hardy's characters very well— exploding out of convention to die, alone, in the wilderness. "Have you ever been to England?" he asks.

"Never," she says. "Have you?"

"Once." Mohr sips his whiskey, is about to elaborate, but then thinks better of it and changes his mind.

"I would love to go there someday. To Nottingham, where my father was from."

Mohr perks up at the mention of Lawrence's hometown. "Your father is from Nottingham?"

"He was," Agnes says. "He passed away ten years ago."

"I'm sorry." Mohr would like to learn more, but is reluctant to ask, uncertain how he would respond himself to questions about Käthe and Eva. Once lines are crossed, there is no going back.

Agnes seems to sense something of this as well, and with slightly affected cheer adds, "He always said he'd take me there someday. My mother was never interested. She said the English here were quite enough for her."

"You were close, you and your father?"

"Very close," she says with a slightly defiant glance around the room. "He was a special man."

Suddenly Mohr realizes what he has done. He downs his whiskey and stands up. "Come." He offers his arm. "Let's go for a walk."

They make their way to the lift together, striding arm in arm. The room seems stifling, precisely the sort of oppressive elegance he has always avoided. Going down, he begins to apologize, but she cuts him off. "It's all right." She pats his arm as if he is the one who needs consoling. How stupid he feels, horrible and stupid, as they push through the heavy revolving glass doors and out into the humid night. It is early evening, and Nanking Road is teeming.

"I'm sorry. I wasn't thinking."

"You have no idea how little it bothers me." She shrugs, but he can see that she is not telling the truth. "Not too long ago I wouldn't have even been allowed in there with my father."

Mohr's discomfort grows as they start walking in the direction of the river. How could he not have realized? He should have known immediately. That look from the waiter.

A minute later, they arrive on the Bund. To the left, the enormous Sassoon House and Jardine Matheson buildings, hulking, American-style skyscrapers. The brightly lit jetties along the water's edge are as busy at night as during the day, ferrying passengers and goods from ships anchored in the middle of the Whangpoo. They stand together at the railing along the promenade, taking in the view. Points of light float in a wide, slick blackness. A smell of diesel and coal hangs permanently in the air. The warships anchored out in the middle of the river seem to multiply daily. Just the day before, he had watched from the steps of the Hong Kong and Shanghai Bank as a Japanese military transport ship docked at the wharf. *Shiretoko*. Coolie porters unloaded, supervised by Japanese troops. He counted the Japanese flags flying from ships up and down the river. Dozens and dozens. He had been at the bank to cash the check from Nagy and cable half of it to Käthe. The cashier, an Englishman named Mr. Arnold, had said that all money transfers to Germany were going through without any problems. "The money will get there, Dr. Mohr. You can rest assured."

Standing now beside this pretty woman with his foot up on the railing, he dreams of pushing the horizon back as far as it will be pushed. He feels her presence next to him, a strong soul, natural and yet unfamiliar. He would like to ask more about her father, what had brought him to this city, and about her mother. In his mind he has a clear picture of mother and daughter, their apartment on Avenue Joffre, Agnes stepping out with friends, *chi-pao* evening dresses slit to the hips, rickshawing and taxiing to visit acquaintances across the Settlement and French Town, restaurants and nightclubs, passports and visas and telex addresses in London and Hong Kong and Singapore. He wishes for some way to assemble it all, integrate and bring everything together, but no sooner has the thought occurred to him than he feels stupid for having it. Assemble what? He reaches for his cigarettes. His bucolic idylls, mountain adventures, his middle European *sitten?* The dizzy skyscrapers behind him clattering and clanging with teletypes and telephones and radios? How can anything be assembled from descriptions and anecdotes—from atmospheres? What is there to bring together? What has he lost that he wants to recover?

He turns to Agnes, offers a cigarette. "Do you know what I would like to do?"

She casts a sidelong glance.

Match after match blows out in the breeze. After several attempts, he manages to light hers, then his own, cupping the match in his fist. "I would like to climb Mount Fuji."

"You want to go to Japan?"

"Have you been there?"

"No, Doctor," she says, holding her cigarette urbanely at the corner of her mouth. "I have never been outside Shanghai."

Back home a few hours later, still in his tuxedo and sitting at his desk, Mohr writes to Käthe:

Oh my dearest, I'm completely worn out. A heat wave. Bills bills bills. I'm going to Japan. Yes. For a vacation! I need it badly. Nagy advanced me a month's pay, and I'm using it to escape from the grind. Am now working from morning until late at night. I cabled $200 to you yesterday. Should be there by now. I can't write. Have to fight just to get in five hours of sleep. This heat! The odds on the street are 50/50 on war with Japan. I don't believe it, but signs are everywhere. Have dreams about Fujiyama. Strange. They say you can walk right to the top. I don't know that I can take another month of this city. Maybe a drive out into the countryside between now and then.

He folds the letter and encloses a photograph of himself taken recently by Wong: standing behind the portrait of Eva. If Käthe had included a picture of herself in that last letter, he could have composed a kind of long-distance family portrait. The three of them, separate, yet pictured magically together. But he doesn't have a recent photograph of Käthe. She has never sent him one.

A summer downpour has flooded the streets. In front of Vogel's iron-gated house, Wong honks a second and a third time. At last, the bandy-legged gardener opens the gate, then returns to his work, squatting like a crab and shearing the grass with a hand scythe. The tranquillity in this farthest western part of the Settlement is always a shock. The mock-Tudor houses, surrounded by manicured lawns and well-tended flowerbeds, songbirds, rustling trees, all part of an elaborate self-deception, an illusion of peace and contentment—a protection and a prison.

A pigtailed servant escorts Mohr through the house and into the back garden. He has always thought of the place as the work of a man with-

out fantasy. It is a more polished, worldly variation of the Würtzburg house he had grown up in, Rottendorferstrasse 1. *Jugendstil* leaded glass, neoclassical sculpture, Persian carpets, porcelain, pre-Impressionist paintings, decorative objects scattered on tabletops and in cabinetry, a grand piano. Hedwig would have declared it *sehr elegant*.

Vogel is sitting in a reclining chair, shaded from the morning sun by an enormous parasol. He drops his newspaper as Mohr tromps across the flagstone patio. Vogel is just five years older than Mohr, but already frail and aged. His thinning hair has gone entirely gray. He combs it back over the top of his head. Sullen, red-veined cheeks scraped barber clean. As always, he is smartly dressed, a man for whom even a hint of illness is bad form and vaguely distasteful. "Have you read the news today?"

Mohr helps himself to a slice of bread from the breakfast tray on the table. "I make it a point never to start off the day on a bad note."

"The Japanese are closing in on Peking and Tientsin."

Mohr pops the bread into his mouth, reaches for his medical bag. "Is that why you called me here? To tell me what's in the newspapers?" He puts the stethoscope around his neck. "Let's have a look at you."

They've seen very little of each other in the past year. Although Vogel has always worked under great pressure and strain, Mohr has begun to suspect the pressure is of the bottled variety. Last time he visited— just before Christmas—Vogel had kept a bottle of brandy at hand, sipped and refilled his glass during the entire visit. He'd never been a drinker. Back in Munich after the war, he had sworn an oath of abstinence, and lectured Mohr about the veterans dissipating all over Germany. Even as a prisoner of war Vogel had been fastidious, played the captured officer to a tee, never deviated from the officer's code. He kept himself scrupulously neat, mended his clothes with meticulous care. Mohr played a much looser game, and charmed the guards with his easygoing humor and occasional outbursts of Shakespeare and Wordsworth. In the prison camp, the two had not been close at all, and had never set out to become lifelong friends. The friendship had evolved by accident. Shortly after the war Mohr ran into Vogel by chance on the street. They detoured to a restaurant, where, down to his last three marks, Mohr insisted on buying. He'd just finished a new play, *Dadakratie,* and watched Vogel leaf through the typescript, page by page. "It's funny," Vogel admitted, without a trace of amusement. Then he put the manuscript aside. "I'm a lawyer, Max. Not an impresario. Have you shown it to anyone else?"

"I sent it to Max Reinhardt. The Deutsches Theater in Berlin."

"What happened?"

"I haven't heard anything."

"It's for the best, Mohr. You're wasting your medical education."

He can remember the scene well. Vogel had a toothache, exuded a strong clove aroma as he went into an intricate and long-winded analysis of the Bavarian political situation; the Räterrepublik. Kurt Eisner had been assassinated a few weeks earlier. Finally Mohr cut him off. "Ach, Vogel. Will you please shut up? I'm finished with all that. Politics. War. Medicine. I'm finished with all of it."

"And what do you propose to do? While everyone else is struggling you're going to—what? Write amusing comedies?"

"That's exactly right, friend. I'm going to write amusing comedies." He smiled.

Vogel snorted.

Mohr stood up, defensive, but hardly offended. "I'm going to find a house in the country, and get a dog, and do lots of hiking and climbing."

Vogel dismissed him with a wave. "Go ahead, Mohr. Get a dog and go climbing. You selfish bastard."

"And I'm getting married." Mohr grinned.

Vogel burst out laughing. "You? Married?"

Now, a much older man unbuttons his shirt and submits to an examination. In spite of Vogel's cranky nature, it is nearly impossible for Mohr to be unhappy around him. By some strange chemistry, Vogel's grumpiness usually has the effect of increasing his cheer. That they are friends these twenty years hence, on a hot morning in a well-tended garden in China. What is not to be grateful for?

Mohr completes the exam, tugs the stethoscope from his neck. Vogel buttons his shirt and walks across the flagstone patio. He stands at the edge, surveying his large lawn. The grass is wet with dew. Mohr picks up the newspaper, reads the headlines: fighting around Marco Polo Bridge, on the outskirts of Peking; a photograph of a derailed trolley car on the Boulevard de Montigny—"A Ricksha Caused This," and an account of injuries sustained—by the tram passengers.

"I suppose the rickshaw coolie just ran up and knocked the tram car right over on its side," Mohr remarks.

Vogel snatches the paper away. "Come inside, Max."

Slightly put off, Mohr takes his bag and follows Vogel into the house. Upstairs to the study.

"Have a seat." Vogel unlocks the drawer of his desk and takes out the little envelope Mohr had left with him on the day he arrived in Shanghai. The diamond from Käthe's wedding ring. She'd given it to him as an emergency security. He'd refused, but she had insisted. With tears in her eyes, she'd insisted. Only after he'd gone did it dawn on him that it wasn't simply financial security she had in mind. Vogel passes it across the desk. "You'll need to find someplace else to keep it," he says. "I'm leaving Shanghai."

"Leaving?"

Vogel nods.

"Where are you going?"

Vogel removes a sheaf of papers from the drawer, quickly leafs through them, then passes the whole stack across the desk. Mohr fans through the papers, stamped *Secret* in bold red ink. "What are these?"

"Read them," Vogel says.

SHANGHAI MUNICIPAL POLICE REPORT

S.1 Special Branch
Subject: Arrival and Departure of Japanese Naval Transport "Shiretoko."

The Japanese Naval transport "Shiretoko" berthed at the
S.K. Wharf, 184 Yangtzepoo Road, at 3 P.M. 300 sailors
landed and proceeded by Landing Party motor trucks to the
barracks on Kiangwan Road. The following munitions were
also unloaded from the same vessel:

300 boxes rifle ammunition

100 boxes each containing 8.75 mm shells

160 drums of kerosene oil

30 bicycles

100 gas drums

91 aerial bombs

220 light gun shells

4000 sandbags

3000 winter uniforms

1000 summer uniforms

100 machine guns

4 motorcycles

"Well, I knew they weren't carrying geishas." Mohr tosses the sheaf
of papers onto Vogel's desk, shakes his head in mock dismay. "And all
these years I thought you were just a simple lawyer."

Vogel picks up the papers. He selects one from the middle of
thestack and hands it across the desk. It is also stamped *Secret*. Mohr
scans the document, which lists the movement of Chinese and Japanese armies, division by division, around China, then hands it back
to Vogel. "Very impressive. But what, exactly, are you trying to
tell me?"

Vogel returns the papers to the drawer, closes and locks it. "Don't
be an ass, Mohr. You know perfectly well."

"That there is a war going on?"

"That the war is coming! Here! To Shanghai!"

"I would say it's already here. If you ever left your house, you might see for yourself. The city is filling up with refugees. Or have your spies over at the SMP not mentioned them to you yet?"

Vogel leers. It's a look Mohr has seen many times: arrogant worldliness blended with something a diseased gland might secrete. "I don't know how to say it more plainly."

"Say what?"

"Get out of here."

It's Mohr's turn now to be irritated. "And where, exactly, would you suggest I go?"

"Palestine."

"And Käthe and Eva? What do I tell them? Put your furs in storage, girls, and meet me in Jerusalem? Or do I have to start up a new practice first? Send for them in another five years?"

Vogel's expression softens. He pushes himself back in his chair. "The war is coming to Shanghai, Max. I can't predict what the course of it will be. All I can say for certain is that it will be bloody and dangerous, and the smartest thing to do is get out of the way."

"And go to Palestine?"

Vogel nods.

"Is that where you're going?"

Vogel shrugs. "Not just yet, but perhaps soon."

"Where are you going?"

Vogel places his hands flat on the desk. "Max. Please trust me. The situation here is going to get very bad."

"What kind of answer is that? Why are you telling me this?"

"Listen, Max. I wish I could go into detail, but I can't. There's nothing for you here in China. Go to Palestine. You can play a role there, not just stand to the side watching events you don't understand unfold all around you."

"Who says I need a role to play? Or that I'm just standing around here?"

"You know perfectly well what I mean, Max."

Mohr looks away, not in the mood to debate. He has Vogel to thank for helping him at so many turns. But there are only so many emergencies a man can face, and only so much help a man can accept in one lifetime. "You know I'm not a Zionist," he says at last. "I don't want to play any roles. I'm a doctor. Just a doctor. I don't want to be anything else but that." He slips the envelope into his pocket. Vogel's place has always seemed so permanent, a house nestled among all the other houses in this moneyed oasis, this city of four million people, of skyscrapers and slums, ringed by factories and warehouses and fed by ships and rail and air. Nothing comes of exile but the object lesson of exile. And here he is, once again, uncertain. "Why should I go to Palestine?"

"I have contacts, Max. They can help you."

Mohr stares at his worldly old friend. Vogel doesn't live. He machinates. "Thank you for the offer." He picks up his medical bag, stands. "But I don't see myself starting all over again. I don't see myself anyplace but here."

"It's not a question of where you *see* yourself, Max."

"No? What is it, then?"

Vogel stands and walks over to the window. "It's a question of safety, Max. And also responsibility. What business do you have here? Are you going to help fight the Japanese? Or join the Red Army? You're a Jew, Mohr. Right now, your place is elsewhere."

"So now you're a Zionist. I hadn't realized."

"No, Max. Just another Jew trying to defend himself."

"What better form of self-defense is there than simply refusing to be provoked?"

Vogel rolls his eyes. "Mohr, you are an escapist."

Mohr's pulse rises. "I am nothing, Vogel. I didn't come here to escape anything. I came because I wanted to come. I banished myself here."

"You banished yourself?" Vogel laughs. "And would you mind telling me what it is that you banished yourself from, Max?"

"The odium of the times," Mohr replies evenly, returning the sarcasm.

94

Vogel's laughter is hearty and derisive. "Odium of the times! That's good. Odium of the times. I'm going to write that one down! Max! Where did you learn to be so pompously naive?" He takes a handkerchief from his pocket, blows his nose, wipes his watery eyes. "You're the biggest ass I have ever known, Mohr! I suppose that's why I like you. It takes courage to be such an ass."

IN MORITZ & SONS, the steamship ticket agency on Canton Road, Mohr listens as the bald Russian ticket agent describes the differences between first-class and tourist on both the NHK and the Dollar lines. He can't make up his mind, asks for a moment to decide, and sits down in the waiting area. An American couple are now at the counter discussing their itinerary with the agent. Vogel is right. Getting out of this fata morgana of a city would be a good thing. But to Palestine? He thumbs through a stack of brochures. Imperial Hotel, Lake Yamanaka: *a most beautiful setting for the viewing of Fujiyama.*

The gay unconcern that Vogel provokes—it isn't a game, just the effect on Mohr's nature of a man for whom everything is overdetermined, and on whom the world wreaks permanent havoc. Why suffer disasters in advance by living in continual anticipation? If suffering is the one thing we can count on, isn't it better to leave the suffering for when disaster really happens? Furthermore, what is luck if, having escaped disaster, you haven't been spared from suffering?

Mohr turns to look out the window. Wong is waiting across the street, lounging against the front fender, fanning himself with his cap. A line of parked cars stretches all the way to the intersection, shimmering in the summer heat. Traffic today is horrible, worse than usual. He's never been so late getting to the hospital. On the table are scattered brochures for the American Mail Line, Dollar Steamship Line, Hamburg-Amerika, Far Eastern Mail. A large bulletin board behind the ticket counter lists arrivals and departures. Hamburg via Port Sudan, Alexandria, Casablanca. Liverpool. Bombay. Hong Kong. Sydney, Genoa, Rotterdam, New York, Kobe, Yokohama—the whole world shriveled to a tightly observed schedule. His stomach feels hollow. Hands begin to tremble. Everything dissolves. He feels pulled the way thread is spun onto a spool, drawn into a larger, massing entity, takes off his glasses, wipes his eyes with the heel of his hand.

The American couple and the ticket agent break off their discussion, turn to look, then glance away again. Mohr leans over, takes the handkerchief from his trousers pocket, wipes his face, replaces his glasses. Twisting the gold wires around each ear makes him feel frumpish, dowdy. The woman turns to look again, mildly sympathetic. A steady breeze blows down from the ceiling fan. Palestine? Why not Egypt? Alexandria. There is a ship leaving tonight. Would Käthe agree to meet him there? Or Palestine?

NO. NEXT SPRING you'll meet just across the Austrian border, in Tyrol. Yes. That's what you'll do. A long summer in the mountains. Achensee. Remember your last breakfast in Wolfsgrub? Delft-ware, fresh coffee, tins of preserves, a round red ball of Dutch cheese. You think back to that day whenever you try to imagine your future together. But there is no such thing as the future. The earth stands still and floats: today, today, today, nothing but today.

"Two tickets," you tell the agent.

"First class or tourist?"

"First class," Mohr says without hesitation; then he watches the forms being filled out, then stamped, itineraries checked, carbons stapled. The office boy is called to fetch receipts, make change.

"TO JAPAN?" AGNES stares at the ticket in her hand. Shanghai-Nagasaki-Shanghai. "With you?"

"Separate berths, of course."

"I can't go to Japan with you!"

"Why not?" Mohr struggles to maintain an impish cheer. "To Fujiyama."

She shakes her head.

"It's a beautiful mountain. Come with me. I want to go to the top."

They are standing at the front entrance of the hospital. He worked late in order to leave with her when her shift ended. She presses the envelope into his hand, looking directly into his eyes. "No. I'm sorry."

"At least take some time and think about it."

Agnes shakes her head. "I can't."

Mohr stands there awkwardly. The silence between them gives way to the clamor of traffic. The Sikh traffic policeman at the intersection blows his whistle. A rickshaw puller stomps past, cursing, barely able to control the momentum of his fat passenger. Mohr smiles; Agnes doesn't. Wong pulls up to the curb. "I simply mean as a friend," he says. "That's all."

"What makes you think I am your friend?"

Mohr flushes. "What makes you think you are not?" He gets into the car and pulls the door shut. Agnes is already walking away as he rolls down the window. Once again, he feels foolish, empty-headed, tangled up in things, his powers gone. He used to think that life here would improve him, that he would grow, and in growing that Käthe and Eva would be inspired, and when they were at last reunited they would all grow together again, and—Germany be damned—their new life here would be richer and he would rejoin the human race, not as a refugee and a has-been but as a free and independent man. Instead, all he feels is lost, without a compass; all he wants is to believe that things could *not* have turned out other than the way they have, that it's not *his* fault he's stuck here, all alone. What happened? Once upon a time he expected only good of himself. He believed in the purity of his heart and all his intentions. But something happened. He was mistaken. No good has come out of anything he has done. Nothing good at all.

On the way home the car gets caught in a parade along Avenue Edouard VII—blue-jacketed sailors and soldiers marching down the avenue bearing banners, drums and horns echoing. His thoughts flitter. Rent, driver, bills, refrigerator, food, cigarettes. Käthe.

Wolfsgrub

rau Mohr!"

Käthe stops scything. How long has Seethaler been calling her? He's down by the house, waving. Sweat drips down her grass-flecked arms. Her blouse clings to her back. She's been mowing a corner of the upper meadow all morning. It's a job she enjoys. It helps ease her lower-back pain. Mohr always said exercise was the best antidote to pain. Kircher, the local doctor, vehemently disagrees, but his advice—rest and more rest—neither is viable nor has helped her much. Only since resuming outdoor work has she begun to feel better. Her growing strength is compounded by a sense of accomplishment. This year, she won't have to buy hay for half the winter. In a few days, Daibler will come by with his new machine and bale what she's cut. Minna and Ziggy can graze the upper meadow through the fall.

Seethaler has been digging all morning. With any luck he'll be finished by evening and she'll have full use of the kitchen again. People are always telling her to update the plumbing in the house, but even if she could afford to, she's used to the simplicity here, likes living in the twilight of a previous age. The old farmhouse is her only refuge from

the half-idea of modernity. In the larger scheme of things, she's only here temporarily—its current guest.

A breeze blows. She puts down the scythe, rewraps her braid, feeling the wind on the back of her neck, a brief shiver of pleasure. Suddenly there are screams coming from the house. She races down the hill; just as she reaches the bottom, Eva and her friends, Lisa and Ursula, burst out the front door and race off, shrieking with laughter.

"Stop!"

Surprised, the children come to a stop.

"What are you doing?"

The girls glance around, sheepish, except for Eva, who is trying to keep from laughing.

Seethaler appears, holding his shovel.

"What happened?"

Lisa and Ursula exchange guilty looks but defer to Eva, whose eyes sparkle with mischief.

"Come here." She takes Eva by the hand. "You're covered in black. Let me look at you."

The girls edge forward, lips pursed tightly.

"You've been playing with the stove."

"No, Mama," Eva says.

"Why are you covered in soot? I've told you not to play with the stove."

"We weren't lighting it, Mama."

"What were you doing?"

"Nothing."

"Don't lie, Eva."

"I promise, Mama. We weren't lighting the stove."

"Then why are you covered in soot?"

As Eva opens her mouth to speak, a banging erupts inside the house. "Who's in the house?"

The girls defer again to Eva. "Martin."

"Martin?"

The girls nod.

Käthe starts toward the house.

"Wait, Mama! We'll get him!" The girls race ahead and disappear inside.

Käthe glances at Seethaler, who is calmly leaning on his shovel. "I'll be out in a minute."

Seethaler nods.

She finds Eva opening the brass door of the big ceramic stove. Martin is shrieking, stuffed into the vent chamber. She sweeps the trio of girls aside, takes firm hold of the little boy's kicking legs, and pulls the terrified four-year-old out of the stove by his feet. The child is covered with soot from head to toe. "Whose idea was this?"

"We were just playing a game," Eva stammers.

The girls are now all on the verge of tears. The little boy's face is smeared with soot and mucus. "Bring me a basin and towel." The girls vanish instantly.

"They said they would leave the door open," Martin sobs. "And they closed it!"

Käthe strokes the boy's hair. "It's going to be all right."

"It was daaaark."

"What they did was cruel, and they are going to be punished."

This seems to comfort Martin, and when the girls return with the basin and the washcloth, Käthe orders them to apologize. The girls begin crying again. "You should be ashamed of yourselves."

"It was only a joke," Eva mutters.

"Do you see anybody laughing?" Käthe finishes wiping the boy's face and arms. "Now, how on earth did you fit inside that tiny space? You're a regular Houdini!"

Martin glances at his tormentors, wiping away tears, shifting nervously.

"What a trick!" Käthe waves an arm. "Like magic. *Simsalabim!*"
Martin smiles.

"You must have rubber bones!" She wrings out the washcloth and
turns to the girls. "Now, take Martin home and tell his mother what
you did. Tell her you are sorry and that I said you must wash his
clothes."

The girls glance at one another with a mixture of skepticism and relief. "Should we bring the clothes back here with us?" Eva wants to
know.

"Of course. Unless she asks you to wash them there. Tell her she
will have them back spotless."

The girls become excited by this new project and lead ever-compliant
Martin away. Käthe sees them to the front gate, then goes around to
the side of the house, where Seethaler is squatting over the narrow
trench he has dug. "No broken bones?"

"Just the usual mischief."

Seethaler points into the ditch. "Ceramic."

The trench is nearly an arm's length deep. Seethaler leans down,
dips his hand into the puddling water, and removes a shard of broken
pipe. "Collapsed all the way to the tank."

"How did it collapse?"

Seethaler leans back on his haunches. His mustache is damp and
flecked with bits of mud. "Roots get inside, crack it. It's old."

"Can you replace it?"

"Of course. With cast iron, too." He reaches into the trench, tugs
out a handful of mucky black vegetation, tosses it aside.

"How old do you think it is?"

"It doesn't matter once the roots get down into them and they begin to crack."

"How long will it take?"

Seethaler reaches for his shovel and stands up. "As soon as I can get
the pipe. That's the hardest part these days."

"And how much will it cost?"

"Was kostet dännn därrrr ganzä Bärg?" Seethaler laughs. He thrusts the shovel into the mound of upturned dirt, then paces off the distance from the opening of the tank. At the kitchen window he turns and repeats the line from Mohr's play, sweeping his arm in mock theater. Käthe can't help smiling at his silliness. *Platingruben in Tulpen* had been a big hit. It had been commissioned directly by the Ganghofer-Thoma-Bühne, a community drama group. The line—How much for the whole mountain?—had become a running joke, locally.

Seethaler slaps his thigh. "The part about the stockings. Remember that?"

"How can I forget?"

Seethaler launches into an impersonation. "'Stockings? Why, they're for catching trout, I tell you! *Zum Forellenfangen!* They swim like the devil—*zack zack*—right into the things!'"

Käthe begins to laugh. He's got it down perfectly. The crusty old mountain yokel confronted for the first time by a pair of women's stockings. *Zum Forellenfangen!* For catching trout! After the play completed its run, a clothing store in Egern had put a sign up on a stocking display as a joke. *Zum Forellenfangen!* Now a new sign in the window reads: *Kaufe nicht bei Juden.* Don't buy from Jews. Last year the store had been Aryanized. The Jewish owner, Leo Wolf, had emigrated with his family to Canada.

"It's Grauvogel, isn't it?" Seethaler says. "The spitting image."

"People say that, but I know for a fact Mohr didn't have anyone specific in mind when he wrote it."

"Doesn't matter. Everybody thinks its old Grauvogel, and that's all that counts." He laughs, swipes his forehead with a sweaty forearm, pulls the shovel from the mound of dirt. Then, as if seized by a sudden change of heart, he thrusts the shovel back into the ground and turns to Käthe. "Dr. Mohr is never coming back, is he?"

The question catches her by surprise. She brushes back a strand of hair.

"He's still in China, isn't he?"

"That's right."

Seethaler plunges the shovel into the dirt and pulls it out and plunges it in again. Käthe resists the urge to say anything more, or to appease his creeping embarrassment. She wants him to know that she is bearing her husband's absence just painfully enough to make the subject off limits. To him and anyone else. Mohr must not become a topic of local gossip. Best of all would be for him to be forgotten completely. She glances into the trench. "How much do you need for the job?"

"Was kostet dännn därrrr ganzä Bärg?" Seethaler repeats, as if granting the change of topic.

She obliges him with a slight smile. "Take as much time as you like," she tells him. "I'll be in the stalls."

She has put off cleaning Minna's stall all morning. The cow has been grazing in the upper meadow since sunrise. She is close to the end of her productive years and Käthe has already decided not to replace her, and to start getting milk from Berghammer.

Midday sunlight pours through the open doors of the barn, narrow slivers of light filter through gaps in the siding. She takes down a shovel and a large metal pail. How will she manage this new domain, this secret life? How will she maintain the distance she must now keep—from friends, neighbors, and acquaintances, people she's never once felt oppressed by? She has become the custodian of a secret. It's frightening.

When the stall is finished, she sits down to eat an apple on an old stump that serves as a doorstop for the barn. Particles of straw and dust float through the open doors on beams of light. In the distance, she can hear the girls returning from Martin's. She owes Otto a letter, and a birthday card to Tante Elisabeth, who is turning seventy-five. The old woman still lives in the Heilwigstrasse house. After the war, the house was sold with the stipulation that Elisabeth would keep the upstairs floor for herself. Käthe has always felt sorry for the old woman. She admires her strength, her independence, but also wonders if love—the capacity for it—can be eroded by loneliness. When Mohr left, he took something of her away with him. Maybe that was what he took—her capacity for love, and the rest of her that remains here is incomplete, has no relation to what was before. She bites into the apple, chews slowly, deliberately. No. If Tante Elisabeth has remained alone all her life, it isn't because she *couldn't* love.

Finishing the apple, she drops the core into the pail, and stands up. As she is emptying the pail onto the compost heap, Seethaler appears.

"Should be about two weeks," he says, pulling a rag from his rear pocket.

"Two weeks? Is that the soonest?"

"If we're lucky."

Another two weeks using the outside privy and hauling dirty water. At least it's not the middle of winter. "How much will it cost?"

Seethaler occupies himself with getting the dirt off his hands. He smiles, stuffs the rag back into the pocket of his trousers. "Nothing, Frau Mohr. I'll do it for nothing."

"That's impossible."

"Yes yes yes. I won't take any money from you, Frau Mohr."

"I can't have you doing it for nothing." Käthe turns to leave, swinging the pail for emphasis.

"Wait," Seethaler calls. "I am not a plumber, Frau Mohr. I am an engineer." He pulls the rag from his pocket once again. She has no idea what the man is getting at. Seethaler rubs his hands vigorously with the cloth. "My father became sick and I had to come back home to help him with the business."

"All the more reason why I must insist on paying for the work."

"May I sit?" Without waiting for an answer, he sits down on the chopping block next to the woodpile. "I never thought I'd be stuck back here. I went to school so that I could have a career, something my father could only dream of." He continues working the rag between his hands. "And here I am. Right back where I started."

"Is your father's health improving?"

"As much as it ever will. That's not the point. The problem is finding work. I can't leave now because I don't have a job to go back to."

"I'm sorry."

"Nothing to be sorry about. It's just how things worked out."

Käthe's unease begins to dissipate. "I must still insist on paying you."

Seethaler glances up the hill in the direction of the grazing cows. "May I speak personally for a moment?"

"I thought you already were."

He leans to one side and stuffs the rag into his pocket. "I have always admired you and Dr. Mohr. The way you live here."

She looks at him, puzzled.

"I mean, as outsiders."

"We're hardly outsiders! We've lived here in this house for nearly twenty years."

"That's what I mean. You live here, but you are also outsiders, and have all your connections."

"Connections?" Once again, she becomes uneasy. "I wish I knew what you were talking about."

"Dr. Mohr was always away traveling. Now he is in China. Those are all connections."

What is the man going on about? "If you want to call being halfway around the world a connection, I won't argue."

"And the visitors that have come here to see you," Seethaler continues. "Heinrich George. Elizabeth Bergner. You think people didn't notice when film stars came to visit?"

Käthe laughs. "That was years ago."

"Doesn't matter. People remember. Look, Frau Mohr. I swore I would never come back here except to visit. I had a job in the city, a good job. Now here I am, stuck right back in the middle of nowhere! As Dr. Mohr would have said, 'What a swindle.'" He shakes his head. "'What a swindle, to search for life on the back roads when there are only highways.'"

The sudden earnestness is embarrassing. Käthe swings the pail.

"I'm not just some yokel, Frau Mohr. I've read your husband's books."

"Then you would also know that he hates highways." She smiles, trying to think of a way to extricate herself. The trio of girls appears at the far end of the garden. Käthe calls, "Eva! Go and fetch Minna down from the field." She watches the girls start uphill toward the pasture, wishing for a quick end to the conversation.

"I will not take money from you, Frau Mohr," Seethaler says with finality.

Käthe turns to him sharply. "Theo Seethaler, please, just tell me how much for the job so I can get back to my work."

"Then pay for the pipe," Seethaler says, backing off. "I won't charge you to put it in."

She flushes, wanting to get rid of him and return to work. "Name your price and I will pay it."

Seethaler smiles as if he has won something and goes off to gather his tools. "I will send the bill next week."

Käthe is shaken, and considers calling the job off, hiring someone else. What does he want? What is he trying to prove? The last thing she can afford now is to draw attention. People remember, he said. What she wants is for them to forget. She returns to the stall and tries to busy herself, waiting for him to leave. *Oh, Mohr! The time has come. I am so tired of waiting.*

"Mama! You're crying!" Eva leads Minna into the barn. Käthe sets the broom aside and opens the door to Minna's stall. "What's wrong, Mama?"

"Just a little dust." She wipes her eyes.

Eva puts Minna into the stall and closes the gate. Käthe is overwhelmed by a strange sense of disembodiment, as if she has lost her power of self, is merely observing it from an uncertain distance.

"Lisa says Minna's nose is too dry," Eva says. "Feel it, Mama."

Käthe places a hand on the cow's nose and lingers for a moment, feeling the animal's breath in her cupped palm. She strokes Minna's head, pats the broad white patch between her eyes, struggling to regain equilibrium. "Yes, she's fine."

"I knew it," Eva shouts to her friends loitering in the doorway, waiting for her to rejoin their game. "Mama says she's fine."

The girls run back outside together. Käthe sits down on the chopping block just inside the barn door. She feels distances and distances, a long ribbon drawing apart inside her of empty distances, and remains in the barn with Minna until Seethaler drives away in his truck.

"WHY DO PEOPLE sleep?" Eva wants to know.

Käthe turns out the light and opens the windows. Eva insists on keeping the windows of her room shut until the lights are out. To keep out bugs, she says. But the house is full of crickets and little moths and other flying insects. How many times has she explained that it really makes no difference whether the windows are open or closed? She sits on the end of the bed. Why do people sleep? A good question. She squeezes her daughter's feet underneath the covers. "I think it must be so that we can dream."

"You can have dreams without being asleep."

"But there's a difference between daydreaming and the dreams you have when you're asleep, don't you think?"

Eva considers this for a moment, then nods in agreement. "Tell me another story about Papa."

Käthe leans against the wall and gazes out the open window. The sky often becomes slightly cloudy around sunset, the air more humid. If it rains overnight she will have to wait another day to finish mowing the top meadow. At supper it occurred to her that she didn't have any luggage, at least not the sort for a trip halfway around the world. What does she need? Hiasl and his wife have agreed to care for the house while they're gone. Käthe has no idea how long that could be. The old woodcutter and his wife aren't concerned. They're more than happy to

come and live in Wolfsgrub—forever if necessary. But luggage. You need luggage.

"How long was it before he could walk?" Eva asks.

Käthe isn't listening. Her thoughts have a way of wandering off in all directions at bedtime.

"How long was it?" Eva asks again.

"How long was what?"

"Before Papa could walk."

Käthe smooths her skirt, tries to gather her thoughts. "Well. The pain lingered for a long time," she begins. At bedtime Eva's eyes always seem bigger, browner, wonder-filled. "Then a great big help arrived. *Improvisationen im Juni* was accepted by the Residenztheater in Munich."

"Papa's play." Eva pulls up the covers.

"That little six-*pfennig* postcard with the signature of the director scrawled at the bottom—I can't tell you how much it meant. It was an indescribable feeling for both of us, but especially for Papa, because it meant that at last he would be able to provide for us. I think that was even more important to him than having his work accepted."

"Mama?"

"Yes?"

"I'm thirsty."

Eva dashes to the bathroom. A wedge of yellow light from the hallway falls across the floor. Käthe slides forward, lies flat on her back, hands folded across her stomach, looking up at the ceiling. She can hear the tap running as Eva fills a glass with water and drinks in little sighing gulps, wipes her mouth on her sleeve, sets the glass down on the porcelain with a click, switches off the light. When she returns, the silence in the house seems denser. She slips back underneath the covers and they lie quietly in the dark for a time before Käthe resumes the story.

"Soon everything began to take shape. Stieler, the director, came down to discuss production. The premiere date was set. Papa was so filled with joy that his pain became more bearable—even though his feet remained black and blue, and hard."

Wutzi, asleep underneath the desk, lets out a little yelp that causes looks to pass between mother and daughter. Eva's questions about sleep and dreams seem funny now, pertinent as they are to dog life. They watch for further signs, propped up on elbows, tired out from a full day of work and play. There was a time when Käthe avoided going to bed too early, and enjoyed the quiet late-night hours. Now she looks forward to sleep, is wary of the night, avoids it the way, as a child, she avoided strangers. Eva sinks back onto her pillow and waits for the story to resume.

"In February the cold broke and the snow began to melt. Stieler came again. Papa got himself all worked up about the direction, was worried that the pace would be too slow, not enough tempo. 'It's too slow,' he told Stieler, 'too drawn out! The audience will get restless.' And Stieler would say '*Mensch!* Don't worry, I'll give you tempo!'

"Our excitement grew and grew, and one day Papa said to me, 'You go to the premiere.' 'I can't leave you here alone,' I told him. 'Of course you can!' he said. 'No. I won't go without you. We always talked about how when your first play was performed, we would sit together in the theater! I can't go.' 'You must.'" She clasps her hands, makes pleading gestures, hither, thither, as a great smile spreads over Eva's face. "'Please! You must!' 'No. No. No.' 'Please!' 'No!' And back and forth and back and forth it went. He pleaded and pleaded until, finally, I agreed to go."

"You and Papa like to argue," says Eva, still amused.

"And it didn't stop there. The next day we were arguing again because Papa said he didn't want anybody in the house while I was gone. Would you believe it? He was just being impossible. He couldn't get out of bed, but insisted on remaining alone in the house until I came back. By then I was too tired to argue. I put food next to the bed, closed the house up, and walked all the way to Tegernsee."

"You walked?"

"There wasn't a bus in those days and we didn't have bicycles yet. I took the train with nothing but the house keys in my pocket."

"Were you scared?"

"Not scared. Nervous."

"Because of the train ride?"

Käthe laughs. "Not the train ride! The opening of the play. Would the audience come? Yes. The audience came. A full house. The curtain went up. A beautiful set. The old duchess looked enchanting, they picked just the right woman for the part. And the butler, well, he seemed a little too old and rickety. Na, I thought, doesn't matter. And then the old Duchess started to sing, '*Brüderlein fein, Brüderlein fein, einmal muss geschieden sein.*' Much too sweetly."

"How was she supposed to sing?"

"I thought it should be rougher, more cabaret style."

"Like how? Show me."

"You want me to sing?"

An eager nod.

"I don't know if I can."

"Try, Mama."

Käthe clears her throat, attempts the growling Marlene Dietrich tenor. "*Brüderlein fein, Brüderlein fein, einmal muss geschieden sein.*"

"Sing the rest, Mama."

"I can't remember the rest."

Eva begs, "Come on, Mama!"

"I can't." She touches her fingertips to her throat. Singing was something she had once enjoyed. With Mohr playing the accordion. "Anyway. It had become real. Papa's play. I was seeing it, hearing it. There it was."

Eva sits up. "What did you do?"

"Well, I didn't cry. Everything was too real. The audience was absorbed. But, for God's sake, it was too slow! They were drawing it out. Stieler promised tempo. Your father drove himself crazy worrying they wouldn't get it right. 'Tempo! Tempo!' He told Stieler. 'Make sure to get the tempo.' And here they were slogging out every syllable, endlessly dragging. Trying too hard! For God's sake! The audience was fidgeting, squirming in their seats, rattling their programs. Oh, dear God, I thought. It's all over."

Eva is fully engrossed, legs crossed beneath the sheet, hands in her lap.

"A flop! It's a flop!" She slaps her hand on the bed. "How could they? How could Stieler? Dragging slower and slower. It's all over. Finally the prologue ended and the story began. Hohorst as the duchess. Faber as Tomkinow. Both were beautiful. The curtain fell at the end of the first act. Cheering. Tremendous applause. Oh, I thought, if only it could just stop here. It can't keep on like this. Can't it just be over now?"

The animated storytelling has roused Wutzi from his slumber under the table. He ambles over to the side of the bed, accepts a pat on the head from Eva, and sits. Käthe reaches out and gives him a pat, too. Funny how excited she's become, a rising chorus of bottled-up memories. Even the dog is listening.

"Then the curtain rises. Act Two. Everything quicker. Good. People are laughing. They feel more comfortable with the piece. They're enjoying themselves, not bored. Curtain. Intermission. All talk, laugh, are happy. I stay in my seat, sink down into it so nobody can see me. I don't want to see anyone, either. Stieler comes up. 'It's going wonderfully! Just stay calm. Don't worry. If they can pull off the third act.' And then, again, they're back on stage. Now they'll get bored. Everything's been laid out. There's no more suspense. Endings are always hard. Oh, please! Please, dear God. Just this one last act! The audience was quiet, inscrutable. The scene went quickly, and no mistakes. Then the curtain fell."

She brings her hands together in front of her face to describe a closing curtain.

Pause.

"And then?" Eva wiggles. "Go on! Don't stop!"

"And it was over."

"No, Mama. What happened then?"

"What happened when?"

"When the curtain went down!"

"Then they went wild!" Käthe throws her arms up. "They shouted, they whistled, they clapped, called for the actors, the director, called 'Mohr! Mohr! Mohr!' The curtain parted. The players came out holding hands. They bowed. Then the leads, alone, one by one. The duchess and Stieler, hand in hand. Applause, whistles. And then they began to chant, 'Mohr! Mohr! Mohr!' Stieler appeared on the stage. The audience fell silent. He said that, unfortunately, the author was not present due to a bad accident, but that he would surely be pleased to know how well his play was received. Then he withdrew behind the curtain. And the audience would not stop clapping."

"What did you do then?"

"Me? I put my head in my lap and cried like a baby. The purest joy. Some friends were sitting behind me in the loge and they took me back to the hotel. Rote Hahn in Stachus. I couldn't go out, couldn't celebrate. All I wanted was to go straight to bed. And the next morning I got the first train and raced home."

"What did Papa do when you gave him the news? Did he really jump out of bed and try to do a jig? Did he do that?"

"Who told you that?"

"You did! You said he jumped up and tried to dance around the room but then fell down and you had to help him back into bed."

"Well, then, I suppose that's what he did." She pauses here, searching for the next thread. Strange how the theater of memory brightens in places, dims in others. "All I see now is Papa lying in bed, beaming, his feet high up on cushions. I can't really remember much of what happened afterward."

"Did you have a celebration?"

"Not really. People telephoned. Papa asked for endless details, every little thing. There was no end to it. Then came the reviews. And they were all good. One said, *Hosanna! A new poet!* Papa immediately started writing a new play. *Das Gelbe Zelt.* It was a complete and total failure. But *Improvisationen im Juni* was performed all over Germany. Rave reviews everywhere."

The moon has risen over the Wallberg, and the room is brighter. There are so many tiny details. Her thoughts return to Seethaler and his strangeness. The closing of the school, finding a tutor. She yawns, glances at Eva, who is still wide awake. Wutzi has gone to sleep again at the foot of the bed. All of it is dear to her, and precious; everything now, and everything that is gone.

Outside, an evening breeze; all around, everything is ripening. The delphinium crop this year will be the largest ever. She is selling bulbs as well as flowers now. She closes her eyes, leans her head against the wall. How badly she misses him. She misses the sweet names he called her, and even the not-so-sweet excesses—of love, of anger—that sometimes overcame them, and left each quieter afterward, and a little frightened. Also closer, more soulfully knit. Now he wants to climb Mount Fuji. Why? She sits for a few moments longer, then opens her eyes. Moonlight. How much does a half-decent trunk cost these days? She gets up, kisses Eva on the forehead, astonished at how beautiful her little girl has become, then crosses the hall to her room and falls into bed.

Shanghai

ong has finally asked if he may bring his wife to stay in the apartment and Mohr has agreed. Although he knows full well she has been living there for some time, he's pretended not to notice. All through June and July, there has been heavy fighting near Wong's village in Hopei. His daughter is now living at a Catholic mission. His son, a corporal in the 53rd Army, is stationed in Paoting. The plight of Wong's family is troubling, and so is the expanding war in the north. The streets of the Settlement are crowded with refugees streaming in from all parts of China. Last night gunshots during a police eviction in the courtyard behind the apartment building. Whole families, squatting there for weeks.

For a week now, Mohr has been taking foxglove. *Digitalis purpurea.* A Chinese apothecary in Foochow Road prepared a tincture according to his specifications. An 0.17 percent solution he takes in doses of four drams per day. The results have been good. No morning flutters, no shortness of breath. His pulse is now quite regular. He feels alert and energetic. Even his shoes seem to fit better.

Last night he telephoned to check on Vogel, who is still feeling ill. "Some kind of intestinal thing," he said.

"Drink plenty of fluids," Mohr advised, then told him about his plan to visit Japan.

There was a brief pause. "Why Japan?" Vogel asked.

Mohr couldn't help smiling to himself. "I've always wanted to climb Fujiyama."

"Are you out of your mind? This is no time for vacations. You don't even have a passport."

"My identity card from the Municipal Police is all I need."

"Who told you that?"

"The Municipal Police, and the agent at the steamship company. Nothing to worry about. Completely ordinary."

"Completely ridiculous is what it is. Really. Why are you doing this, Max? Why won't you listen to me?"

"Just a short vacation. I plan to come right back."

Vogel grunted and didn't pursue the topic. They talked for some minutes longer. Vogel seemed frailer than usual. "Should I come out and check on you?" Mohr asked.

"Don't bother."

"I can be there first thing in the morning."

"Not necessary, Max. It'll take more than medicine to cure my problems."

And with that the conversation ended.

Today is Sunday and Mohr has decided to go for a drive in the country. In the rear seat of the car, map open in his lap, he watches the passing landscape. Next to him is a basket of food prepared by Wong's wife, and *The Prose Poetry of Su Tung Po,* which he bought a year ago and has been reading in bits and pieces. The perfect guidebook for traveling in China—not by palanquin, but by V8 Ford.

"Wait! Stop!"

Wong glances into the mirror. Mohr gestures behind them, to a copse of bushes and some sort of earthworks set among the fields. Wong pulls over, puts the car into reverse with a look of mild bemuse-

ment. It is a cemetery. Unlike the usual tumbledown interments he's seen and photographed on earlier excursions, these graves are presided over by clay horses, bigger than life, spotted with lichen and dirt-blown. He stalks among them with his camera, patting their flanks as if they are living creatures. An old man appears. Wong shouts to him from over by the car. The old man shouts back in a gravelly voice that seems blown straight off the fields.

Wong saunters over, exchanges a few words with the old man, then turns and says to Mohr, "Master pay looksee."

Mohr hands over a few coins, holds up the camera. The old man looks on with a tinge of disgust.

"No wantchee. No can do," Wong says.

The old man stumps off. Mohr puts his camera away, resumes his inspection. He lights a cigarette, and asks Wong to photograph him standing next to one of the clay horses, smiling at the thought of himself as a tourist. No, not a tourist. A tramp.

They return to the car, resume their drive. Mohr stretches his legs across the backseat and watches the countryside fly past. For the moment, he has no worries; is looking forward to packing up and living out of a suitcase—even if only for a few weeks. What made him think Agnes would come away with him to Japan? The whole thing makes him feel bad now. To whom should he apologize?

To Käthe.

The car speeds along in the direction of Soochow. The previous year, he had had dinner there with Vogel at the Garden Hotel restaurant, served by the most obnoxious maître d'hôtel outside Paris. This time he'll have lunch in the open air. A picnic. Mohr wonders what Wong thinks about this little expedition. Drive to Soochow, eat, return to Shanghai. Does Wong wonder why he would want to take photographs in a graveyard? Does he wonder what amusement there is in driving all this distance? Mindless motor touring.

"Stop!" Mohr calls again. Wong slows the car with a "Now what?"

glance in the rearview mirror. On the outskirts of Soochow, the fields are ripe with watermelon. The harvest is in full swing; melons are being loaded onto carts and wagons. Mohr approaches one of the carts, covered by a film of reddish dirt, waves to a young boy hoisting two large yellow melons. An elderly man shoos the boy away with a flap of his hand, and gestures for Mohr to select one. The melons are stacked precariously high. He selects a medium-sized one, wipes the dust from it, and presents it. The man holds up five fingers.

Mohr shakes his head, holds up one finger.

A group of boys has stopped to watch the transaction. Mohr is thinking of the vendors at the corner of Yates Road, how they spray their stacked wares with water to keep them looking fresh, a fine, expert mist—from the mouth. He can't count the cholera cases he's seen in the last two years, but the piles of glistening watermelon slices are what come to mind every time he treats one.

The man holds up three fingers.

Mohr shakes his head again, determined not to be taken for an ignorant tourist. He knows exactly what a watermelon costs on Bubbling Well Road, after it has made the trip down Soochow Creek, been unloaded directly off the barge onto a pushcart and tugged through city traffic by a shirtless coolie. He can buy a large, uncut melon directly in front of his apartment building for three *tael*. He holds out one finger.

The man holds up two. The sooty-faced little boys stand behind him, craning. Mohr's resolve vanishes. He digs two tael from his pocket and hands them over to the man, who shoos the boys away, back to work. With the fruit tucked under his arm, he returns to the car. Three little boys are merrily inspecting the front grill. The radiator is steaming in the heat. Wong opens the door. Mohr sets the melon on the rear seat, is about to get in, but notices the trio of boys standing off to the side. He beckons to them.

Wong frowns.

"Have looksee," he tells the boys.

Wong disapproves, shaking his head vigorously.

Mohr laughs. "Maskee. Maskee." In an instant the three boys are in the back of the car, tumbling and bouncing and peering into the frontseat. Wong refuses to let go of the door. He calls the boys out, barking angrily as they tumble off with waves and backward glances, then climbs behind the wheel.

Mohr pats the dust from his trousers and stands for a time by the roadside, watching the harvest continue. Flat fields shimmer in the heat. Birds reel overhead. A thousand little pictures of summers past— of cows and sheep and goats standing at the trough in the meadow, the slopes of the Wallberg. Käthe's delphinium. The mere thought of those blue flowers is enough to make him feel that he has received his due, everything he deserves. Why China? Käthe asked up on the roof. He has an entire list of reasons that, taken together, yield a bundle of complexes that can only be disentangled slowly, and with reference to ever-larger turning wheels. He smiles to himself. Käthe says he's complicated, but he's not complicated. It's the world that is complicated. All he wants is to be reunited with his family; he wants it so badly he can already see the breakfast tray and flowers and singing magpies and folded newspapers lying on the table, a succession of trouble-free todays where before and after have merged with one another.

All at once an idea for a poem springs to mind. Excited, he returns to the car, digs into his bag for pencil and paper. As they drive on, Mohr scribbles.

The path that leads from my door to your door
winds through a busy world where everyone is a stranger
and when at last I arrive on your doorstep
to find that you have set out to look for me
the world will, for a moment
seem small

Near Soochow, the traffic becomes dense. Roadside shacks, tea-houses, little hotels. They arrive, at last, in the center of the compact, canal-webbed city. Traffic is at a standstill. Mohr considers the situation, then takes the map and camera bag and gets out of the car. "Drive hotel-side, Wong. *Dung o li.* Wait my come."

"Garden Hotel?" Wong asks.

He leans into the window and repeats. "Garden Hotel. *Dung o li.* Hotel-side. *Dung o li.*"

Wong shoos him off with a friendly wave. The car jolts forward. Mohr stops at a tea stall to get his bearings. A man pokes him on the shoulder, points at his dust-covered shoes. Mohr shakes his head, and the man quietly withdraws. It was autumn when he was here with Vogel. The city hadn't seemed all that crowded. They'd driven straight to the Garden Hotel, walked along the canal after lunch. It had been a pleasant afternoon, and how familiar everything had seemed—the cobblestone alleys lined with one-story, tile-roofed buildings, latticed woodwork, shops open onto the street. A picture postcard. Vogel had said something to the effect that if it weren't for the Garden Hotel there would be noplace to eat anywhere. Mohr had rebuked him by detouring down every little side street.

He makes his way through crowded alleys and narrow lanes to the North Gate. The smell of joss sticks, heavy in the air. The area around the gate is packed with shrines and crowded with peddlers, beggars, and ragged children running in all directions. On a low wall near the gate, he sits down to catch his breath, begins to photograph. He takes in the entire scene through the camera lens—not in large sweeps but in isolated moments: A woman holding a young child by the hand, an old man in a long, quilted coat leading a goat on a rope, a Taoist monk in a tall conical hat, porters with poles across their shoulders, rickshaws going in all directions. A large black Packard shoots out of a side street, honking the horn and scattering people. A tea cart is upended, hot coals spill onto the pavement, which the angry vendor picks up

and hurls at the passing car. Excited by the commotion, Mohr starts
down a side street, and is stopped short at the sound of a gong being
struck. The sound blossoms into a steady, deafening crash. Nobody
seems to take much notice. He steps under the awning of a shop and
glances around. A man eats a bowl of congee, blowing steam and slurp-
ing spoonfuls of the hot rice gruel into his mouth with grunts of satisfaction. Mohr is short of breath again. He takes out a handkerchief,
wipes the sweat from his forehead, lifts the camera again. A sudden
touch on the shoulder makes him jump.

"Dr. Mohr?"

He spins around.

"I'm sorry. I didn't mean to startle you."

Mohr recognizes his bruised young neighbor from downstairs and recovers his composure by wiping his forehead again. "You surprised me."

The man squatting against the shop wall glances up, then returns
to his congee.

"I saw you across the square, photographing," the man says. "You
didn't you see me? I waved."

"No, I didn't."

"I was standing right over there." He points. Traces of his injuries
are still plain to see. His nose is bent. Slight yellow bruising remains
around his eyes. He is wearing a Panama hat, a blue cotton suit and tie,
and in spite of his dress he seems scruffy and unkempt.

"I'm sorry. I didn't recognize you. And I don't believe I know your
name."

"Granich. Konrad Granich."

They shake hands and Mohr asks, "Did you ever go to hospital? Has
anybody looked at you?"

Granich casts a few darting glances—across the square, toward the
gate, then shakes his head.

"I tried looking in on you once or twice, but you were never at
home."

Granich seems preoccupied, makes no comment.

"Your nose was fractured."

Granich touches his nose, shrugs. "It doesn't hurt."

"Well, there's not much that can be done about it now." Mohr looks in the direction Granich has been glancing. "Come. Walk with me."

Granich waves, backs away.

"Come on. We're both tourists here. Let's walk."

"I can't. I have no time."

"No time?" Mohr laughs, crosses his arms over his chest. "This isn't Berlin. I should think you have all the time in the world!"

With another glance around, Granich shrugs and gives in. A short time later they have walked the entire distance to the Garden Hotel. As they approach the front gate, Mohr spots his car parked near the top of the long driveway. Wong is wiping the windows with a large cloth. "Do you like watermelon?"

Granich is amused. The walk has eased some of his reserve.

"Come and have some with me."

"Not in there," Granich says. "I will not go in that place."

"Why not? It's the finest in Soochow."

Granich shakes his head. "It caters to imperialists."

"Well, as it happens, I hadn't planned to go there, either." Mohr smiles. "I have brought my own watermelon and some food and am going to find a shady spot and sit down for a very unimperial picnic."

Wong acknowledges Granich with a friendly salute, then unpacks the car and leads them to a patch of grass along the banks of a canal. He seems slightly bemused as he helps Mohr spread the blanket in the shade of a tree. "Mister b'long bottom-side Master house," he smiles, by the by.

They sit down only to discover there is no knife to cut the melon with. Wong goes back to the car, retrieves a large cleaver from the trunk. Mohr has never seen it before, wonders what other surprises are hidden away in the car. Wong makes short work of the melon, hands it around. His wife packed a British-style feast of cucumber-and-butter sandwiches, which he proudly offers around, balking at Mohr's insistence that he take one for himself, then giving in with a contented smile.

It's a pleasant setting. Mohr is happy for the company. A slight breeze is blowing. Birds swoop along the canal banks, where the grass is greenest. The heat is bearable in the small patch of shade. Granich removes his hat and his jacket, rolls up his sleeves, and stretches out on the blanket. He begins talking about the situation in Spain, the buildup of German naval forces in the Mediterranean, and then turns to what he terms the "capitulation of the Chinese worker's struggle."

"Capitulation?"

Granich peers up. "To the war against the Japanese. The only salvation of the workers and peasants of China is to struggle independently against the two armies, against the Chinese army in the same manner as against the Japanese army."

Mohr takes this in, slightly curious. "Is that the Party line?"

Granich nods.

"But won't the Chinese have a better chance if they aren't divided among themselves?"

"Chiang Kai-shek is no ally of workers and peasants," Granich protests, sitting up. "He'll betray us at the first opportunity!"

"Us"? The fervent solidarity is amusing. Granich is about to continue, but Mohr cuts him off. "That beating, it wasn't bandits, was it?"

Granich shrugs, doesn't answer.

"How old are you, Granich?"

"Twenty-five," he answers moodily and puts his hat over his face.

Mohr fishes his cigarettes from the pocket of his shirt, then stands up and strolls down to the edge of the water. A group of coolies taking a midday break has been watching, fascinated at the sight of two Europeans sharing a meal with a Chinese. Mohr nods to them as he passes, then continues a short distance along the canal. In the distance he can see the Tiger Balm Gardens, another of the places he visited with Vogel. A barge passes, loaded with produce. A little boy sitting on the gunwales waves, and Mohr waves back. Contentment is an enduring and unchanging sufficiency. He recalls the line from Lao Tsu, and wonders how long twenty-five-year-old Granich has been involved in politics. At his age, Mohr was stuck out on the front line of an insane war, and already disgusted with ideology. Poor him, poor you. What prospects among scattered fragments, missing links, lost connections?

Suddenly he is restless, and wants to start back.

Granich is sitting on the blanket, knees pulled up to his chest, puffing on a cigarette. Wong has repacked the basket and returned to the car. "May I offer you a ride back to Shanghai?" Mohr asks.

"No. No, thank you. I still have things to do here." Granich rolls down his sleeves, puts on his jacket and hat. He seems nervous once again.

"Can I drop you someplace on the way?"

Granich's features contract. "No." He shakes his head. "That wouldn't be a good idea."

"Oh? Why not?"

Granich ignores the question, stands up.

Mohr picks up the blanket and begins folding, eyeing Granich. "You have nothing to fear being seen with me. I'm not mixed up in politics."

"Oh? Just another innocent victim," he quips.

The sarcasm rubs Mohr the wrong way, but he won't be drawn into an argument. "I couldn't have put it better myself." He smiles, and finishes folding the blanket.

Granich softens, seems to appreciate the neutral remark. He puts on his hat, tipping the brim slightly forward and down. "Thanks for the picnic," he says. "I've enjoyed myself."

"Are you sure about that?" Mohr tucks the folded blanket under his arm.

Granich nods. "I'm sure, Doctor." He manages a smile, and starts off with a wave. Mohr watches him descend the little slope to the canal path in his ill-fitting, crumpled suit, waits to see if he'll turn when he reaches the footpath—but he doesn't. Without breaking stride, he slips his hands into his trousers pockets and saunters away, a proud young man, shaken by hatred. Mohr wonders where else their opinions may have collided, what they might have argued about in the car on the way back to Shanghai. Perhaps they wouldn't have talked at all. That would have been best. Better to keep quiet than express yourself feebly.

In the car he remembers an old folk song. Returning Wong's delighted rearview glances, he sings:

Müd bin i, müd bin i
Leg i mi nieder
Packt mi die Lieb
Auf muss i wieder

Tired am I, tired am I
I lay me down
When love comes over me
I must get up again

"You enjoy taking pictures, Dr. Mohr," observes the clerk.

Mohr places the rolls of film on the counter. It's the third time this week that he's been to the shop—Eos Film & Photo—just a short distance down Bubbling Well Road from his apartment.

"If I could fly, I would fly." He smiles, watching as the clerk busies himself making out receipts for each roll of film. Burton is his name. He is freshly combed, crisply attired in a Shantung silk suit, and gives the impression of having come straight to work from a night out on the town.

"Photography is certainly different from flying," he says, keeping up pleasantries.

"You don't think flying and photography have anything in common?"

Burton shakes his head, bemused.

"Gravity is defied. Light is captured."

"Contact sheets or prints?"

"Time also."

Mohr pats his pocket, takes out his cigarettes. The shop smells of film and developing chemicals mingled with tobacco. The plate-glass window, boldly lettered in gold paint, frames the street beyond; a cabinet along one wall contains the newest in camera and photographic equipment, securely locked. He enjoys it in here, a pleasant diversion, a little world apart. "Contact sheets," he says, lighting a cigarette and stepping over to the camera case. "The new Leica?"

"Model G. With Xenon lens and Rapid Rewinder."

Mohr blows a stream of smoke against the glass. On a lower shelf are exposure meters of various makes. He reads the printed advertisement out loud: "Whether shooting in deep shaded woods, or shipboard, or indoors. It will enable you to bring back a perfect photographic record of every trip." He stands, turns. "What do you make of all this picture-taking?"

Burton shrugs. "It keeps us in business—with good customers like you."

"I mean one hundred years from now? When every person living on earth today is dead, and the world has been transformed." Mohr's thoughts begin to race. He glances at the advertising placard. "Will it matter that we made a perfect photographic record of every trip?"

The clerk regards him with bemused caution and shakes his head. Mohr steps back over to the counter. "Have you ever asked *why* you take pictures on holiday?"

"I would say to remember."

"To remember what?"

"The holiday."

Mohr smiles. "Yes. But, isn't it to remind you of the joy you felt on holiday? That's the essential thing. What you *felt*. Can a feeling be preserved in a photograph?"

"I don't know," Burton says in the way clerks have of politely dividing their attention. "Can it?"

"I think so."

"Is that why you do it, then?"

Mohr laughs, shakes his head. "No. I take them to send to my wife. Proof of my existence." He crushes his cigarette into the ashtray at the side of the counter. *"Einmal jedes, nur einmal. Einmal und nicht mehr. . . ."*

"I'm afraid I don't understand German, Dr. Mohr."

"Everything just once. Once and no more. From a great German poet, Rilke."

A polite nod tells him the young Englishman doesn't know who or what he's talking about. Never mind. His thoughts continue to wander. Can feelings be preserved in photographs? The way love letters can be written on a typewriter? Remember those last weeks in Berlin, Lindenstrasse, looking down on the tram stop? A thousand telephone calls to blasé consular officials who wouldn't follow up, who made him wait on the line and then simply hung up? He called to tell Käthe he was coming back via Prague, where doors were still open, and Eva came to the telephone and said, "Papa, please come home soon!" After that all he could bring himself to do was sit at the window and watch the trams. He sat there all day, alone and helpless, trying to talk himself into feeling big and ambitious once again.

Burton passes the receipts across the counter. "Your photos will be ready on Wednesday morning. Should I charge to your account?"

Mohr slips the receipts into his pocket, feeling slightly absurd. "Please," he says, and leaves the shop.

On the way home he stops in at Café Louis. They make a delicious apple strudel, a large slice of which he buys to take home. The Viennese owners are pleasant and friendly. He's never lingered there the way many of the clientele do, discussing events and news and passing along job tips and jai-alai odds. Talk today is about the sinking of the *Deutschland* off Ibiza and the subsequent German bombardment of Almería. A shame it had been merely the ship called *Deutschland,* he'd like to say. He's begun to feel not only anti- but *un*-German, and hearing his native tongue spoken on the street now places him at an odd distance—from himself. He is learning to feel more comfortable in the English-speaking world, but it will never be a home to him. He's glad for the anonymity this big city offers, accepts the boxed pastry from the anemic-looking woman with a polite *danke schön,* and shuffles out the door with a sense of having eluded her questioning one more time.

Even in early evening it can be brutally hot this time of year. Mohr holds the neatly tied box in both hands, making sure the warm pastry doesn't come through the bottom. He walks quickly, threading his way down the crowded sidewalk. At Yates Road, the sweat-drenched traffic policeman blows his whistle furiously as Mohr dodges a trolley car coming around the corner. Horns blare. All he wants is to get back home, take a cool shower, eat the strudel, read the evening newspaper, and go to bed.

As he enters his apartment building, a strange man approaches.

"Dr. Mohr? May I have a word with you?" The man displays a brass, star-shaped shield; he is thin, pale, and gives the impression of having been made to wait far too long. "My name is Stubbings, C. I. Stubbings of the Shanghai Municipal Police, Special Branch. I would like to ask a few questions."

Mohr doesn't try to hide his surprise. "You want to talk to me?"

"Just a few questions." The policeman glances up the sidewalk. "Do you mind if we talk upstairs?"

Mohr beckons him in, too tired to play the game of cheerful insouciance he usually likes to play with authority. He's late paying Settlement taxes, should have sent Wong to deliver the checks last month. But wait, the police don't collect taxes! He ushers the policeman directly into his sitting room. Do they know he is sheltering refugees in the apartment? Zappe is asleep on his perch.

"You were in Soochow yesterday, Doctor."

Startled, Mohr puts the strudel on a side table and sits down behind his desk. "I was, yes."

The policeman smiles, fingers his trim mustache. There are traces of sadness in the man's red-ringed eyes, something that has been driven assiduously away by regular habits and membership in a club.

"Visiting friends?"

Zappe lets out a sudden squawk and begins to peck at the bars of his cage. "No." Mohr shakes his head. "Just tourism." How forthcoming should he be? "And a picnic." He gestures to the chair across the desk. "Please, sit down."

The policeman pulls out the chair, sits down. "A pretty little town, Soochow. Used to go there quite often myself."

Mohr take out his cigarettes, offers them.

Stubbings accepts with a polite nod, and produces a shiny silver cigarette lighter. He leans across the desk, lights Mohr's, then his own. "Let me get right to the point, Doctor." He plucks a fleck of tobacco from the tip of his tongue. "How well do you know Konrad Granich?"

Once again, Mohr is startled. "My neighbor from downstairs?"

The policeman nods.

"Whom are you following? Me or him?"

The policeman gives a slight smirk. "I am merely curious to know how well you know him."

"Not well at all."

"Would you call him a friend?"

"Not exactly, no. But he's a likable enough fellow."

"So, your little picnic together—" Stubbings picks another fleck of tobacco from his tongue. "It wasn't a friendly affair?"

"We met by coincidence, and I invited him to share my lunch."

"I understand." The policeman nods graciously.

"I'm happy to tell you everything I know about Herr Granich. But I'm afraid it won't be of much interest."

"Perhaps not."

"A few weeks ago I patched him up. He'd been fairly badly beaten. His nose was broken."

"Did he tell you what happened?"

"He was robbed."

"Anything else?"

"No. And I don't imagine that is why you are interested in him."

The policeman squints. "Can you tell me anything else? How he came to you? How you left him?"

Mohr repeats the story, crushing his cigarette into the ashtray as he finishes.

"And you didn't see him again until yesterday in Soochow?"

"That's correct. It was pure coincidence."

"And you asked him to join you on a picnic?"

"Correct."

"Just like that? May I ask what you talked about during your picnic together?"

Mohr folds his hands on the desktop. "I can assure you that it was quite banal and uninteresting."

"Perhaps, Dr. Mohr. But banalities are precisely what I am most interested in. Did he tell you where he was going? Did he say what he was doing in Soochow?"

"No."

"Did you discuss politics?"

"Not in the sense you are thinking, no."

"Oh, and what sense would that be, Dr. Mohr?"

"In the police sense, of course. Conspiracies, plots. I'm afraid I can't tantalize you with anything of the sort, Officer."

"So. You talked as fellow countrymen together." Stubbings smirks again. "The Fatherland, that kind of thing."

Mohr does not rise to the bait, and smiles pleasantly. "Let's say, we spoke as citizens of the world, grateful to be living in the International Settlement under the benevolent protection of the Municipal Council."

"Very nicely said, Doctor. I will make a note of your loyal sentiments."

"Thank you, Officer Stubbings. Now, if you will excuse me. It has been a long day."

The bird squawks. The policeman remains in place. "You know that Granich is a communist, then? A Moscow-trained agent?"

"I don't bother with politics or ideologies. I find it all too confusing."

"Well, perhaps I can unconfuse you. Have you ever seen a magazine called *Voice of China?*"

"No."

"It's printed right here in this building. Downstairs. By Mr. Granich himself, as a matter of fact. Do you remember the Canton uprising in 1927?"

Mohr shakes his head, a little surprised by the thought of young Granich covertly churning out pamphlets and manifestos just one floor below. "In 1927, Canton could not have been further from my thoughts." He pries another cigarette from the tin on the desk.

Stubbings produces his lighter again, fixes Mohr with an appraising look. "I wonder, Dr. Mohr, if we aren't working at cross-purposes here."

"Cross-purposes?"

"What I mean to say is that, perhaps, our interests are not quite so far apart as you might think." The policeman stands up and crosses the room to the window, then turns and folds his arms over his narrow chest. "Did you read about the rioting in Chapai yesterday?"

Mohr shrugs, says nothing, conscious now of lying. In fact, he not only read about the riots but had treated some of the injured who turned up at the hospital.

"Communist agitators," Stubbings pronounces. "At the American–Far Eastern Match Company. The riot squad finally restored order. I'm sure I don't need to get into details. The situation in the city is bad. Very tense. Let's just say that your picnic yesterday. It's the timing of it, that's all." He stops, as if to let everything settle. "Fourteen people were killed. Many more wounded, Dr. Mohr. Your picnicking friend belongs to a group of terrorists who are planning riots, a whole series, in commemoration of the uprising at Canton in 1927. Not just strikes but military operations, coordinated and supported by the communists."

Stubbings jingles his keys in his trouser pockets.

"Why are you telling me this? Are you looking for an informant?"

Stubbings laughs. Rash, a little frightening. "So! You are a fan of the cinema, Doctor! I must say, I enjoy a good picture, too." He shakes his head in mock indulgence. "I'm afraid you have it all wrong. It doesn't quite work that way. Sorry to disappoint."

At last, Mohr loses patience. "What do you want from me?"

Stubbings flaps his arms. "Nothing at all, Doctor. What you have told me has been quite enough. Very helpful. I appreciate your candor."

"Then I'll see you out. I'm afraid that is all the time I have now. It has been a long day. I still have work to do."

"Patients? At this hour?"

"Just paperwork."

As he escorts Stubbings to the door, Wong appears. "Master catchee chow?"

"Chow? Ah, yes, Wong, yes. Chop chop."

"Number One?" Stubbings asks.

Mohr nods.

"Working late as well, I see."

Mohr lets the remark pass, opens the front door. Stubbings pauses on the threshold. "Keeping up with all the various elements pitching up here in the Settlement is quite an impossible job." His glance lingers just long enough for Mohr to catch the drift. He offers his card.

Mohr slides the card into his pocket. "I am sure you are doing your best," he says, and shuts the door.

. . .

AT THE JAPANESE silk factories in Pootung, children work plucking silk cocoons from boiling vats with their bare hands, and Chen Siu-fang had three burned children in her car with her this morning. She pulled up to the hospital entrance just as Mohr arrived. He helped them out of the car. All three were under ten years old and in various states of shock. One was burned up to the elbow. Agnes was waiting in the emergency room with rolls of tea-soaked lint. For nearly a month now Chen Siu-fang has been driving to Pootung to pick up burned children (and their mothers, if they can be located) and delivering them to the hospital in her car. Agnes explained it to him as they began their rounds together.

"She fetches them on her way in to work."

"Every day?"

Agnes nodded. "Her father gave her a car. He owns hotels."

"I wish I had known," Mohr said under his breath, remembering the wrong impression he'd had of the young woman, a spoiled rich girl.

Now, back home and reading the newspaper all these hours later, he is still distracted by the events of the day and suddenly recalls the visit from the SMP the night before. Will the police begin following Chen Siu-fang now? It hadn't occurred to him to make the connection. Should he say something? As much as a desire to help, it was to undo his mistaken judgment that he went looking for Chen-Siu late that afternoon. She was surprised by his offer. "You're offering me your car?" She looked at Mohr dubiously. "That's very kind of you. But what I really need is a driver."

"You may have my driver, too, of course." He felt her sizing him up. Even in her nurse's uniform, she exuded an air of privilege. He extended his hand, and only when she shook it—letting go at once—did he realize how young she was. Once again, he realized how unfairly he'd judged her.

Shortly after nine o'clock the telephone rings. Mohr hesitates, then picks it up. It is Agnes. "I'm calling to thank you," she says.

"Thank me for what?"

"For your generosity. Chen Siu-fang told me that you are giving her the use of your car and driver."

"I wish I had known earlier. I'd not have waited this long to help." Mohr pauses. "Did she ask you to call me?"

"No."

"You and she are friends?"

"Yes."

There is a brief silence, almost as if she has her hand over the mouthpiece. Old friends? He is about to ask, but Agnes cuts him off. "I've been thinking about what you told me the other night. That you are impulsive."

Mohr laughs. "I told you that?"

"I think I misunderstood you."

"That's perfectly all right. I misunderstand myself."

"I'm serious." The sudden tremor in her voice takes him by surprise. He presses the telephone to his ear. "You see, when Chen Siu-fang told me you wanted to help her, I could only think of the offer you made to me."

His vision narrows to the circle of lamplight on the cluttered desktop. "To come to Japan?"

"Can you understand my difficulty?"

He squeezes his eyes shut, says nothing.

"I'm sorry. This is embarrassing. Perhaps we should talk another time."

"No. Please. Go on. I'm glad you're telling me this."

"I feel stupid. I don't know what I'm trying to say."

"About Japan. Your difficulty."

The sound of a match being struck, a cigarette being lit, relieves some tension. He reaches for his Chesterfields. "I don't quite know how to say this." She exhales. "When Chen Siu-fang told me you'd offered her the use of your car and driver, I suddenly realized something I hadn't understood before." A nervous puff. "It's the occasion. That's it. The occasion."

"I don't follow. Which occasion?"

"What I mean to say is, well, when you offer your car—or a steamship ticket to Japan—a person has a right to ask, why is he doing this? When it's charity there's no question. A person gives when they are moved by some reason to give. The occasion of the gift is irrelevant. Nobody thinks twice about it."

"And you want to know why I asked you to come to Japan with me."

"I think I have a right to ask."

Mohr taps his cigarette ash. "I don't know."

"Don't know or won't say?"

"I don't know."

A long exhale. He can see the great cloud of blue smoke rising into the air above her head, the telephone pressed to her ear. "I believe you, Dr. Mohr."

"It's my honest answer."

"You know why I have to ask, don't you?" Her voice is suddenly different, completely changed, a tone she has never used before.

He is shaken by her nervous frankness, the dropped pretense. "Can you tell me?"

"I have to know that there is a difference between the use of your car and an invitation to go away with you to Japan."

Mohr is ashamed, and rolls the ember of his cigarette in the little ashtray, searching for the right words. "It's not all the same." He hesitates, still caught short, then finishes in a rush. "My invitation was sincere. I'm sorry if it came across the wrong way. The truth is, I wasn't thinking of you at all but only of myself."

A long pause. "I prefer to believe you didn't know what you were doing." There is a hint of humor in her voice now. She seems pleased to have arrived at a new level of intimacy.

"I have embarrassed you, and I am very sorry."

"You have no idea how glad I am to know that, Doctor."

What's this? She's pleased? It's an odd position he suddenly finds himself in; can't say what it reminds him of. Being Chinese and English, she must be keenly sensitive to every slight and insult. As a German and a Jew, he has some insight into the self-negating nature of this odd dialectic, a potent admixture of inferiority and superiority complexes muddled and mixed together—not at all noble or easy to live down. He imagines her at the other end of the line smoking her cigarette, wrapped in something luxurious and silky, with the radio turned down and cosmetics strewn about the table. Now that she has him wondering, he is more drawn to her than ever. Her frank way of speaking, leaving him to make connections. He's glad she is taking him to task, and feels suddenly pardoned for the anserine introversion that has kept him home night after night, burrowing into himself.

For an hour after Agnes's telephone call he paces his room, stands at the window with Zappe on his shoulder, smokes. He misses seeing the stars, makes do with the flickering, blinking neon of the city. Sleep has been difficult lately. Tonight there seems no chance of it at all. He returns to the desk, touches fingertips to the keys of his sturdy Remington—and waits. When nothing comes, he sits back and stares at the cluttered desk as if hidden there are clues to what is inaccessible in his thoughts.

Before turning in for the night, Wong brings him a pitcher of water and a small bowl of rice, egg, and diced green onion. Mohr sips the water but can't bring himself to touch the food. No appetite. On the desk is a collection of Lawrence's writings called *Phoenix*, just published in America. He and Lawrence had often discussed the phoenix myth, and he's been thinking of ways to make use of it in the novel he has just returned to. It's been a slow return, and he has doubts. Can a novel called *The Unicorn* also have a phoenix? Would too many mythological creatures in the same book be overbearing? But why shouldn't a book be overbearing? What should a book *be*, if not overbearing?

"I don't much care for it," he can hear Lawrence saying. It is what Lawrence said of all his work; claimed it "too modern" and himself "too *altmodish.*" Everything Lawrence said to him has become grist for a counterturning millstone, his works in progress. After the conversation with Nagy, he decided to resume work on the book, and in spite of Lawrence breathing down his neck—he has gone ahead and done it, put a phoenix into his novel.

How old-fashioned.

He picks up the camera lying at the corner of the desk, recalling his little outburst in the photo shop; turns it over in his hands, wipes the lens with the end of his shirt. Does he think of Wolfsgrub only in pictures now? Views through the trees, the house far below. Unlike the resurrected phoenix—*es scheint nicht wiederrufbar*—appears beyond recall—there is so much to recall, and so many photographs to pick over, leftovers of long-forgotten moments.

The clock on the wall is ticking, but he couldn't be less concerned with the time. His thoughts always seem to run counterclockwise to events, to spin off in a different direction. That's how it feels now— trying to write once again. There's no hurry. Tomorrow always comes soon enough. Käthe always said that when he seemed in a rush— buzzing around, in Lawrence's words—and usually suggested they go for a walk. She would fetch the perambulator and wrap the baby up, tuck it in, and they'd set out on the usual route across the valley toward Angermaier, Käthe pushing the carriage. Along the way, Mohr would stop here and there to frame a photograph—then decide not to take it. The real buzzing years began in 1927, the year he met Lawrence, and five years after *Improvisations in June.* Money remained the big problem. Publishers blamed the economy, said they couldn't advance, though they continued to publish. Theater producers claimed to be on the verge of bankruptcy, yet the theaters were full, night after night. Then came *Ramper.* Simultaneous openings in Hamburg, Mainz, Bochum, Karlsruhe. A hit! Now, suddenly, everybody wanted something from him. A radio play. A film script. A short article for the *Berliner Börsen*

Courier. "Something short," the editor suggested. "'What Does the Public Want from the Theater?'"

"I can tell you in two words. Free tickets!"

People urged him, "Come to Berlin!"

"I can't come to Berlin."

"*Mensch!* Mohr! Are you crazy? You *must* come to Berlin. You're completely out of touch. Now's your big chance."

The words rang in his ears, appalling and appealing, in nearly equal measure. For a time he was able to ignore the temptation. The years in the country had done Käthe and him both good—physically, emotionally. He cut his own wood, mowed his own field, kept a cow and sheep. He delivered babies, treated ailments, vaccinated the neighbors and their animals. He helped pull broken machinery out of muddy fields and delivered intoxicated men home to their wives—had been brought home drunk himself once or twice with slaps on the back and much laughter. The war slipped into the past. Life was quiet and good. He wrote plays and they were produced. He wrote novels and somehow they got published.

But then he began to feel restless. Difficult to say exactly when. The friendship with Lawrence accelerated it. He still doesn't understand why, except to say that Lawrence acted on him like a leavening agent that made everything seem urgent, more vital. Lawrence even noticed it himself. "You must learn to be more peaceful inside yourself or one day you'll just explode like a rocket and there will be nothing left but bits," he wrote to Mohr. "My cough, like your restlessness, is a good deal psychological in its origin. A real change might cure us both."

A change! Of course! How perverse, but also how right!

He was out walking with Käthe one afternoon when it all came out. The fresh air felt good; to be outside after a heavy rain. "I think I should go to Berlin," he said.

"What for?" she asked, struggling to keep the wheels of the baby carriage from running into the muddy ruts in the road.

"There are things I can only do there, in the city."

"What things?"

"Radio. Film." He hated having to spell it out to her, but as he did he felt that he was simply being practical.

Käthe looked at Eva, asleep under the blankets. "You know the field that Berghammer wants to rent?" she asked, stopping suddenly.

"The one over by Sonnenmoos?"

"I was talking to Marie the other day and she says they can rent it only if they promise to use manure. No chemical fertilizers."

"What does that have to do with anything?"

She wasn't smiling exactly, though her eyes were shining as though she might be, someplace inside. "Cultivate and culture. Isn't it funny that both have the same Latin root?" She resumed pushing the carriage.

Mohr stumped along sullenly behind her for the rest of the walk. The weather changed and the sun broke out, bright and clear and crisp on the wet mountainsides. He went to Berlin later that year, began a period of shuttling back and forth between misconceived and steadily eroding notions of what was necessary and what was merely possible. What happens is always different from what is dreamed—yet all that matters, in the end, is vision: how one sees. He sits at his desk, spends his evenings sorting and sifting through notes and scattered scraps. He is surrounded by countless bits of paper. What an absurd pastime, putting things down on paper—in words, in pictures; inducing dreams in others.

A KNOCK AT the door.

"Captain Brehm!" Mohr stands up, beaming. "What a great surprise! When did you get in?"

"The day before yesterday," Brehm says, entering. "I would have telephoned first, but . . ."

Mohr claps the captain on the shoulder as if to hold him in place. It has been nearly six months. Wong appears in the doorway, smiling. "*Gee o pow* whiskey, Wong!" Mohr tells him, pull some bills from his pocket. "Number one bottle. Chop chop."

Brehm looks unsteady in street clothes. He tosses his hat on the table and sits down on the sofa. He seems grayer and thinner since his last visit. The ruddy face that once could be read like a navigational chart now seems all folded up. "Where have you been, Captain? You had me worried."

"A leave of absence," Brehm says flatly. He accepts a proffered cigarette, taps it once, twice, then, instead of putting it to his lips, rolls it contemplatively between his fingers.

"And have you returned from it yet?"

Brehm manages a smile.

"Well, it's good to know you weren't lost at sea! Last time the *Saarbrücken* was in port, I went looking for you. They said there was no Captain Brehm aboard. They were completely unhelpful, told me there was a new captain. I don't remember his name."

"Henkel."

"Right, Henkel. He'd gone ashore so I wasn't able to learn anything."

Wong returns carrying a tray with a bottle of Red Lion Whiskey, a pitcher of water, and a bowl of salted nuts. "Only two glasses?" Mohr asks as he sets the tray down. "Catchee three piece glass!"

Wong bows tolerantly, goes off to fetch another glass. When he returns, Mohr pours out the whiskey and hands the glasses around. Wong accepts with some embarrassment. He touches the glass to his lips, sips tentatively. "B'long number one whiskey," he smiles.

"Doctor talkee gut?" Brehm asks in his flatfooted, German-inflected pidgin.

"Number one," Wong answers.

Mohr laughs, begs to differ. "*Shun mo hwah! Boo yow hoo schwo!*"

"*Oh dien buh tso!*" Wong insists politely. "*Shih dzai hao kan.*"

"What did he say?" Brehm wants to know, holding his glass out for a refill.

"He says my Chinese is unmistakably grand."

All laugh. Mohr refills Brehm's glass. Wong excuses himself with a polite bow, takes his drink with him. Zappe begins to squawk—*Brüderlein fein Brüderlein fein. Einmal muss es sein.* Mohr has been trying to teach it to say that for weeks. He coaxes it to keep on, but the bird will not repeat.

In short order, the bottle is almost gone and the afternoon with it. Mohr calls himself a wanton and a drunk as Brehm brushes the notion aside with slug after slug of whiskey. What Mohr wants to call himself is unfaithful, but in spite of being drunk, he manages not to mention Agnes. He has Brehm's predicament to distract him. The captain is distraught. His wife came down with shingles during his last return home, suffered terribly for weeks. Then, just before he was scheduled to set sail, a further complication developed. She began going blind. "How is that possible?" he asks repeatedly. "I don't understand."

Mohr tries to console by saying not much is known about the disease, that sometimes it can lead to neurological complications.

"But to blindness? Permanent blindness?"

It's already six o'clock in the evening. They are in the captain's Norddeutsche Lloyd company car, being driven to an address in the French Concession where Brehm has some sort of gathering to attend. "I'm away for half the year, already feel like a guest in my own house. And now my wife can't take care of herself, let alone the children."

"You'll have to hire a housekeeper."

The captain's eyes grow dark. He shakes his head. "What I would rather do is . . ."

"What would you rather do?"

The captain seems to think better of what he is about to say. "I don't know. In fact, there aren't very many options."

"Do you love her?"

Brehm is startled by the question, and turns away without answering.

"Oh, come now, Brehm, don't be offended." Mohr smiles extravagantly. "When spring is lovely, it's lovely, lovely, lovely. The organ grinder stands on the street corner, dragonflies swoop over the pond. Birds sing and dogs bark and everywhere the songs of love, love, love. Don't make yourself sick over it. You'll figure out what to do in time."

Brehm doesn't find the attempt to humor him very amusing. A short silence ensues. Mohr turns to look out the window at a passing chaos that seems already to have woven their private miseries into its sprawling web.

"Well," Brehm sighs after a while. "For now they're staying at her brother's. The children don't seem to mind living with Uncle Jürgen while Papa is away at sea."

"See. Already you've managed. Life is long, my friend."

Brehm mutters something unintelligible under his breath.

"Cheer up, Brehm. You're halfway around the world. Try not to be so glum."

"Would you stop trying to humor me? What am I supposed to do? Pretend there's nothing wrong? I'm not like you."

"Oh? How is that?"

Brehm flushes, half in anger, half in embarrassment. "With your head in the clouds."

Mohr grins at the captain. "Sometimes it's good to have your head in the clouds. Especially when you don't know where you're going and your ass is stuck in third class."

Brehm turns away again to look out the window. Mohr feels close to him in a way he never has before. Partly, it's the idea that the man has not a clue how drastically different their misfortunes are. On a private, complicated level, Mohr is amused by the thought that Brehm's wife symbolizes all Germany. A slow, painful descent into permanent blindness. "At least you can go home," he says finally, and leaves it at that.

Brehm snorts, picks the lint from his trousers.

"And still, there are people who want to live a hundred years!"

A dubious look from Brehm.

Mohr chatters on drunkenly, trying to change the mood. "People think they can cheat nature, find lasting happiness. They go on diets, don't drink, don't smoke, avoid coffee and tea, become vegetarian, wear special underwear, eat vitamins. And if they're lucky and don't get hit by a bus, maybe they *will* live a hundred years."

"What in God's name are you talking about, Mohr?" Brehm glowers.

"Medical science is dedicated to tricking the body. Someday it will succeed and we'll all get to live one, two, three hundred years. Can you imagine anything more miserable?" He takes a last, deep drag from his cigarette. "Have you ever been seasick?"

"Never."

"Not once?"

Brehm shakes his head and grabs the leather strap as the driver swerves around an overloaded cart. "What about you?"

"Also never."

"You're lying, Doctor. I've seen you puking over the rail."

"It wasn't over the railing. It was all over the deck. Where are we going, anyway?"

"To a cocktail party." Brehm is now holding the strap with both hands, face turned to catch the warm breeze coming through the window. "You're a goddamned hypocrite, Mohr. You know that? You talk as if you're somehow above and beyond banal little problems."

"Do I?"

"Life is long. Cheer up. You talk as if nothing could be simpler. Don't be glum. And look at you! Have you followed your own advice?"

"No. But there's an important difference."

"There is? You think your unhappiness is different from mine?" Brehm shoots back.

"Oh my, Captain. Your face is swelling up. You're turning red!"

"Shut up, Mohr," Brehm snaps, turning away in disgust.

Mohr becomes serious. "Yes. It is different, Captain. Fundamentally and completely different. I left my family behind. *They're* the ones who must cheer up, try and forget *me.*"

Brehm keeps his gaze fixed out the window.

"My biggest fear is that they will," Mohr adds quietly, feeling suddenly light-headed. "Where did you say we're going? A cocktail party?"

Brehm nods.

"We can't do that!"

"Why not?"

"Look at you! At me! We're drunk! Wearing dirty clothes."

"You look just fine."

Brehm reassures him again as they enter the sixth-floor flat of a Mr. K. De Sailes, a Shanghai Municipal Council board member. Mohr remains at the captain's side, casting glances around the large room—brightly lit and expensively furnished in mahogany and chrome and thick slabs of architectural glass. Nobody seems to notice or to mind their disheveled appearance. Attentive Chinese waiters in starched gowns ply the room with trays of hors d'oeuvres and drinks. Brehm helps himself to champagne, passes a glass to Mohr. "Once a sailor, always a sailor." He winks. "To the cocktailing class."

Mohr's instinct is not to mingle but to stand apart. But isn't everyone in the room standing apart? Confident and singular and self-assured; each an elite unto himself. He glances about, imagining the remarks that will be made later this evening as ties are unknotted, shoes kicked off, stockings rolled down—How ghastly boring. My God, could you stand it? I nearly died. Each vacuous moment swept away, of no concern. An elephant storming into the room would hardly break the surface. Maybe if he fell asleep on a chair in the corner, and began snoring.

A German voice attracts his attention. A few paces away, a small group pays court to a young man who looks like a bank cashier recently promoted to manager. A Nazi. Mohr taps Brehm on the shoulder. "Let's go."

"We only just arrived!" Brehm says, and ambles into the crowd, clutching his glass in his fist.

Mohr can't help but admire him—the most charmless, unaffected person in the room. He steps over to the corner, exchanges a few pleasantries. A gray-haired and very alert French lady protests the public executions of opium addicts. "I've read they are given opium to calm them down beforehand," Mohr can't help observing dryly. "They are?" the woman gasps, moves on. An American businessman sidles up and asks, "So, how you do you like Shanghai?" All the while, Mohr's attention is drawn to the German, the way he is attended to and openly admired by certain of the guests, the way he listens with one ear, eyes roving. "Why should it matter if the Japanese quarrel with the Chinese?" The man flourishes his cigarette. His glance skims the room, alights momentarily. Mohr averts his eyes, wishing he could tuck his head in like a turtle, peer out at all the peach and pear shapes gaily mingling.

"You can buy hundreds of them on Foochow Road. Any time you like!"

"Best of luck!"

"Thank god, my children are in England."

"Rather hot, isn't it?"

"We had lunch in Bernard's swimming pool yesterday. Oh, there wasn't any water in it."

Mohr holds his glass in his fist. The conversation is light, the odors slightly stronger: whiskey, eau de cologne, cigarettes.

The hostess suddenly materializes at his elbow. "Oh, Herr Fuchs!" She beckons the German over. "Allow me to introduce you to Max Mohr, the German writer."

Her dowdy pomp is immediately overshadowed by the Nazi's suave prominence. Up close, Mohr recognizes a midlevel functionary, Party pin neatly attached to the lapel of his suit. The man steps forward, inclines his head. "Fuchs," he says. "Ministerialrat, Deutscher Botschaft."

The woman smiles nervously as Mohr steps back, out of handshake range. The man parries with a sidelong glance at the hostess. "A German writer, you say?" He sniffs. "Mohr? I don't believe I recognize the name."

The woman is caught off guard, then recovers. A shadow of a smile. "Oh, well, I'm sure," she flutters.

All at once, Mohr's stomach unknots. "There's no reason why he would know it," he says, taking a step forward. "Even if he *could* read, his government has burned all my books."

The words linger. Then, in one smooth, unwilled motion, Mohr tosses his champagne into the man's face, turns to the stunned hostess, places his empty glass in her hand. "Please, excuse me, Madam."

Fuchs sputters. Guests part as Mohr walks away. At the door, a welter of protests, Fuchs's outraged voice. Mohr's pulse pounds, ears ring. Down the corridor to the lift. He jabs the button, surging with pleasure—one, two, three times. Then Brehm has him by the elbow, is pulling him toward the stairway. "You idiot," he repeats all the way down the stairs. "Idiot, idiot, idiot!" All traces of alcohol evaporate as they descend the six flights. By the time they reach the bottom Mohr feels gloriously sober and clear-headed. "I'm hungry. Let's go to Delmonico's for eggs and onion soup!"

"I don't know what to say to you, Mohr," Brehm says, shaking his head. "That was an idiotic prank."

Mohr laughs. "What's he going to do? Revoke my citizenship?"

The captain doesn't share Mohr's high spirits, isn't feeling well at all. He wants to be taken directly to the pier. In the car, he leans his head against the window, closes his eyes. "Heine said a country that burns books ends up burning people." Mohr glances over but the captain doesn't respond. "I wish I had thought of it back there."

They drive in silence, all the way down Avenue Joffre to the Bund. The *Saarbrücken* isn't the largest passenger liner at anchor in the river, but its single stack and twelve tall funnels rising in threes from the foredeck and amidships give it a sturdy appearance. Mohr can't help feeling awed by the sight, even as a silhouette of twinkling lights in the distance, moored to buoys in the middle of the Whangpoo. He feels a twinge of nostalgia for the idle hours he spent walking its decks, gazing up at kilometers of rope and cable suspended from its towering masts. On the open ocean, seabirds would perch up there for days at a time. A slight breeze blows off the water, sounds of boat traffic, smells of diesel and garbage.

"When do you sail?"

"In two days."

They shake hands. Brehm is smiling again; all is forgotten. "Can you come aboard tomorrow? For breakfast? I'll send a boat to fetch you."

"I have no time."

Brehm looks Mohr directly in the eye. "I'm sorry for calling you a hypocrite."

"And I'm sorry about your wife," Mohr answers. "I hope she recovers quickly."

Brehm nods, stops short of saying anything else.

"May I give you a package to take back? I can send Wong with it tomorrow."

"Have him leave it at the Nanking Road office. My steward will bring it to the ship."

"When do you return?"

"In November." They shake hands again. "Enjoy your visit to Japan, Mohr. I wish I could go with you."

Mohr laughs. "As it happens, I have an extra ticket."

The jetty is guarded by Settlement harbor police. Brehm shows his identification. One of the *Saarbrücken* crew salutes, opens the gate for the captain to pass through. Two sailors are waiting, ropes in hand. The captain waves a final good-bye, then steps aboard the tender. Mohr watches the little boat churn away, remembering the day he walked up the long gangplank in Hamburg, to board the ship that separated him from his past and stranded him in the future.

Wolfsgrub

ook, Mama. It's Hartl!" Eva points to the rear door of the bus, where passengers are struggling with their packages and bags. Käthe is seated on a bench under an awning just outside the post office. The driver steps from the front door of the dusty old omnibus, pushes his cap back, lights a cigarette.

"I don't see him."

"There!" Eva points to a young man struggling with a rucksack. He slips his arms through the straps, ambles over. He is wearing an armband with a swastika. "*Grüss Gott,* Frau Mohr. Hello Eva," he says, smiling.

"Hello, Hartl," Käthe replies sternly. "Your mother said you were coming home for a visit."

He nods politely, adjusts his pack.

Eva points to the bright red armband. "What's that?"

Hartl glances at his arm. He smiles self-consciously. "That, Evalein, is a symbol of the future."

Käthe frowns, feels a pit in her stomach. How can this young sprout talk of the future when he has no idea what is being destroyed of the present? How is Marie going to react to her boy's newfound ideology? "You must be excited about starting your *prakticum*."

"Very much, thank you, Frau Mohr."

"We're going to Munich," Eva announces.

He jounces once, twice, to settle his pack. He has grown in the half-year since they last saw him. It would be natural to comment, but Käthe is having trouble digesting his unfortunate political transformation, would rather scold him the way she once did for cutting the bark off the old larch tree at the back of the house. She hugs the bag in her lap. It contains the buttered rolls and cheese she packed for lunch, a book to read on the train, and nearly all the money she's saved over the past year.

"Have a good trip." Hartl turns to leave, then hesitates, takes out a small packet of sweets. He offers it to Eva. "For the trip."

Eva accepts eagerly.

"Save them for the train." He saunters off with a wave.

Hartl's symbols of the future present themselves all the way to Munich, beginning with the confusion of some passengers between the new second-class and the first-class cars. "This can't be second class," a woman insists on entering the compartment. "The seats, they're upholstered!" When the conductor assures her that it is indeed second class, she seats herself next to Käthe. "Renovated," she says, beaming with satisfaction.

"You should see what first class looks like now," mutters a sour-faced man sitting by the door. "Soon the entire Reich will be upholstered."

"That would be just fine with me," the woman returns.

The small talk subsides as the train leaves the station. Eva turns her attention to the bag of candy. Käthe opens her book—Robert Walser's *Jakob von Gunten*. Alternately absorbed by the book, the passing landscape, and a sense that this excursion they are on is practice for something larger, she can't escape anxious thoughts of the future, which remains a disturbing dream. On the outskirts of Munich they pass by the zeppelin fields. The woman leans across to Eva. "Look at that! How lovely. Imagine what it must be like up there." She points out the window to the three large airships tethered by their noses to huge iron towers, each at a different angle to the passing train.

"They look like sausages," Eva announces. "Flying sausages."

The woman laughs. "Marvelous."

Käthe closes her book. She sees nothing marvelous about the sight. She reaches into Eva's candy bag and takes out a gumdrop. Why do certain people assent so readily to so many things? Upholstered seats and mammoth airships? If they would only stand back, allow themselves time to think, the moment would not be so dreadfully devalued, the mad rush into the future slowed.

Eva offers the woman some candy.

"Oh, how sweet!" The woman helps herself to a gumdrop. "May I ask where you are going?"

"Munich. Do you like the green ones?"

The woman nods. "I do."

"The red are my favorite. What about you, Mama?"

"Red." Käthe rolls the candy on her tongue, and regards the woman as neutrally as she is able. A host of assumptions: small town, grown children, a dog, a balcony, a neighbor she complains to. As they draw closer to Munich, she becomes nervous. The way she compensates is to project an exaggerated version of the edgy, urban indifference that offends her in others, and is the reason she's grown to dislike the city in the first place. Passing through the suburban train stations, the billboard advertisements draw her attention. *Makedon Perfect, Odol, Continental,* and the latest Claudette Colbert movie all urge themselves on the commuting population. She scoots closer to Eva, whose nose is pressed against the window. She has been more subdued than usual on this trip, hasn't once asked to explore the rest of the car or be taken for a snack. Käthe draws her onto her lap.

"What's wrong?" Eva wants to know.

She leans forward to whisper. *"Buden angst."* Claustrophobia.

Eva twists around. "What's that?"

"Nothing to worry about."

The woman in the hat is pretending indifference, gazing out the window. Holding Eva is a kind of protection. But it is also a subtle act of rebellion—to be so demonstrative in public. How silly that this little act of affection should make her feel so proud. Eva senses something of it, too, nestles closer. "What is claustrophobia?" she asks again. The woman's eyes dart. Käthe blushes. The sour-faced man sitting by the door takes out a handkerchief and blows his nose loudly. The woman has stiffened, the gumdrop in her mouth long since dissolved. If her gaze were any more distant, her eyes would harden into glass. "I'll tell you later," Käthe whispers, then closes her eyes and tries to drift off.

A sudden change in the weather greets them on their arrival in Munich. As they leave the train station, Käthe scans the sky. "It doesn't look good for a picnic."

They cross the street to wait for the tram. For the briefest instant she considers calling Bertl Schultes, the film director. He has dropped by Wolfsgrub twice since Mohr left, is the only person in Munich she would still consider visiting. He lives within walking distance of the train station, but a call there would mean a detour, and the last thing she wants is to stay in the city any longer than they have to. She runs down a list of all the people here she once knew, those who have emigrated, those who have remained. Ten years ago it would have been impossible not to run into an acquaintance on the street. Now, the thought of it scares her. Ah, look! It's Käthe Mohr. Käthe! How good to see you! How are you these days? And your husband? Where is *he?*

The first thing she notices on boarding the tram is all the Party pins in people's lapels. It is ten o'clock and the car is crowded. They move toward the rear, where a young man stands up, offers his seat. Käthe thanks him and takes Eva on her lap. It is overwhelming, to be in a place at once so familiar and so completely alien. It isn't just the buildings, bedecked with banners, posters, and flags, but the feeling of losing herself in the flow, of becoming a part of it. No easy thing to sidestep or get out from under. She is reminded of a horrible image in a letter from Mohr just over a year ago, of floods and bodies floating down the Yangtze River. A nauseating image of water thick with decomposing humanity. Oddly, in the very same letter, he described the jacket and shirt he had just ordered from an English tailor. She found herself agreeing with his little quip, that man is not descended from gods or from primates but from plants—each new generation dependent for its nourishment on the decomposition of the previous one. But what if the mulch turned toxic?

Outside the Haus der Kunst hangs an enormous banner for an exhibition called *Entartete Kunst,* Degenerate Art. *Deutsches Volk, komm und urteile selbst!* They step from the tram and cross the street, pause to look up at the museum entrance. "Detrimental and of no lasting value to the culture of the German people" was the wording in the letter from the Reichsschrifttumskammer announcing the ban on Mohr's work.

"We're not going here, are we, Mama?" Eva protests. A queue has formed at the museum entrance. Eva tugs at her mother's arm. "Mama, come on. It's down *there!*" She points to the enormous department store on the next block.

Käthe feels a small, subversive pleasure in being tugged away from such an enormous propaganda exercise by a twelve-year-old. But she also can't help feeling curious. What effect might it have on her to go inside? An act of solidarity with the banned artists? Or would going in only contribute to the force majeure of Nazi propaganda? Some months ago she forwarded a letter to Mohr announcing a new Zurich-based literary journal. A joint statement from Thomas Mann and Hermann Hesse. *We wish to be artists and antibarbarians, to observe moderation and defend values, to love what is free and daring, and to despise philistinism and ideological rubbish—to despise this last most thoroughly and deeply where with contemptible hypocrisy it postures as revolution.*

Mohr's clipped reply from Shanghai had been: *"Ich bin mit allem quitt."* Finished. With Germany, with everything. Käthe had expected him to say as much. Sadly, it was also not quite what she had hoped for.

Eva's fatigue evaporates the moment she enters Kaufhaus Beck. Her bubbly curiosity is just the right foil for the salesman who materializes the moment they step onto the polished floor of the luggage department. It is brightly lit, decorated with travel posters and travel placards showing airplanes, steamships, and well-dressed travelers. A large placard for the Deutsche-Afrika-Linie is on conspicuous display behind the sales counter—a gleaming luxury liner—*30 Ports of Call. 33,000 kilometers.* It makes Käthe feel queasy, unable to imagine herself anyplace but back home.

"Is there something specific you are looking for?" the salesman asks. He could have stepped from one of the posters himself.

Käthe hesitates, scan the displays. "A bag. Some luggage."

A clipped smile, an indulgent glance at Eva. "Of course." He has the full measure of the situation. "How will you be traveling?"

Käthe takes Eva's hand, draws her away from a gleaming glass case. "Rapidly." She smiles. "As rapidly as possible."

The man chuckles. "What I mean is, will you be traveling by land or by sea?" He clasps his hands. "Or by air? We have a full selection of luggage for the air passenger."

"By sea," Käthe answers, feeling slightly absurd. Another poster has caught her eye, of an airboat, and in the background the skyscrapers of New York or some other gleaming American city. Eva has noticed it as well. The salesman gestures for them to follow. "Flying sausages," Käthe whispers. Eva snickers with delight as they traipse behind the salesman through the fog of merchandise. The smell of new leather and canvas reminds Käthe of her grandmother's house: the old steamship trunks with their drawers and compartments and the very important-looking brass plates that read, "Madame Kämmerer." Family legend had it that these were the second of three demands she had made before agreeing to marry Grandfather Kämmerer—not the trunks, just the brass nameplates. The first demand was for a honeymoon in Spain, and the third was that she be allowed to bring her dolls. Just the story for the way home. Käthe smiles at the thought of her grandfather begging for the sixteen-year-old girl's hand. "If you don't, I'll shoot myself," he is supposed to have said. Grandmother Kämmerer, who was a great beauty—the spitting image of Empress Eugénie of France, it was said—put down the doll she was playing with and replied, "Well, I guess I'll have to do it, then."

The salesman gestures to an enormous leather trunk with two handles. Flashing a smile of satisfaction at the loud clack of brass clasps, he opens the trunk and points out its features. "English," he pronounces. "Top craftsmanship."

"It's a little large," Käthe tells him. "I could never carry it."

"It's not meant for a woman to carry."

"What about that one?" She points to a bag on display across the aisle.

"That is airplane luggage."

"May I see it?"

The man leads them to the display. "Weight restriction on airplanes means lightweight luggage. The limited size makes it completely inappropriate for long voyages."

Käthe lifts the bag. "It's light."

"As I have described."

"May I open it?"

The man nods. Käthe opens the clasp. The interior of the case is simple. Two silk-lined compartments, a single cloth divider with brass clasps "It's nice. I like it."

"Allow me to show you something more appropriate for sea travel," the man insists, and disappears into the next aisle.

"What do you think?" she asks Eva.

Eva runs her hand along the silk interior, fingers the clasps. "It's a funny color."

"I like that I can lift it."

The salesman returns with another trunk, slightly smaller than the first. "You will fit twice as much in here," he says.

Käthe barely manages to lift it. "Too heavy."

The man shrugs. "No luggage is truly light. Even women's luggage is not meant to be carried by women. May I ask where you are traveling?"

"China!" Eva says proudly.

"To China! Then by all means you must go with the first one. The coolies there will carry it for you." He laughs. "And they'll carry you with it!"

Käthe distracts herself by examining the clasps and hinges. The prices are much higher than she imagined. "May I look around a little?"

"Of course! Take your time. I'll be right here if you need me."

She takes Eva by the hand and walks down the rows of display cases, overwhelmed by choices she suddenly feels incompetent to make. A light bag or a heavy trunk? How much do they need? Or want? All of Mohr's traveling over the years, his coming and going, his tramping around, hasn't furnished her with the practical example she needs just now. He took all the luggage with him when he left. Even if there were some way of gauging what they need in luggage by what they have of possessions, of knowing exactly what to expect in the new life ahead . . . But these are all questions she can't answer. Deep inside, she expects that, yes, they will return one day. Should they leave some things behind? What if they don't return? Shouldn't she take as much with her as possible?

She glances helplessly at all the shapes and sizes of luggage. Buzzing. It was the word Lawrence used to describe Mohr. Buzzing around. An English expression. It seemed to amuse him to think of Mohr in some sort of dizzy, perpetual motion, whereas it only made her sad. To her it just looked as if he were always uncomfortable and trying to get away.

"Are we going, Mama?"

They are moving in the direction of the large glass doors at the front of the store. A man wearing a frock coat with rows of brass buttons and white gloves bids them good-day and holds open the door.

"Aren't we going to get anything?" Eva wants to know.

"Not now, sweetheart. I need to think about it." Outside, the weather is changing again. The clouds are lifting. "Let's walk a little."

"Where?" Eva wants to know.

She can't decide, and glances up the street to the tram stop. There is no longer a queue to get into the museum. She starts off in the direction of the National Theater, but after a few paces stops and changes direction. How will it feel to pass by the place? Will she feel anything at all? A worrisome prospect, to feel nothing, to be left cold.

It isn't until they cross the Maximilianbrücke, are making their way down the steps to the footpath along the river, that she begins to feel easier. The air is cooler down by the water, the summer canopy a rich and luxuriant green. They pass a group of young boys splashing at the water's edge. "Shall we have our picnic?" Käthe points to a small patch of grass just a short distance ahead. Eva races to claim it and sprawls out in the grass.

"Tell me what claustrophobia means," Eva asks as Käthe unpacks their lunch.

"Claustrophobia is when you are afraid of being closed up in a small space."

"Like Martin when he was stuck in the stove?"

"For example. And now that you know what claustrophobia is, I'm sure you won't do it again. That was a mean trick you played."

"Do you have claustrophobia?"

Käthe bites into her roll. "Sometimes."

"What does it feel like?"

"Hard to describe." The bread is slightly stale, but delicious. "Like you need more air. Just a little more room to breathe."

Eva twists open her roll, examines the butter spread thickly inside, then twists it back together. "Did you have claustrophobia in the train?"

"Maybe. A little."

"And in the store?"

"Maybe."

"Mama?"

"Yes."

"Are you afraid of going to China?"

A shy smile. "Maybe. A little."

"Me, too."

They eat in silence for a time. The boys throw stones from the riverbank. The sun breaks through the clouds. A breeze picks up. Sound of traffic on the Maximilianbrücke. "Did you and Papa take trips together in the old days?" Eva asks.

Käthe adjusts her skirt, stretches out in the grass. "Yes, we did. We took some wonderful trips together."

"Where did you go on your honeymoon?"

"We walked to Innsbruck."

"All the way?"

"And back again."

"Where else?"

"We went to Berlin quite a lot. And Hamburg."

"Did you go to foreign countries?"

"Yes, we did. After Papa's feet healed. We wanted to recuperate."

"Where did you go?"

"Well, *I* wanted to go to Italy."

"And Papa didn't?"

"No. Much too tame for Papa."

"Where did he want to go?"

"Somewhere in the desert. Arabia. Across Morocco, up into the mountains to the Berbers. Algiers. Something like that."

"What did you do?" Eva asks, looming over her mother, eating her roll.

Käthe closes her eyes, feels the warmth of the sun directly on her face for the first time all day. *"I wanted something else. Especially after the year we had just been through. I dreamed of deck chairs and Italian balconies, arm in arm through narrow streets, of being close together, strolling around, eating sweets. But I didn't want to be some sort of ball and chain, some shrew who didn't know how to have fun. Gaurisankar and Klotz am Bein."*

"What's that?"

"I've never told you about Gaurisankar and *Klotz am Bein?*"

"No. It sounds funny."

"Gaurisankar is a mountain in Nepal, one of the tallest in the Himalayas. Papa always dreamed about climbing it one day. It's a symbol, a place where you go to see life clearly. You know what a *Klotz am Bein* is."

"Someone who can't walk properly?"

"It's a joke Papa and I had together. Gaurisankar and *Klotz am Bein*. You want to climb up Gaurisankar, but there's *Klotz am Bein* always holding you up, pulling you back. Anyway, I didn't want to be Papa's *Klotz am Bein*."

"So what did you do?"

"What you always have to do when you're stuck between Gaurisankar and *Klotz am Bein*."

"What's that?"

"Compromise. Papa said, 'How about this. We'll do it your way for the first two weeks. Nice and cushy and comfortable, places where there are other people, tourists. And then we'll split up. I'll bring my gear along with me. My saddle.'"

"A saddle?"

"So he could ride. Up into the Atlas Mountains of Morocco.

"At any rate, we eventually arrived in Genoa. I still remember the lights. We arrived late at night. Stars shining brightly overhead. Palast Hotel Miramar. I was trembling with excitement, visions of silk sheets and breakfast in bed. Would Papa go for it? I wondered. The Miramar?

We arrived on the platform. 'Where are you going? Which hotel?' the porters asked. 'Come. Come, follow me.' The hotel touts descended on us. Papa shooed them all away. We came into the main terminal of the train station. 'Oh, there,' said Papa. 'That's the one.' And he steered straight toward this cripple standing there with a hungry-dog look on his face. *'Albergo?'* Papa asked. He liked to think he could speak Italian, or any language he felt like. We followed the man down a series of dark, narrow streets, and into a dingy old building. It stank horribly. An old, bedraggled woman led us inside. 'We'd like a room, please,' he said to the old lady, politely, as if it were the Miramar. She looked at him like he was loony. The room stank even more than the lobby downstairs. Two narrow, iron-post beds, dirty linen, a tiny metal basin on a wobbly old stand. 'Prego!' she said. *'Bene, bene,'* said Papa. 'Perfect! Just the place. Let's go down and see what's happening. Looks like there might be a nice, cozy trattoria downstairs. Or maybe we should go out and find someplace to eat?' A trattoria? In this dump? Wait a minute, I wanted to shout! This is my ten days! What about *my* Gaurisankar? I was too tired to go out. We stayed in our fleabag hotel. All night long I heard strange noises. And the door wouldn't even close properly. I tried to be optimistic. The glass is half-full, I kept telling myself. Don't leave the toothbrush on the washstand. Better not get undressed for bed. 'Do you hear those noises?' I asked Papa. 'Nah.' He slept right through the night, and was bubbling with excitement the next morning. 'Isn't it beautiful? What a beautiful city! Look at the wonderful shops. Oh, look! There *is* a Miramar here! I'd rather die than stay there, wouldn't you? What a bunch of snobs. Palast Hotel, *pfui!* Are you hungry? Me too. Let's find someplace to have breakfast. Croissants and coffee.' In the main shopping street we stumbled into this Swiss hotel that was just wonderful, and so we moved there right away. Silk sheets, blue. Just clean and simple and not a trace of the obnoxiousness of the Palast Hotel. We stayed two nights. Very grand. Then a little way outside the city we found a really nice place, a real *albergo*.

At night people came out from the city to dance there. We stayed a few days and then Papa said he wanted to go back to Genoa, to the harbor to find a ship. 'I'd like to go first to Spain,' he said. 'I'll look for an old freighter, something cheap. From Spain maybe on to Tangier, something like that.' So, we went back to Genoa to look for a boat, stood around the harbor day after day. Can you believe it? The two of us just standing around the harbor? Finally he found just what he wanted and he put me on the train."

"Were you sad?"

"No. I was thrilled to be back home. It was springtime. Just lovely."

"You came back all alone?"

"Sure. He wanted to go off like a tramp, and I wanted to come back home. It was a practical solution, don't you think?"

Eva shrugs, unimpressed.

"Every day I got a telegram from him. Barcelona: 'Thinking of you.' Madrid: 'Not much to report. Missing Wolfsgrub.' Pamplona: 'Bull-fighting is cruel. Not in the mood for Africa.' A few days later, Paris: 'Nothing.' And then about a week later, he showed up at the door, as glad to be back home as ever."

Käthe gets up and stretches lazily. The afternoon sun has drawn more people down to walk along the river. She picks up her handbag, smooths down her skirt. "That's just the way he has always been. Wanting something badly, and then finding out it wasn't what he wanted after all."

KÄTHE SETS DOWN the new suitcase. "Anyone who hasn't mowed a field with his own hands will never know how big the world is," she groans. She's carried the bulky case all the way from the bus stop. They are at the top of the road leading down to Löbelhof and Wolfsgrub. A cool summer evening. The rain that never came to Munich fell here sometime during the afternoon. The fields are in greenest summer bloom. A few wisps of cloud drift overhead. Eva slept for nearly the entire trip, on the train and then again on the bus. She is still groggy in spite of having walked from the bus stop. Käthe flexes her fingers, stiff from gripping, and sits down on the case to rest. "Anyone who hasn't carried a heavy bag from Rottach to Wolfsgrub will never know how big the world is, either."

"In the store you said it wasn't heavy, Mama." Eva plucks a tall stalk of grass at the border of the field. "Isn't that why you bought it?"

"It wasn't as heavy as the others." Käthe bounces lightly on the case, testing its sturdiness. Less than a kilometer to go, but they're in no hurry. Dampness rises from the surrounding fields. Ripe, cool, quiet. Wolfsgrub lies just at the end of the narrow lane, hidden in a little grove at the foot of the mountain. For seventeen years she has walked down this road. Now, all of a sudden, she is about to walk away.

"Think how heavy it will be with all our stuff in it," Eva says, peeling a stalk of grass. Käthe watches her peel away layer after layer until the stalk is reduced to a bundle of wet strands. She sucks on the end of it, then flings it away and pulls up another. "That man in the store was mean, didn't you think?"

Käthe stands up. "Some people think they know what you need better than you do yourself. Anyway, it doesn't feel all that aerodynamic to me." She lifts the suitcase. "Let's see if we can make it the rest of the way without stopping."

As they draw closer, Käthe begins to wonder what *not* being here will feel like. When does a somewhere become nowhere again? *Can* a somewhere become a nowhere? Mohr believed that somewhere and nowhere were one and the same place. She dismissed it as a fine little romance, an opinion he held for the way it sounded rather than out of any rigorous philosophical conviction. Wolfsgrub was always a nowhere. It was he who had changed. "Let's wander off," he liked to say, "into our own nowhere." She would ask why he seemed so restless and discontented all the time. How impossibly naive such talk seems now, when people are no longer wandering but scrambling—and not just somewhere or nowhere but *anywhere* that can offer refuge.

The Daibler twins appear near the end of the road—on stilts. Eva runs to meet them. Seethaler's truck is parked at the gate. Käthe leaves the suitcase at the front door, finds him and two young helpers working in the ditch.

"*Grüss Gott.*" He climbs out of the ditch. "The pipe came in yesterday."

She peers down at the pipe.

"Cast iron," Seethaler says. "From start to finish." He gestures from the house to the tank, covered with a concrete slab.

"Very nice. It seems deeper than before."

"That's because it's getting dark out," Seethaler says. "The boys'll come back in the morning and fill it in."

"I can use the kitchen sink now?"

"All set to go."

"At last." Käthe sighs happily. "Thank you."

"My pleasure, Frau Mohr." He smiles. "My pleasure."

She shows him to a spigot at the back of the house where they all wash.

"Mama!" Eva shouts, rounding the corner of the house, waving something over her head. "A letter from Papa!" She thrusts the envelope at her mother. "Open it," she demands.

"In a moment. I need to talk to Herr Seethaler."

"Can I open it?"

The Daibler boys are negotiating their way through the garden gate, tottering precariously on their stilts. Käthe hands the envelope back to Eva. "I'll be a minute."

Seethaler wipes his wet hands with a rag.

"I'd like to speak to you about the bill."

"Don't worry, Frau Mohr. The invoice is all prepared."

"That's what I would like to discuss. But first, I owe you an apology, Theo."

"Nonsense."

"I want to apologize for my rudeness the other day."

"Nonsense," Seethaler repeats, then shouts to the boys to gather up the tools and meet him at the truck.

"I'd like to ask if you would consider a trade instead of cash."

"A trade?" Seethaler starts in the direction of the truck.

"Something unexpected has come up. I'm short of cash."

"Frau Mohr, Frau Mohr." Seethaler tugs his mustache, shakes his head.

Her heart begins to pound. What she is about to propose occurred to her only moments ago. The new suitcase cost twice what she'd planned to spend—and turned out twice as heavy, too.

Seethaler climbs into the truck, rummages around on the front seat, then closes the door. He hands a sheet of paper through the open window. "As promised."

Käthe is shocked by the figure. "Theo! Surely this isn't the cost!"

Seethaler smiles. "I found a cheap supplier."

She folds the paper, flushing with embarrassment. She fumbles for a moment, creases the paper with her nails. Seethaler looks past her to the boys still cleaning up. The Daibler boys are teasing them from up on their stilts. "I would still like to propose a trade," she finally says.

Seethaler gazes out the front window of the truck.

She tucks the bill into her pocket. "Before my husband left I had a little cabin built." She points to the woods sloping up behind the house. "Up there, near Kaltengruben. It's just a little hut, really. A place for him to write."

The boys are coming across the lawn. "Don't forget the shovel!" Seethaler shouts.

Käthe puts her foot on the running board. "You can have it."

"Have it?" Seethaler is surprised. "Have what?"

"The hut. Take it away."

"Take it away?"

"The whole thing. Windows, stove, floor planks, roof shingles. There's plenty of good lumber. Just take it away. Whatever you want."

Seethaler seems amused. The two boys stroll up, smoking cigarettes. They put the shovels into the truck and then climb up into the bed.

"Think about it."

Seethaler starts the engine. A blast of black smoke erupts from the clattering tailpipe. He revs once, twice; puts the truck into gear. *"Was kostet dännn därrrr ganzä Bärg?"*

"Theo Seethaler. Stop your games and just do what I say!" Immediately she feels ridiculous.

Seethaler is surprised by the outburst. "I'll think about it, Frau Mohr," he says through the window. Then waves and drives off shaking his head.

Eva calls from the kitchen. "From Japan, Mama! Look. With a photo." She holds the letter out. "Read it."

Fuji New Grand Lodge
Lake Yamanaka
Japan
Liebste Käthe,
Have landed in a wonderful spot. A tiny Japanese cottage on Yamanaka, one of the five Fuji lakes. Was away for three days, up Fujiyama, the most beautiful mountain on earth. Am completely exhausted today, saddle sore and a stiff back. 12,400 feet (4,100 meters), straight up, and down. Did very well. A great view of the Pacific and a deep, dangerous crater on top. Pilgrims everywhere, all slept in the shelter on top together. Just beautiful. But a dangerous mountain, too. You ride for hours and hours and then through the lava fields, like being on snow. Looks just like the Wallberg—but four times as high, and jutting up alone out of the landscape. It was wonderful, but exhausting. I am having a wonderful time. Out on horseback early every morning, then again in the evening. Remember the yellow morning glories you handed to Lawrence the day he left? They are everywhere here, sprouting in glades of tiger lily and more than a thousand species of songbird,

giant butterflies, dragonflies. A dream from childhood, riding through volcanic forests, galloping along the shores of the Fuji lakes. All this beauty, and war breaking out! Everyone is frantic and I feel completely calm, inside and out. They are evacuating Americans to Manila, English to Hong Kong, and Germans here, to Japan. Of course, as a non-Aryan, I am not among them, which is just fine with me. I don't know how I'm going to get back to Shanghai. But I am determined to go back. What's going to happen to my practice? Don't worry. I'm not worried, though I think we can count now on a long and nasty war. Depressing to see how this thousand-year-old silk and garden-house culture is being murdered by technological modernity. This is one of the most beautiful places on earth. I wish the two of you were here with me; then again, I don't, and would rather be back with you in our little nook at the foot of the Wallberg, clear-headed and healthy and awake and able to see the beauty in everything. All my love to you and Eva. MM.

Käthe folds the letter, picks up the photograph. Mohr holds two horses by the reins as they graze in front of a large bush. He is wearing a white shirt with sleeves rolled high up his arm, looking over his shoulder, hair tousled, wind-blown. There are mountains in the background.

"Why two horses, Mama?" Eva asks.

"I don't know," Käthe says, and puts the photograph down on the table.

Part Two

From a distance there is no difference between a rainy and a sunny day.

Emotion toward things of the past is less intense than toward things of the present. That's how Spinoza put it, and his formulation makes sense. But Spinoza had never seen a photograph. To say the rain that fell last week is the cause of your mood today would be absurd. So how is it that looking at old photographs has such intense effect, moves you so strongly?

You put down the picture you've been studying.

It is dark throughout the house but for the yellow cone of light that shines on the center of table, the very same table at which Käthe and Max are sitting, crumpled and unhappy, in the picture you have just set aside. The electric bulb flickers, making the light in the room seem uncertain.

You've been sitting all evening at the old oak table, sorting and arranging, resorting and rearranging photographs. The piles are now all in disarray. You stopped following a time frame. But when, exactly? You smile at the irony of the question, stand up to stretch your legs. The light fixture buzzes. As you leave the room you consider switching it off, then change your mind and linger for a moment.

Mohr used to say that writing was simply the effort of capturing all the various strands of consciousness and putting them into words. But are words precipitated out of experience the way images are precipitated out of the light captured in a camera? Photographs. Do they convey the simultaneity of impressions we have when we see? Of thoughts, when we think? The tune of consciousness? No. They can't. They are a subversion of the moment, the way words are a subversion of what we are really thinking deep within ourselves. The world is always near at hand, yet inexpressible, and the gulf can only be partially bridged in acts of memory.

Take in the setting: a table covered with snapshots; two cigar boxes, lids open; four bound albums, one missing its cover; lengths of ribbon, some old and faded, some still bright; souvenir postcards of the Graf Zeppelin, the Kürsingerhütte on the Gross-Venediger, the Pension Goelands in Bandol, France; a pen-and-ink drawing of the Shanghai Bund; a magnifier; a teapot and cup; an ashtray; a covered butter dish; a plate with a brown apple core and bread crumbs—all lit from above by a small light hanging low over the center of the table.

You step outside for a breath of fresh air. It's a cool, moonless night. The surrounding hills, a line of blackness etched against the starry sky. Everything seems so perfectly familiar and natural. How to know Max and Käthe. Photographs make everything seem recent and vivid, tensed and tenseless, the future past nested in a moment.

You sit on the bench by the front door, light a cigarette. These little breaks intensify the sense of being both lost to and intimately connected to the present moment. Of course, you have your own pictures to pass along, too; someday your children and grandchildren will look back—at you, at themselves. What moves you in looking at these old snapshots of people who were gone long before you entered the world isn't nostalgia, but a thrilling sense of connection, and it makes you both happy and sad to realize that what is keeping you up so late into the night is a feeling not of presence, but of absence.

What can be more natural than going through old pictures?

There you were, Max. Here you are, Käthe.

Which tense to use? How to describe a photograph?

There had been a sack race, seven children hopping across the yard. There is Martin, in last place, and Eva about to tumble over the little girl who has just fallen in front of her. Their joy is plain to see, not only in their faces, but in the blur of motion as they tumble forward, giddy, hopping and falling in their sacks. The photographer intrudes into the foreground of the scene: Mohr's shadow on the grass, a reminder of what is and is not present. The narrator. Other photos were taken that day, but this sack race is the one that carries the fullest measure of the moment. On that day, as Mohr chased around, photographing the children's games, had he already known he would leave? Had he told Käthe yet?

She must have wondered herself. Perhaps even as she sat up at night, looking at the very same picture. Why do people keep photographs? To remind them of the past, or to guard against the future? "I've had enough of the future," Mohr told her shortly before he left. "Especially a future where all everybody talks about is the future."

She had taken to following their conversations with her eyes more than her ears. In the weeks leading up to his departure, he was easily excited, but on their last night together, he was quiet. The weather had grown cold and damp. They were lying in bed. It was late at night. "You want to stay, don't you?"

Mohr looked away. "I don't know what I want." He said it as if the choice were between this house in the country with goats and chickens or a tobacco shop in the city selling lottery tickets and magazines. "You can't run away from the times," he said at last. "You can only turn your back."

"Is that what you're doing? Turning your back?"

They went to Munich together and said good-bye at Stachus. Mohr didn't want to say good-bye at the station, bundled up against the cold, struggling with luggage and waving his final wave to them from the train. In the end, he just wanted to get it over with, and carried himself as if he'd developed new muscles in his legs. Käthe felt as if she were just recovering from something. When they said good-bye, it was with the feeling that they'd never loved one another more than at that moment. Or ever would. Mohr turned and walked away quickly, gripping a bag in either hand, leaning forward with his hat slipping back on his head, overcoat flapping, unbuttoned. He stopped at the station entrance, turned and waved, then disappeared through the doors and was gone.

It is brisk now, and dry. Your eyes have adjusted to the darkness. A refreshing breeze blows from the north, the direction of the lake. High up in the forest, elk are calling. It is mating season, and the hills reverberate with their lowing cries. Should you go back in and continue looking at photographs? Or put them away? It's not an easy thing to decide. What right do you have to intrude into their lives like this? How can you presume to be so intimate? Or is it simply *the past* you are looking at—empirical, true, and over? You don't know what to do. The further back one goes, the more blurred the days and years of a lifetime become until, finally, it merges into the homogenous infinity of not-being.

There you are.

What was the past before photography? Was it easier to face when there was nothing to look at?

Shanghai

series of loud explosions awakens him shortly before dawn. It is followed by a barrage of naval guns from the flotilla of Japanese warships in the Whangpoo. Mohr sits up in bed, rests his chin on his knees listening to a symphony of air-raid sirens, clattering machine guns, and antiaircraft fire. Yesterday a stray shell landed in the middle of Yates Road. He was on the other side of the Settlement when it happened, overseeing the transfer of medicine and supplies from a hospital being evacuated in the war zone. The time might have been better spent at Lester Hospital, but Timperly wouldn't risk losing a whole truckload of free medicine, and Mohr was dispatched with a Chinese driver and a Sikh NCO to fetch the precious and perishable cargo to safety. It took eleven hours.

He gets out of bed, marches across the room, and lifts the telephone from its cradle. He pauses before putting it to his ear, as if his hesitation might miraculously restore the dial tone. It doesn't. He'll have to wait until later to find out how the night went for Agnes. With a glance at the cluttered mess on his desk, he lifts the cloth from Zappe's cage, lights a cigarette, and steps over to the window.

It is just after five o'clock. In thirty minutes the curfew will end. There is something reassuring, if also surreal, about the sight of the deserted street below. A bunker of sandbags has been built in front of the apartment building, a snail-shell shape, open at one end. The rickshaw pullers have turned it into a sort of staging area from which they dart across crowded lanes of traffic.

He opens the window. A sudden breeze blows the ash from his cigarette. He steps on it. A bizarre voyeurism has overtaken the city, combined with a peculiarly British civic-mindedness. Yesterday a cartoon by Sapajou in the *North China Daily News* mocked Shanghailanders as camera-touting tourists flocking to their rooftops to watch "fly fly eggs"—pidgin for bombs—fall from the sky. In the same edition was a notice from a local housewife on how to keep tomato juice, unrefrigerated, for up to a week (lemon juice).

He picks up Käthe's letter.

The distance between us seems greater than ever, darling. You're so difficult to reach and the mail has become so uncertain. The birthday telegram did come through. Thank you so much. At least I know you're still all right. I can't imagine what you must be going through. It's impossible to get much of an impression from the newspapers. Are you working as a doctor? You'll laugh at the question, since there must be nothing but wounded and war and every sort of horror. Are you allowed to help? As a German, I mean? I so desperately want to be there with you now, if only so you can tell me that there was once something pure and true between us. It could turn out that we'll never see one another again, or that you love another woman—I don't know where I'm going with all this— just tell me that something lives within us that was once beautiful and real, okay? Tell me, if ever we see one another again, that there will still be this connection, apart and separate from everything else. I sound dumb now. Pardon. I enclose photos of Eva, but for all I know this letter will be lost somewhere on the border of Manchuria, or be burned. Now you're

surrounded once again by grenades and exploding bombs. When will I have news? Everyone here asks about you, but I don't know myself! How far we've been driven apart! You are all I can think about, and how close we once were. Now there is nothing but silence. I feel so peculiar today. What we had was real and beautiful and unforgettable, wasn't it? Tell me you think so, too. We are fine. Eva is big and strong and happy. There is nothing left in Germany that would interest you. We hope that the war ends soon. God protect you from illness and war and want. I can't think of a single happy thing to say today, nothing to make you smile. I don't know why. You'll just have to take this letter as is, okay? K.

He folds the letter and puts it aside. Once again, everything and nothing has changed.

Returning from Japan six weeks ago, he had stood at the railing of the *Satroclus* and watched in amazement as a Japanese destroyer fired shell after shell into the skeleton of the Chapai Power Station. Agnes and the other five passengers who had come on the British boat from Nagasaki were belowdecks. Mohr chose to ignore the warnings of the officer in charge and came up for a look at the devastation that had been wrought in the short time they'd been gone. Japanese warships were arrayed up and down the Whangpoo as far as the French Bund. The flagship, *Idzumo*, was dressed for war and hulked in the middle of the river. They passed close enough that he could see its sandbagged sides, its bridges strung with hammocks, and even make out the shapes of individual soldiers pointing antiaircraft guns to the sky. A sudden burst of gunfire erupted from one of the cruisers lying along-side the *Idzumo*. He dropped into a crouch behind the rail and watched in disbelief as machine gunners fired on a tiny flotilla of sampans try-ing to cross the river about three hundred meters upstream. Spurts of water erupted in ever crueler arcs until the fishermen, heaving their oars, swung their little boats around and headed back toward Nantao.

He retreated from the railing in a crouch, his stomach knotted tightly, his shirt soaked in sweat. The punc punc punc punc of the machine guns continued. He returned below. Agnes was in one of the tiny galleys on the lowermost deck. Her eyes were closed.

"I've never felt so sick," she groaned.

She had been crying. The sound of engines and the dull, gray-metal atmosphere made talk unnatural. He brushed the hair from her cheek and she made room for him on the narrow berth. He lay down beside her, drained by the ordeal of the last thirty-two hours, but also suffused with the exhilaration of having made it safely back.

His thoughts drifted to the little cottage on the gently sloping hill just above Lake Yamanaka—another cosmos, entirely. He'd never felt more out of touch. They'd arrived late at night, been shown to the cottage by a lantern-toting porter from the New Fuji Grand Hotel, which owned a string of cottages on one side of the lake. On that first morning, he woke up slowly, gradually taking in all the new sounds and fragrances. The waxy light filtering into the room through paper screens was like nothing he'd seen before, soft and opaque and also clear and transparent. He slipped out of bed and went to look out the window. "There it is!" He couldn't contain himself. "Fujiyama." The mountain rose up across the lake. Right out of a dream. Agnes tugged the sheet over her shoulders and sat up. "Come look," he insisted. "There it is. We're going to climb it."

She smiled, shook her head. "First things first," she said.

He left her to get dressed, went outside and stood on the cottage's front stoop in his undershirt and shorts, exhilarated by the sight of the mountain, the fresh morning air.

Later that day, on their first ride around the lake, he felt a similar exhilaration. It was the freedom to go—and to *be*—wherever he pleased. As they stopped to take in yet another magnificent view of Fujiyama, Agnes said, "Hiroshige painted right here where we are standing."

Mohr was embarrassed not to know Hiroshige. "How did you learn to ride so well?" he asked.

"My father taught me." She flicked the reins and trotted off. He watched her round the bend, feeling strangely, wonderfully disoriented. The day was hot and humid, but the air along the lakeshore was refreshingly cool. They rode in silence for a long time, Agnes leading several paces ahead. Mohr's exhilaration began to fade; his freedom began to feel dubious, counterfeit. Was it right that he was here with her? How was it wrong? He tried to think of Agnes and Käthe as spokes meeting in the nave of a wheel—and himself as the hollow hub, the empty place on which everything turned.

"What are you thinking?" she asked.

"I don't know," he answered, feeling right away that his evasion somehow violated the serenity of the setting. They'd gone nearly halfway around the lake and it was time to decide whether to continue all the way around or turn back. Mohr patted the animal's dusty neck. "Let's stop for a rest."

They dismounted. Mohr tied the horses. Agnes took the camera from the saddle pack and made some photographs. They were a short distance above the lakeshore, in a small meadow surrounded by a dense thicket thrumming with summertime: calling songbirds, chirruping cicadas. A carpet of wildflowers spread out in all directions, buzzing with bees and fluttering with butterflies. The horses grazed, flicked their tails. Agnes walked down to the water. He lay down in a soft patch of grass, closed his eyes, and drifted off, feeling transient and singular, like a passing cloud.

Some time later, Agnes returned. She sat down in the grass beside him, holding a bunch of wildflowers she'd picked. "I like the sapphire ones," she said, slipping a stem from the bouquet and offering it.

He rose on his elbow, accepted the tiny flower. "Do you know the name?"

She shook her head. "Do you?"

"No."

She gazed out across the lake from under her hat. The hunting-club outfit she had on seemed oddly out of place in this landscape—cream-

colored jodhpurs, tightly wrapped leggings, and a white summer shirt. He put his arms around her and kissed her, then lay back down in the grass. "I'd like to come back here," she said. "Right here. To this very spot." She looked down at him. "I'm going to do it. I'm going to come back to this exact place every day."

"Every day?"

"Every day."

"I'm sure there are other places that are just as nice."

"But here, we are exactly halfway." She pointed to the cottage, just visible among the trees directly across the lake. "And being halfway, the farther away we ride, the closer we come to home."

Mohr laughed. "The same way that if you keep going east, you eventually end up in the west?"

"Yes," she said. "Just like that."

It wasn't until evening, as they sat together on the steps of the cottage, that he began to understand what she meant. The night air was humid but cool. A mild breeze. The moon rose in a yellow sliver over the lake. He sipped his tea, slowly rolling the perfectly turned porcelain cup between his palms. Rolling and sipping, rolling and sipping. He became conscious of the touch of her thigh against his—sitting on the narrow step, unsure what closing this half-distance would mean, and if it were even possible.

"What are you thinking?" she asked, lighting a cigarette.

"I don't know," was his answer for the second time that day. Another evasion, but also a truthful reply, one that needed no clarification. He reached for his cigarettes and stood up, walked a few paces into the shadows, beyond the cottage's lamp glow. "I haven't heard silence like this for a long time." He remained in the shadows, taking in the cozy lamplit cottage silhouetted against the night sky. Agnes bent forward and stubbed out her cigarette, scattering the glowing embers back and forth until they disintegrated in the gravel. Then she stood up and went inside, leaving him feeling suddenly shuttered in and grown over by vines.

His sense of isolation seemed to grow rather than diminish during the weeks they spent together, as if each were seeking the other on a plane beyond everyday life. It had been that way with Käthe, and with Lawrence in the end, too: a contradictory sense of intimacy and isolation that somehow resolved itself into something beyond, and possibly other than, friendship. Mohr thought of Lawrence frequently in Japan. They'd met almost exactly ten years earlier, on a bright October day in 1927. A broad terrace in Baden-Baden. Lawrence had been waiting for him and waved at an empty chair. "Frieda has left me here and gone off for a nap." He said it the way an old man might rue an inconvenience. "I have never understood why people insist on sleeping during the day." Then he fixed a look on Mohr, his aqueous eyes neither smiling nor frowning but radiating illness and frank appraisal. His red beard was freshly clipped against his hollow cheeks. "Sit down," he said.

Mohr sat. He immediately felt too large, was embarrassed by his brand-new tweed jacket, and his good health. He leaned forward, elbows on his knees, clasped and unclasped his hands self-consciously. Lawrence had answered his letter immediately, which had caught Mohr off guard, made him feel as if he were being granted an audience. He wasn't certain if he should take the initiative and begin a conversation, or simply sit and admire the view, as Lawrence seemed content to do.

A deer emerged from the wood and began to graze at the far end of the lawn. "How tame," Lawrence said and coughed, passing his fist across his mouth as if repressing something foul. More deer emerged from the wood. "Eden is so badly lost," he went on, watching the deer.

"Lost or tamed?" Mohr ventured.

Lawrence thought for a moment, then said, "The question is not only how to prevent suburbia from spreading all over Eden, but also how to prevent Eden from running into a great wild wilderness."

"I would not mind Eden returning to wilderness." Mohr came forward in his chair. "Where can you find *real* life in all this goddamned civilization?"

Lawrence put his fist to his mouth again, but did not cough. "Are you married?"

"And I have a daughter named Eva." Mohr smiled. "Speaking of Eden."

Lawrence did not return the smile. "I meant are you *happily* married?" The question was neither offhanded nor intended personally.

Mohr paused to consider his answer. "When I am in my little house in the mountains, all I can think of is getting out. And when I'm away, all I want is to return."

Lawrence cocked his head. "I have always said that the Eden between a man and a woman has always been a matter of either love or of understanding. It can never be both."

Mohr was puzzled, not certain he understood what Lawrence was saying. He recalled the quasi-platonic flavors in Lawrence's books, terms such as *sex-circuit,* the idea of separate beings perfectly polarized, a cosmic duality that was not the result of a broken, fragmented whole but, rather, *the singling away into purity and clear being of things that were mixed.* He was tempted to quote this, but was constrained by self-consciousness and the feeling that it would have the wrong effect.

"I don't think I can agree with you," he said at last. "But maybe we use the words differently. I would say that love and understanding must always go together—and I am not thinking of Kant, but of my wife and child."

"Herr Doktor, let's be honest. Understanding comes *always* at a price. It is very difficult to preserve one's central innocence without becoming bitter. Especially in a relationship between a man and a woman." Lawrence frowned. "Love *and* understanding? I don't know anyone who has managed it—and anybody who claims to have is a swindler or an idiot."

A period of silence fell. Mohr felt strangely weakened. All the heightened sensibility, all the infirmity. The *Kurgäste* came and went on the terrace, elderly ladies, mostly. He was surprised to find this radical Englishman so comfortable amid all the *Bürgurtum.* Lawrence sputtered once or twice, ever on the verge of eruption. At last, Frieda appeared with the announcement that it was time for his *Inhalationskur.* She was bright and friendly and simply dressed, a lapsed aristocrat, whose airs Mohr was all too familiar with. A web of family connections had gotten him there, and he found himself immediately at ease with her.

"These cures will kill you," Lawrence grumbled to no one in particular. "Really, in Baden one ought to be at least seventy-five years old, and an *Exzellenz,* or at the very least a *Generälchen.* The place is such a back number."

Mohr chuckled, suddenly at ease, and at last found his balance describing his life in the mountains.

"It sounds lovely," Lawrence said. "I haven't been in Bavaria since before the war. Isartal. It was lovely."

"Then you must come and visit me at Wolfsgrub. You don't have to be a *Generälchen,* and the mountain air will be good for you."

"My sister tells me you are a medical doctor as well as a playwright," Frieda cut in.

Mohr smiled. "Which means only that I will play my accordion for you rather than promise a *kur.*"

Lawrence lit up. "At last, a man who doesn't make promises! Oh, I should love to set out with an accordion and turn my back on the world! As soon as this beastly cough goes down, we'll do it, shall we? To Greenland. Like your Captain Ramper."

Mohr laughed, pleased to learn that Lawrence had read his play.

"With an accordion!" Lawrence continued, then nodded at Frieda. "I'm afraid if there's a sound of accordions anywhere, the beloved women will not be left behind." Frieda smiled indulgently, pleased by her husband's sudden change of mood. Lawrence continued, "If we set out with music and light heels, how can you expect the women to let us go alone? *Aspettiamo pure!*"

"We can pretend we are going to a gathering of the international Pen Club," Mohr joked.

Lawrence groaned. "How awful!"

The attendant, who had been standing discreetly aside, came forward with a wheelchair. Frieda touched her husband on the arm. "I can manage by myself just fine, thank you." He waved away the wheelchair. "I will walk," he growled and stood up. "I look forward to reading more of your work," he said, and they were gone, all talk of Greenland and escape and light heels vanished into a tedium of scented vapors, where the poor man was reduced to a paper silhouette of himself.

The ship lights flickered. Mohr raised himself on an elbow, anticipating a plunge into darkness. Instead, the lights glowed brighter. Agnes was curled next to him, breathing softly. Belowdecks in the warship was a purgatory of artificial light. There were no portals, no openings to the outside. He felt strangely vulnerable and exposed; couldn't imagine ever actually sleeping inside the steel hull of a warship. Nevertheless, he took off his glasses, held them on his chest, and tried to rest his eyes.

"What about Käthe and Eva?" Agnes suddenly asked. She rubbed her eyes, a little disoriented, as if she had been dreaming.

Her question startled him. "What about them?"

"Do you still plan to bring them?"

He dangled an arm over the edge of the berth, traced his fingertips along the steel floor, eyes fixed on the ceiling. He wanted badly to explain his predicament, but so far, in his effort to find just the right words, he'd succeeded only in keeping silent about it. He felt helpless and inarticulate. "I suppose they're better off where they are, for now," he said at last.

"Do you miss them?"

He closed his eyes again, feeling for the first time since boarding the ship that he might actually want to try to sleep after all. "Yes, but what should I do?"

The engines surged. The whole ship began to rock, as if suddenly changing direction.

"In China, we believe everything is predetermined," she said.

"In China, a man can have several wives." It was an attempt at humor but came out sounding cruel.

"I am not your wife," she said and turned to the wall.

"Don't be angry with me."

"I'm not angry," she said.

But she was. He lay for a while listening to the straining of the ship's engines, the sound of frantic activity above deck. The sound of footsteps just outside the doorway made him sit up. A few minutes later they were stumbling with all their bags behind an English sailor, down a narrow gangway that, by some miracle of the British Navy, deposited them onto the very wharf from which they'd embarked just three weeks earlier, aboard the NYK Express Lines *Nagasaki Maru.*

They returned to a completely broken city, and stood on the jetty, dumbstruck, disoriented, and out of breath, clutching their luggage. It was shocking to see the swarms of people trying to leave—the sheer numbers—families of all nationalities being evacuated, pushing past them at the customs shed, waving their anxious good-byes from beyond the barrier fence.

What to do now? Mohr offered to drop Agnes off at home. She refused; insisted on taking a separate taxicab. His protests were mild, distracted as he was by the chaos all around; shouting customs officials, police. A pit opened in his stomach as he kissed her good-bye. It felt different. She had changed, but not just her, him as well. She slid backward into the taxi. Mohr leaned into the window. "I need some time alone. To make sense of things."

"Please," she cut him off wearily. "No more explanations."

"Will you call me when you get home?"

She nodded, her smile a little too dark and uncertain for parting to be easy. Going home separately was more natural than dragging out good-bye. What other option was there? To make matters worse, he'd made her angry with his stupid quip back on the boat. This was not the time for talk. She was tired and worried about her mother, alone these two weeks.

Turning onto Nanking Road from the Bund, he saw the badly damaged facades of the buildings. Sandbagged machine-gun emplacements and barbed wire at every intersection. Military vehicles and people moving along the streets. At the hotel lodge in Yamanaka he'd read the newspaper accounts of the August 13 bombings of the Cathay and Palace Hotels and New World Amusement Center—dropped not by Japanese but by Chinese airplanes. By accident! Thousands killed. The bombings had happened on the very day they climbed Fujiyama.

Wong dissolved into tears when Mohr walked in the door. *"Ó kán ni kó lee 'en,"* he kept repeating. I am so sorry for you. Mohr was alarmed. He took Wong by the hand, tried to reassure him. *"Bùh bìh gwá nìen."* You needn't be anxious. "See? All one piecee!" Wong's wife was standing in the hallway. Looking haggard, she greeted Mohr nervously, then fetched a pitcher of water. Wong dragged the bags in from the landing. He was unshaven, barefoot, wearing a dirty tunic. It looked as if he hadn't been outside in days; he could not stop apologizing as he tried to fill Mohr in on all the horrors of the past two weeks. It took some time for the picture to emerge, all that Wong had seen and done. Evidently, he had been doing a fair amount of ambulance duty with the car. "Every day hospital-side, Missy Chen Siu-fang. Every day."

Mohr was too tired to absorb it all and went to his room. In spite of the summer heat, the windows were shut tight. The air was stale. The entire apartment smelled like bird shit and old cooking oil. He threw open the windows, let Zappe out of the cage, took the bird on his finger. Wong began unpacking but Mohr stopped him. "Not now. *Hóu lài yé kó i,* Wong. Afterward."

He took a bath—a long, hot bath. In the tub, a revelation of the sort that only comes in moments of quiet exhaustion: that in coming back he had finally made this city his home, could never have felt truly settled here until he'd left and returned.

AND NOW IT is November.

The war has been grinding on, but the Japanese have not yet sent their troops to occupy the International Settlement or French Concession. In the last few weeks, Mohr has visited every refugee collection point in the Settlement, knows the conditions firsthand. There are now thirteen thousand in the New World Theater alone. The area has become a slime pit, an incubator of cholera, dysentery, tuberculosis. In his report to the Chinese Red Cross, he said it should be evacuated immediately. An impossibility, clearly, but also the only way to minimize the death toll of the coming epidemics. A few days ago, he tried to get places for two more of Wong's family at the Girl's School on Thibet Road, elderly cousins of his wife. It was the best refugee facility in the city—or, rather, the most exclusive, as he'd remarked acidly to the King's Daughter Society ladies, who refused to take them. He tried two more places after that, but conditions in both were simply too appalling, and so he ended up bringing them back home.

Today, a consignment of smallpox vaccine is due in from Hong Kong. The chances of it coming in on time, if at all, are slim. Lester Hospital has become a collection point for food and medicine donations from all over the city. Wong makes regular use of the car, picking up and delivering supplies and people all across the Settlement. Chen Siu-fang is no longer cruising Pootung godowns and silk factories for patients, but has been put in charge of a small ambulance corps, with three donated Red Cross vehicles at her disposal. In compensation for the use of the car and for Wong's efforts, Timperly has given Mohr permission to supply himself and his burgeoning household from the hospital's stock of milk, eggs, rice, cod-liver oil, and whatever else there is to be had at the end of the day.

A light knock at the door. Wong materializes carrying a tray.

"*Dzáo dzáo an* Wong." Mohr beckons him in.

Wong clears a place amid the clutter of the desk, sets the tray down, and with a nod toward the open window says, *"Ni yáo hsíao hsin!"*

Mohr shakes his head. No. Closing the window is out of the question. He pulls the tray closer, inspects. Tea, a small bowl of rice—there hasn't been bread anywhere in the city for three days—and a boiled egg. Wong steps to the open window, gingerly touches his fingertips to the panes as if they could shatter at any moment. "All night *fang fang fang,*" he says, and in an unprecedented act of boldness pokes his head out and peers into the street. "No wantchee Master hurt."

"No wantchee anyone hurt," Mohr says, peeling the egg and slicing it in pieces over the rice. Disregarding what he has just been told, Wong closes the window. Mohr lets it pass, will open it again just as soon as Wong leaves the room. The business with the windows has become a ritual between the two of them: Mohr tries to persuade Wong to keep the windows open—especially in the claustrophobic little room he and his expanding family now occupy. Wong refuses. There are now seven people living in the former waiting room. The air has become fetid. Mohr would like to put a limit on the number of people he will allow into the apartment, but realizes he can't. The situation in the city has become too desperate. Even the Municipal Police can't keep out the masses of refugees pouring into the Settlement. In spite of checkpoints and barricades and barbed wire, the streets are choked with humanity fleeing the war zones.

"My come Master hospital-side?" Wong asks.

Mohr glances at his wristwatch and nods.

Wong leaves him to finish his breakfast. Their communication has taken on a telepathic quality. Straitened circumstances have lent an immediacy and an urgency to the smallest interaction. There is little to discuss, but also a heightened awareness of things. The presence of rice and eggs. The availability of coal. Hot water. There is so little left that can be called normal; yet in spite of all the hardship, Mohr feels unusually contented. He is working around the clock, feels completely drained and empty. Smiling at the thought (can a person really be empty who is aware of it?), he stirs the sliced egg into the rice and begins to eat, holding the bowl under his chin, Japanese style.

Lawrence used to talk about counterfeit peace, the empty egoism he said was the essence—or lack of it—of modern man. Mohr remembers feeling badly stung by the remark, and becoming increasingly unsettled during their daily chats out on the veranda of Lawrence's rented villa at Bandol, just months before he died. They'd been enjoying the warm afternoon sunshine and discussing a popular English novel by a writer named Walter Wilkinson called *The Peep Show*. Frieda said, "Speaking of peep shows, we watched you swimming this afternoon, Max," and she pointed down to the rocky stretch that Mohr swam from every afternoon.

"Like a bewildered seal rolling around," Lawrence sniped.

Mohr felt his temper rise. "Who can be anything *but* bewildered in this crazy world?" he returned with forced composure.

"You needn't try to idealize it," Lawrence came back. "As long as the quick of the self is there, your bewilderment is counterfeit." He lifted a finger from the armrest and pointed at Mohr as if giving him permission to examine himself. Counterfeit, authentic; emptiness, fulfillment; connection, annihilation; male, female. Mohr was fluent in Lawrence's language, but was wary of his mania for dividing the world into oppositions. What was the opposite of swimming? Drowning! And it wasn't "the quick of the self" that kept you afloat. To stay afloat you had to swim in all directions at once, toward ever-receding shorelines.

Yamanaka had reminded him of Bandol in so many ways: a temporary idleness shadowed by tortuous indecision. As the days there stretched into weeks, the journey with Agnes had begun to seem a sort of reverberation of that earlier one. Marriage had been a central theme of both trips—his marriage. Specifically, his condition as a married man. With

Agnes, it had gone largely unspoken. But it was all Lawrence would talk about. "Promise you'll return with Käthe in February," he insisted, close to death and yet bent as ever on extracting pledges and promises. He had a right to all his demands, not just because he was dying, but because his dependence on others had taken its toll, and dignity required it.

Mohr ignored the request, continued with the task at hand.

"What are you doing?" Lawrence asked after some minutes.

He was sewing lavender and uncooked rice into a small sachet. "Something for you to put over your eyes when you sleep. I picked it in the fields over there." Mohr pointed in the direction of the hills, where he walked every morning with the proprietor's dog, Rabelais.

"More of your Bavarian quackery? Sometimes I think I should call the health authority." Lawrence cracked a smile, passed his hand across his mouth. "I suppose it must be something potent."

Mohr waved the sachet under his nose. Lawrence sniffed, then sat back in his chair as Frieda breezed back onto the veranda. Mohr offered her the little purple pillow to smell. "The smell makes me think of sleep," she said.

"Then you must have one, too. I've made one for myself already."

"What is it that *you* need medicine for?" Lawrence frowned, then turned to look over the rail of the veranda to the Mediterranean shimmering in the sunlight.

"It's not medicine," Mohr replied. "Just something to relax and calm you down." The point was taken. Lawrence continued to look out over the water. The sparring between the two of them had become tedious in those last weeks they were together. It was partly Mohr's fault for sharing so much of his personal troubles, but Lawrence liked to draw them out, was ever eager to examine. That Mohr should feel confined by married life bothered Lawrence to the point of anger. "Is it a doom to you?" he would demand. "Do you feel condemned to it?"

Mohr tried to explain it as a question of separate destinies, how to be together and apart at the same time. "What you have called mutual union in separateness."

Lawrence reacted as if the words caused him physical pain. "You must be her man, utterly." He scowled. "Anything less is not worth a forked radish."

There was some element of vengeance in it, of the sick man envying health. A man who feels cramped by married life will always be an irritation to a man being nursed by his wife and who is contented with the simplest domesticities—regular meals, a comfortable bed, a window that lets in the breeze. Why are the healthy man's discontents viewed as spiritual failings, but the sick man's cantankerousness merely as lapses of spirit? Why not the reverse? Why not call the dying man to judgment and allow the healthy man his lapses? Eventually, Lawrence stopped berating and took to teasing instead, calling him *der schwarze Ritter*, the black knight.

Mohr feeds Zappe the last bits of rice, and watches as they are picked away, one by one. The bird has fallen quiet lately, rarely even squawks. The sounds—bombs and artillery in the distance, the whine of airplanes—seem to have rendered the poor animal mute. When he opens the cage now, the bird will not be coaxed out. "Zappe, my little friend. You've stopped talking." He fetches the cover and drapes it over the cage.

UTILITY WORKERS ARE restringing downed wires along Shantung Road. Mohr watches their acrobatics from the car. A maze of ladders and large coils of wire have made an obstacle course of the entire street. An English foreman on the ground in pith helmet and kneesocks directs the activity with an aggressive, self-conscious authority that seems more desperate than reassuring. Wong navigates the clogged and crowded street with telepathic assurance. Driving in Chen Siu-

fang's ambulance corps has made him a confident—if slightly aggressive—driver. He also enjoys showing off the clever alternative routes
he has learned all across the Settlement and French Town. "Who
taught you this way?" Mohr asks as Wong makes a sudden turn down
a narrow alleyway.

Wong smiles into the rearview mirror. "B'long my pidgin."

"Your pidgin b'long your pidgin. My pidgin b'long everybody
pidgin."

Wong hangs his arm out the window to signal a turn. "Everybody
pidgin b'long, Dr. Mohr!" He laughs, pushes his cap back on his head.
Wong is right. Mohr's business is everybody's business, and everybody's
business is his business. He has precious little privacy these days, keeps
no secrets. Wong has begun showing a dry, ironic side that seems to be
a consequence of his total dependence on Mohr. The humor suits Mohr
well. In fact, the more cramped the situation in the apartment becomes,
the more he enjoys his wry, impertinent "Number One."

A group of Red Cross volunteers spills out of the main entrance just
as they pull in front of Lester Hospital. Mohr hauls his black medical
bag across the seat. Wong opens the door, salutes with a grin. He is
wearing a newly cleaned uniform. It has never quite fitted him properly.

Inside, Mohr finds Timperly talking to two doctors about cholera in
the refugee camps. "We can't bring them here," Timperly is saying.
"The isolation ward is overflowing." He acknowledges Mohr with a nod.

"And beriberi?" one of the doctors asks.

"Send Marmite," Mohr suggests. "There are dozens of donated
crates piling up downstairs."

Timperly lets him know with a patronizing nod that the subject is
already well in hand. In spite of arriving ambulances and pandemo-
nium outside, the doctors calmly continue their discussion. Mohr scans
the lobby for Agnes.

Timperly concludes with the other doctors, and turns to Mohr. "I
expect you'll be off to the Country Hospital later today."

Timperly no longer bothers hiding his resentment of the foreigners-only hospital out on Great Western Road, and his impatience with Mohr's divided loyalties. Mohr would like nothing better than to devote himself exclusively to the Lester Hospital, but with war and the collapse of his practice, he's become more dependent than ever on the other hospital for income.

"No. Today I am all yours."

"Are they even taking soldiers there?"

"Not yet. But they're assisting at the Red Cross camp along the Nanking rail line. Supplies and medicine."

"To keep the wounded from being brought into the Settlement. How orderly."

"The wounded get quicker attention near the front."

"No doubt they do," Timperly says acidly.

Mohr can only shrug. He isn't especially proud of his arrangement with the Country Hospital. The place is emptying out, part of the general evacuation of foreigners from the Settlement, a slow attrition of doctors and staff. Last week even Nagy packed up and joined the British evacuation to Hong Kong. It came as no surprise, and Mohr wished him well. There was something hollow in all the Shanghailander "solidarity" being trumpeted in the local press—as if there were something epic and heroic in the forbearance of inconvenienced colonials.

"You realize, Mohr, I would prefer you to remain here. This war is only just beginning. And now to make things worse, Chen Siu-fang is missing."

"What do you mean, missing?"

"I mean that she left here at six o'clock this morning with three ambulances and Dr. Soo from Chun-Teh Hospital and has still not returned."

"Where were they going?"

"To collect wounded up in Paoshan, near the North Railway Station. The fighting up there has been heavy since yesterday."

Mohr leans against the banister, suddenly light-headed and slightly sickened. He had been with Chen Siu-fang at one of the refugee stations just last week, spent the entire day with her. "Nobody has gone to look for her?"

"We're too short-staffed and it's too dangerous." He fixes Mohr with a hard look. "I want you to make this hospital your only commitment. At least for now. You're one of my best doctors."

A surge of emotion prevents him from answering. The news of Chen Siu-fang mixes precariously with Timperly's compliment. "Very well," he says at last, not as much in consent as in recognition of something all too familiar: the point where the living must begin filling in for the dead.

They shake hands a little awkwardly, and Timperly starts up the stairs. Suddenly he turns and says, "I forgot to tell you. I had a visitor the other day from the German Embassy. Some man named Fuchs."

Mohr is puzzled, then rolls his eyes, recalling the name and the incident at the cocktail party. "What did he want?"

"It was very unpleasant. He told me about an inquiry that came into the embassy about you from the Municipal Police. He seemed particularly interested to learn that you'd gone to Japan."

"What did he ask you?"

"He wanted to know how long you have worked here. How did I hire you." Timperly clears his throat. "He asked me if I realized you were a Jew. Said there was an inquiry under way."

"What sort of inquiry?" Mohr would be angry but for the tinge of bemusement in Timperly's voice.

"He wasn't too clear. Something about Jews and false claims to military service. He asked if you'd claimed to be a veteran."

"What did you tell him?"

"I said yes, indeed. I told him I also knew that you had been a prisoner of war, and had received the Iron Cross." Timperly's eyes twinkle. "You should've seen him. He went red in the face, insisted I was mistaken, that you'd never been in military service, that you'd misrepresented yourself in order to get the job here. He said it was these sorts of falsehoods the German authorities were investigating. Not only that, but he told me he was unable to find any evidence that you had ever attended medical school! And suggested that I fire you immediately!" Timperly laughs. "Don't worry, Mohr. I know a doctor when I see one. And a Nazi, too, for that matter."

Mohr is not amused. He goes to the dispensary to see if the vaccine has arrived from Hong Kong. An investigation! He should've expected it. Start with burning books, end with burning people. The man in charge of the dispensary shrugs indifferently when he asks about the shipment, leads him out to the loading dock at the rear of the building. Crates and boxes of donated supplies are piled up everywhere, guarded by three Chinese men in Red Cross volunteer whites. They watch as he fills a wooden crate with eggs, two containers of Milco powder, cod-liver oil, Rexona ointment, Monsol disinfectant, Cenovita yeast, and two woolen blankets.

Wong leaps from the car as Mohr struggles up with the crate. He tries to relieve him of the load, but Mohr nods for him to open the door. He sets the crate on the rear seat, is about to tell him about Chen Siu-fang, then decides to wait. No point saying anything until they know more. Wong ticks off all the things that he has heard are available at the market today.

"*Pin-go, hung-tsai-tou!*" Wong says.

Mohr digs into his pocket for money, understanding that Wong means to buy fish, apples, and beetroot on the way home. "*Dang hsin,*" he cautions.

"*Ní djao hu dzï gí yào dang hsin!*" Wong shoots back. "My come by'm-bye," he says, and hops into the car.

"Come *ye-ye lí shí,*" Mohr tells him, pointing to the glove box where the extra curfew pass is kept.

Wong drives off, smiling and shaking his head. Mohr repeats the words, *ye ye lí shíh,* realizing he's just spoken complete nonsense. Grandfather mile time, something like that.

Agnes suddenly appears at the hospital entrance with a group of volunteers. He hurries to catch her. Beside the parked ambulances some sort of effort is under way to assign and coordinate volunteers. In his haste, he trips over a newspaper boy hawking the *North China Daily News.* The boy falls with a yelp, and drops his bundle. He is no more than ten, barefooted and wearing a tattered cap with a faded and indecipherable insignia. "Pay my pay my!" the boy shouts.

Mohr grips him by the upper arm, looks him over, then presses a few coins into the boy's hand. The road is clogged with cars, rickshaws, clanging trams. A motley of military police, Red Cross, and hospital staff work to clear a path for the wounded Chinese soldiers being unloaded from ambulances. A shortage of stretchers and an oversupply of stretcher bearers only adds to the confusion. He presses forward, thoughts careening: bacon and sardines are good to have on hand. Chemistry is interesting. Subclinical avitaminosis. Rilke: *Geh in der Verwandlung aus und ein*—Go with change, out and in. . . .

"Max!"

It is Agnes. She runs toward him up the steps, taking them three at a time. "Chen Siu-fang is missing." She is out of breath. Strands of wet hair cling to the side of her face.

"I know. Timperly just told me."

"Nobody has heard from her all day."

The military police guarding the front doors suddenly begin shouting and swinging sticks. Mohr puts an arm across Agnes's shoulders and draws her close. "I've been worried, too. I tried calling you all last night and this morning. The telephones are out."

The front lobby is filled with soldiers, laid out in ever denser rows of folding cots. He leads Agnes over to a corner, glancing around at the mounting chaos inside the hospital. They sit down on a wooden bench. Absurdly, it seems just the time for a private moment together. "A let-

ter came a few days ago," he begins. For days now he's been going over it in his mind. How to broach the subject. He can't see anything clearly.

She stands up and looks squarely at him. "I've been trying to find a way to put this into words, Max. I've been thinking about it since we got back." She sits back down, conscious also of the absurd moment. "This morning my mother was waiting for me at the breakfast table, the way she does every morning. And I realized something. I realized . . ." she breaks off, confused.

"You realized?"

"Well, I realized this is how it has to be for now."

Mohr is unsure what she is trying to tell him. "How what has to be?" His heart is beginning to beat faster. He puts his hand in his coat pocket, feels for the tablets he now carries. He began taking them in Japan, after the climb up Fuji. Glyceryl trinitrate. Agnes procured the tablets with the help of the hotel's manager, who had them sent from Tokyo. It took three whole days to recover, weak, with swelling ankles.

"Everybody must just keep up what they've always been doing," Agnes says, speaking slowly, deliberately. "Especially now, with everything topsy-turvy. Doctors doctor. Nurses nurse. Cooks cook. Shopkeepers keep shop. My mother waits for me to come to the table. Everybody doing what they've always done so things can seem normal." She stands up again.

He is unsure how to respond, and feels overcome by something cold and automatic, something he knows from the last war. It's the opposite of an emotion, a petrifying substance that invades the blood, hardens vision, clogs the heart. He is still thinking about it a short time later, struggling to clamp a bleeding artery in the leg of a Chinese soldier. The tourniquet that was applied by the medic in the field lies in a heap on the man's stomach, where Mohr flung it at the first gush of blood. There are electric fans all around the room to circulate the air. The blowing makes it harder to work. He calls a nurse over, nods at the fan. "Point it away." The soldier's leg is a crimson purple mess of shattered bone and tissue from midthigh to just below the knee. Mohr is soaked with blood to the elbows. The nurse points the fan away, then pats his forehead with a towel as he thrusts his fingers deep into the wound, takes hold of the torn artery, and applies the clamp. The bleeding stops. He stands back, looks down at the soldier, whose pallor is on the verge of chalk. He pries open an eye, feels for a pulse. "Disinfect and wrap the leg," he instructs the nurse. "Then send him up to the second floor." All amputations are carried out upstairs, away from the overcrowded public areas.

He makes his way through the maze of cots toward a washbasin that has been set up at the bottom of the staircase. An orderly pours water from a large jug onto his hands and forearms. He watches the crimson water swirl into the basin, glances up at the large electric clock over the entrance doors. It has a sweeping second hand that is pleasing to watch, not the jerking tick tick tick of old clocks, but a sweeping, continuous movement, inexorable and modern and painless. He suddenly realizes that he is hungry. And tired. The orderly offers a clean towel. Mohr pats his arms dry, looking around to see where he is needed next.

Wounded soldiers arrive throughout the morning. Toward noon, he finds himself involved in a heated discussion with Timperly, two Chinese doctors, and a representative of the National Child Welfare Association. How to handle the tide of malnourished refugees who were bypassing the overcrowded stations and coming directly to the hospital for food?

"There isn't enough space," Timperly says.

"I noticed this morning that the Lyceum Theater up the street has been sandbagged." Mohr offers. "We can try sending them there."

The Child Welfare man perks up. "And you should begin sending the soldiers to the military facility up at North Station. They can be kept there or discharged or sent back to their units, as their officers see fit." He glances around at the doctors.

Mohr lights a cigarette, blows out a thick cloud of smoke. "Sending them up there would be the same as killing them."

The man rushes to object. "The Chinese positions have been consolidated. You can read it in today's papers. This is a civilian hospital. Combatants need to be brought under control of the military authorities as soon as possible."

"They're not combatants. They are wounded." Mohr is astounded by the man's idiocy, and looks to Timperly. Returning wounded soldiers to the war zone was beyond stupid. It was criminal. He waits for someone to take up his argument; then it dawns on him that there are things going unsaid, a bizarre complex of agendas.

"This is not exactly the view of Mr. Kobeyashi or Mr. Takeshita." Timperly's tone is ironically mild.

"Who are they?"

"Mr. Kobeyashi sits on the board of the Municipal Council. And Mr. Takeshita sits on the board of this hospital."

And they are Japanese. The picture becomes suddenly clearer. Tending the Chinese enemy. Mohr puts his cigarette to his lips, glances at the Child Welfare man. "And who sits on the board of your organization? Mickey Mouse?"

A loud burst of machine-gun fire drowns out the laughs of the doctors. It is followed by the high whine of airplane engines. People begin moving toward the doors out of dumb curiosity.

"Get away!" Timperly shouts, and darts into action. "Get down!"

Mohr joins Timperly's example, begins pulling people away from the doors, shouting, "Get down! Get down!" as the machine gun is joined by another, bigger gun and the sound of winding engines. Seconds later an explosion shakes the building. A shower of splintered glass rains down on the lobby. There is the briefest silence, then the room erupts in panic.

Mohr stands up, examines his arms, legs. He is still holding his cigarette. He drops it on the floor, crushes it underfoot, then scans the room. A throng of people is pushing through the shattered glass doors. They are met by an equal throng trying to get out. The electric fans have all stopped, as has the sweeping second hand on the clock. Mohr joins Timperly, who is leading a group of nurses and hospital staff toward the entrance. Someone takes his arm. It is Agnes. "Are you all right?" she asks in a daze.

Mohr nods. "Are you?"

"Yes," she says and, with a firm squeeze, lets go of his arm and disappears into the crowd.

The bomb landed just up the block. Several automobiles are on fire. The air is thick with smoke. Military police blow their whistles and wave their guns, push back the gathering crowd. A group of hospital staff is already pulling the injured from the rubble. Several ambulance corps volunteers brought stretchers and have already begun the grim work of sorting the living from the dead. Mohr suppresses an urge to retch, and pushes deeper into the wreckage.

Timperly appears suddenly. "We need to get back inside," he says, and is gone again. Mohr continues on. An elderly man approaches, leaning on a stick. His face is smeared with blood. Mohr dabs the bloody face with a wad of gauze, revealing a large splinter of glass embedded in the man's scalp, just above the hairline. Gently, he pulls it out, holds it for the man to see. "Glass," he says. "No shrapnel, only glass." The man nods, seeming to understand. Mohr presses the gauze against the wound. *"Du wirst es überleben, alter Mann,"* he says under his breath, guides the man's hand to the gauze, and presses firmly against the wound.

Moments later he is pressing through the crowd at the hospital entrance, rowing with his arms. A group of English soldiers—Royal Welsh Fusiliers—has materialized, and they are pushing at the perimeter of the crowd using batons and rifles. Mohr feels part of a great wounded organism falling to pieces, can see Timperly standing at the doorway, flanked by soldiers. He is pointing out those who may be allowed to pass. The soldiers seesaw with their rifles, clear the area in front of the doors. Glass crunches underfoot and thin trails of blood

streak the concrete. Mohr pauses to catch his breath, hears Timperly's voice. A soldier uses his rifle butt against the crowd. Mohr continues to shove his way through until he reaches the top of the steps. It feels as if his chest is being squeezed by a great hand. Suddenly the soldier butts a bloodstained woman in the stomach. Mohr lunges. The startled soldier steps back and raises the butt of his rifle, lip curling.

"Stop, Mohr! Are you mad?"

And then they are inside the lobby again. Timperly lets go of Mohr's arm with a forceful shove. "What's the matter with you, man?"

Mohr's ears are ringing. He scans the sea of cots, dusted with splinters of glass and fallen plaster, makes eye contact with a Chinese soldier sitting just a few feet inside the entrance. The man had watched Timperly hauling Mohr through the doors. The expression on his face seems divided between mirth at the sight of scuffling doctors and sympathy for the absurdity of their struggle.

WHO IS HE? Did you treat him? How was he wounded? What did the lobby look like just a few minutes ago? What are you supposed to be doing?

"GO AND SIT down," Timperly orders, pointing to the staircase across the lobby.

Mohr marches off like a truant, sits on the bottom step, and reaches into his pocket. As he lights his cigarette, he shakes out two extra and tosses one each to the men on the cots directly in front of him. A sudden rush of clarity. "We'll mow down to the pond," he is thinking. "Until it's too hot."

Bright sunshine, a warm, humid day. They had stopped to sharpen their scythes, were sitting in the grass in the shade of an old chestnut tree at the far edge of the field. Käthe took the whetstone from the pocket of her smock and handed it to him. As he set to work, Käthe began to talk about planting a crop of flowers. "Delphinium," she said. "From there to there." She pointed from the top of the field down to the pond.

"That's a lot of flowers."

"Not for the flowers. It's for the bulbs. People will buy them. They're popular."

He listened as she began to outline her idea. The last few months had been a disaster. Money was getting tighter and tighter. Publishers were purging Jews (Mohr had got by thus far as an *angeblicher Jude*—an *alleged* Jew) from their lists. The radio show he'd done with Heinrich George had not resulted in anything beyond some free dinners and a handful of reviews. He had started making plans to leave. Käthe didn't know yet.

"It'll be hard work," he said, passing the stone along the curved edge of the blade. "I think it's a good idea."

Käthe jumped up happily, brushed the hair from her face, and began to pace as she described her plan. The whole field would have to be plowed under, the soil turned and fertilized. Planting would have to start indoors, in February, and be staggered through the season. As she went deeper into details, a wonderful feeling of relief welled up. His stomach did a little forward roll that he managed to contain by focusing on the long scythe blade. He held it close, sharpened and sharpened, with glances down the gently sloping field to the little pond where Berghammers' cows were grazing at the bank. He could imagine Käthe's delphiniums, row after row of deep blue flowers bending on their stalks, lovely against the deep green of the larches at the forest edge. He could close his eyes and see it all, close his eyes and know that whatever happened to him, everything here would be just fine. He put the freshly sharpened scythe into Käthe's hands. She waded back into the tall grass, swinging back and forth in a wide swath. He swiped the stone over his blade quickly, too quickly to have sharpened it much, then hurried to catch up to her.

He drops his cigarette onto the floor and steps on it, shaking his head. No. He hadn't deserved any of it. The land, the house, the woman. He hadn't deserved a fraction of it. Not a fraction. He glances up at the soldiers, one of whom is pinching his cigarette between fingertips and staring back at Mohr with an open sympathy that borders on tenderness. It is an authentic look, not counterfeit or sentimental, and expresses the exhaustion of the entire city. Mohr shrugs, shakes his head as if to say, I am as befuddled by all this as you are, my friend. The soldier returns the gesture without so much as a smile.

Agnes suddenly materializes with a cup of water. Mohr stands up to accept, but Agnes pushes him back, sits down next to him on the step. "Drink it."

He empties the cup in three large gulps. "It's warm," he says.

"It's clean," she replies, taking the cup back. "You look pale. Are you all right?"

"As fit as ever."

"Do you have your tablets with you?"

He pats his coat pocket. "Right here."

A massive cleaning detail has begun, directed by Red Cross volunteers and public utility workers. The newspaper boy has somehow sneaked past the guard at the front entrance and is scurrying between the rows of cots hawking his papers. Agnes rises to leave.

"Wait." Mohr hesitates, aware of the pathetic egotism in what he is about to ask. "Come home with me tonight."

Agnes regards him for a moment. "So. You're tired of being alone?"

He pulls her down beside him, a little more forcefully than he'd intended. She is startled. Once again, he is on the verge of explaining: that he has no good choices—or, more precisely, no choices that leave him with any vestige of goodness, that no good can possibly come from any path he chooses to take. She looks at him with that familiar, clouded expression, her dark, practical eyes, and he releases her hand. She stands, smooths down the folds of her uniform, and walks away.

He finds himself staring at the soldier again. The man flashes a stupidly presumptive grin. Mohr ignores it, gets up to resume his rounds.

He works in a fog for the rest of the morning. At some point toward midday, the number of wounded begins to slow, but more and more sick refugees are turning up. All but the most badly off are given water to drink, a dose of cod-liver oil—which for some reason there is an abundance of—and sent right back out onto the street. Toward the end of the afternoon Mohr finds himself handing out empty matchboxes. Evidently a call has gone out across the city for matchboxes to put aspirin tablets in, but there is no aspirin, and crates of matchboxes are piling up on the dock, so there is nothing else to do but give them out, empty.

He passes Agnes several times during the course of the morning. They exchange glances but nothing further. He wants a chance to explain himself, to describe his predicament, how he feels backed against a wall, yet also optimistic, and ready for change. He wants her to know that, in spite of their separate lives, he feels a bond. It should not be simply refuted due to complicated and inconvenient circumstances. Smashing human connections is the easiest thing in the world to do. What a pity if they couldn't rise above the level of angry little egotists. But Agnes has every reason to reject him. Perversely, he begins to hope that she will do just that. It will take the decision away, restore his tarnished innocence. In a strange way, she predicted this impasse while they were still in Japan, sitting one evening out on the steps of the cottage. He was stiff in the legs after three hours on the tatami mat, sitting at the lacquered writing table by the window. He had been working on the manuscript. *The Unicorn.* In the very first week he'd felt rooted in a daily rhythm. It had felt right to be there with her. No questions, no vagueness. They just simply got on well together. Her reserve and calm balanced his impulsiveness. Working on the novel felt right, too.

"I can't imagine what writing a book would be like," she said, and drew closer. The horses had been taken back to the stable just before nightfall. The old man seemed too frail to handle such large animals, but he brought them up at dawn every morning, left them tied to the post beside the cottage, and vanished as silently as he came. Mohr had joked that it was not a man at all, but a forest spirit who brought the horses up from underground. "Do you think you'll finish it?"

"I've hardly begun."

"Will you try to get it published?

He shook his head. "I can't really be too concerned about that," he said, taking out his cigarettes. He offered one to her. She put it to her lips, bent toward the cupped flame. "It doesn't really matter if I do or not," he said, watching the ember at the tip of the match extinguish in a tiny curl of smoke that hung for a moment in the still night air.

"You're writing it for yourself, then?"

"I suppose I am."

"And when it's finished?"

"When it's finished? I'll put it away and forget about it."

"Something you've worked on for so long? You think you can do that?"

They smoked in silence, listening to the cicadas in the trees, waves of sound building, shrinking back, then building again like the coda of a sonata that erupts and sinks back again, erupts and sinks, but never expires. He waited for the obvious next question, but Agnes never asked it.

A RUMOR HAS been circulating around the hospital that the Chinese are sending reinforcements into Chapai to stop the Japanese. The troop numbers he's heard throughout the afternoon range from five thousand to twenty-five thousand, but by early evening that rumor is replaced by another, more alarming one: that the Chinese are in fact withdrawing from Chapai, and in their retreat setting fire to everything. It is impossible to know which version of events is correct, but what gives credibility to both is the fact that the flow of wounded to the hospital has virtually stopped.

"It isn't because they've stopped fighting," Timperly remarks. He has asked Mohr up to his office for a short break and a cup of tea. The cleanup of the lobby is well in hand. The glass doors have been boarded up, the floors are free of broken glass. Mohr declined at first, thinking he'd rather find an empty cot and close his eyes, but Timperly insisted. Now Mohr finds himself looking out the window of the superinten-dent's office. The bomb crater up the road has been cordoned off and traffic flows around it at almost the normal rate. "Incredible," he muses aloud. "Really not much different than ants."

Timperly pours tea into two cups from a cracked pot. "As far as I know, ants don't demolish their own nests."

It is nearing twilight. With the office doors closed against the puls-ing disorder of the hospital, the feeling in the room is as close to tranquillity as anything Mohr has felt all day. Mohr sips his tea. Directly across the street from the hospital is a brand-new building that he's never taken much notice of, but which seen now in the twi-light reminds him of Berlin. He feels captured and fixed, split be-tween here and there, now and then. Blue sparks arcing from the electric tram wires overhead suddenly illuminate the facades of Nol-lendorfplatz. Käthe is sitting next to him. She squeezes his arm, rustles closer on the hard wooden seat. The tram squeals around the corner and is gone.

"Has anybody heard from Chen Siu-fang?"

"I have calls in to the SMP, the Red Cross, and about three other places; am still waiting to hear back." Timperly stirs his tea, absorbed, then looks up and shrugs. "There's nothing we can do but wait."

Silence for a few moments while they sip their tea, trying to release some of the tension of this unusually long day. It's the first time he and Timperly have sat quietly together like this. Mohr feels himself un-wind a little, looks out the window and watches the sky, streaked with red and purple. Timperly is preoccupied as well. His hand shakes slightly when he lifts his cup. He is the opposite of the waistcoated English doctors on staff at the Country Hospital. Mohr has come to respect him. So what if he goes about as if his contact with the earth is affected by hidden tracks and wires? Abruptly, he breaks the silence. "Tell me something, Mohr. Do you really believe that a person becomes lost as soon as he begins to worry about how he can help the masses?"

Mohr turns from the window. "Pardon me?"

"Your words." Timperly picks up a book and reads from it. "'Those who force themselves to love the masses are seized by the fearful hatred which lies hidden in every enforced love.'" He shakes his head, puzzled. "*Phillip Glenn.* I've just finished reading it."

Mohr tries, unsuccessfully, to mask his surprise. "Since when do you find time for reading?"

"It hasn't been easy." Timperly's tone is at once confiding and confessional. "I don't mind telling you that, as a socialist, I've been hard put to understand what you mean."

Mohr is suddenly uncomfortable. "It's a novel, not a manifesto."

Timperly turns to another passage and reads, "'As long as he had change in his pockets he would give, but with no more concern than when cleaning his teeth as long as he had toothpaste.'" He closes the book, puts it down, and smiles. "I mean, really, Mohr. Is charity for you merely a question of having the toothpaste?"

Mohr smiles self-consciously, caught off guard. He reaches across the desk for the book, unable to suppress a tiny surge of bitterness in spite of what strikes him as something of a miracle. An English translation of his book, available right here in China. He glances at the translator's name, which has certainly not been lost on Timperly: Countess Nora Purtscher-Wydenbruck. A bloody aristocrat! "The political sentiments belong to the character in the book." He fans through the pages. "Modeled on an old friend. A man whose spirit went beyond ideology."

Timperly takes this in, squinting from behind his steel-rimmed glasses. "Well, I can't speak to the spiritual qualities. But knowing you as I do, I was a little surprised by the reactionary opinions."

"Are you trying to draw me into a debate on socialism?"

Timperly does not answer right away. He removes his glasses, rubs his eyes with the heel of his hand. "I never properly thanked you for the use of your car and driver."

"It was a reactionary gesture, Doctor; you can rest assured." Mohr smiles, still trying to regain equilibrium. He is pleased by Timperly's interest and effort, but also slightly wary of his motives.

"You're stuck here, aren't you, Mohr?" Timperly stops rubbing his eyes, begins to clean his spectacles with a pocket handkerchief. A squeaky cart rolls by the closed door of the office, and Mohr listens as the noise fades down the corridor. He is determined not to be drawn into any traps, glances at his watch with an air of distraction. "I'm not exactly sure how to answer that question."

Timperly continues cleaning his glasses. A silence descends, threatens to become a contest of wills, but Mohr is too tired for that. "If you mean that I am without a valid passport, then yes. I am, as you say, stuck here." He is about to stand up, but suddenly changes his mind and sits back in the chair. "What if I said I've *chosen* to remain here? Would that *un*stick me?" He smiles, turning the tables. "Or in being without a passport, have I somehow forfeited my free will?"

"You're not alone," Timperly states flatly. His tone is sympathetic. He puts his glasses back on. "I know many people in exactly the same position. And not only Jews."

Mohr feels a twinge. It's Timperly's enunciation, as if he were himself offended by having to use the word. In Germany the word *Jude* has always seemed to imply a misfortune of birth. The English, *Jew*, seems imbued with a no less accusatory quality of lapsed decorum, a breech of etiquette. Mohr glances at his watch again, anxious to put an end to the strange interrogation. "I need to get back to the ward."

"I'll get to the point," Timperly says, also glancing at his watch. He

folds his hands, presses his fingertips to his lips. The gesture seems oddly studied and out of character. The rituals of tea have always felt strange to Mohr, English manners in general; a residual effect of his prison-camp experience where, as a medical officer, he'd been subjected to a strange deference and respect. It didn't take long to realize that it was really a form of ridicule. Since then, he's always been wary of trying to share too much of an English joke.

"I am curious about some of your contacts here."

"You can't be serious."

Timperly keeps his fingertips pressed to his lips, eyes set intently. "The fellow from the German Embassy, Fuchs. He isn't the only one interested in you." He stands up, begins to pace. "The Special Branch of the Shanghai Municipal Police have been here as well."

"Stubbings."

"That's the name. He wanted to know about your trip to Japan. And Konrad Granich."

"Granich?" Mohr looks up, startled.

"He's been murdered. In a village just outside Nanking." Timperly crosses the room, and then turns as if ready now to answer any questions Mohr might care to ask.

But Mohr has no questions and stands up to leave. "I'm sorry," he says, feeling sickened for the second time that day, wanting only to go downstairs and finish his work for the day. Then to go home. With Agnes, if possible.

"You knew Granich,"

"Yes, I knew him," Mohr says flatly. "And, evidently, you knew that I knew him."

Timperly acknowledges this with a shrug.

Mohr takes this in, then shakes his head. "I don't care to know any more and I can't think of anything to say."

"You must admit there's a curious pattern here."

"A pattern?" Mohr looks squarely at Timperly, then shakes his head and laughs. "Well, if we're going to play detective, have you noticed that barbed wire seems to reappear in this city in five-year cycles? 1927, 1932, 1937. You could say the real culprit of the situation is— the calendar."

"This issue concerns me, Mohr. You can't expect me not to be curious."

"Sometimes ordinary life is too banal to be believed. Events don't fit into patterns, no matter how wonderfully they seem to align."

"I won't argue the philosophical point with you. I'm perfectly willing to accept, for example, that the reason for your trip to Japan was simply to run off with one of my nurses." Timperly's expression becomes serious. "But the fact is, none of that is of any concern to me, either. Sit down. I have something important to ask you."

Mohr hesitates, then returns to his seat.

"I must ask for your help rescuing a very sick comrade."

"'Comrade'?" Suddenly he realizes he is being taken into Timperly's confidence.

"He's very ill, and I'm afraid I've run out of options."

"Why can't you treat him yourself?"

"It's too risky."

"What is wrong with him?"

"We won't know until we can get a doctor to see him."

"He's a communist?"

"And too well known to travel openly."

"Who is it?"

"Better not to know."

"Where is he?"

"In Hungjao."

"Ah, a well-heeled communist!"

Timperly acknowledges the joke with a faint smile.

"You want me to bring him back here?"

"It depends."

"Depends on what?"

Timperly pauses to formulate. "If the opinion is that he should be brought to hospital for treatment, then . . ."

"Then what?"

"Then by all means, he should be brought here directly. It would be best for everyone involved if he could be treated and allowed to convalesce right where he is. But that judgment has to be made by a doctor."

Mohr regards Timperly skeptically. "I'm no revolutionary. I don't mind saying I'm completely indifferent to your cause. To politics, in general."

"Even those that have oppressed you?"

"Especially those!"

"Well, I trust you. That's good enough."

"Was Granich part of your group?"

"He was," Timperly states without any trace of emotion. "And so is your old friend Vogel."

"Oh, so you know Vogel, too?" Mohr slaps his thigh with an exasperated chuckle, slides back in the chair, hitches his trousers, crosses his legs. "Of course, I should have guessed. Are you also some sort of spy? No, wait. Don't tell me. I want to be the only asshole in this city who doesn't know."

"It was Vogel who suggested that I hire you."

Mohr takes this in, resisting the urge to press for details.

"Will you help us?"

"I should refuse to have anything to do with all of you," Mohr says in disgust, then hauls himself out of the chair and breaks into a sardonic smile. "But what choice do I have?"

Timperly stands up, extends his hand across the desk, as pleased as Mohr has ever seen him. "I will send a car to pick you up in the morning."

"All this time I thought you were just a charity hospital superintendent, Dr. Timperly."

"I could say the same about you, Dr. Mohr."

"Can I ask what Granich was up to?"

"He was delivering a letter." Timperly says it as if all there is to be said about it is summed up in his flat tone.

The corridor outside Timperly's office is being set up with bedrolls and blankets by three Chinese men wearing Red Swastika Society smocks. The building is filling from the ground up with sick and wounded. "Thank you," Timperly calls as Mohr closes the office door behind him.

A LINE HAS formed outside the kitchen, and stretches down the full length of the corridor. It is moving as quickly as can be expected. The hospital staff are fed twice daily according to a schedule that Timperly himself devised. Mohr finds himself downstairs, carrying his camera. There have been two more ambulances since his tea with Timperly. Mohr spent the entire time in the operating room. When he reached the limits of his effectiveness there, he began to wander about the hospital taking pictures. It seemed a good thing to do: ward to ward, floor to floor, clicking away at the fringes of all the misery.

One of the Chinese doctors in line beckons for him to take the place in front of him. Mohr thanks him, and declines. Affable and very young, the doctor had transferred here from a hospital in the war zone that had been evacuated a week earlier. "Come, come. Aren't you hungry?" he asks.

"No, thank you, Doctor," Mohr begs off, glancing down the queue, the length of which is a good indication of how serious the food situation is all across the city. The kitchen at Lester Hospital is notoriously bad even under the best circumstances.

"I admire your restraint." The young doctor laughs.

"Not restraint. Fear. I can't afford to miss a single day of work."

The doctor laughs again.

"You haven't seen Agnes Simson, have you?" Mohr asks, lifting his camera to photograph the line of people queued up for their meal.

The doctor steps out of the picture, shakes his head. "Not since this morning."

Mohr snaps a few more pictures down the corridor, then returns to the first floor via a narrow staircase that is used mainly by kitchen staff. At the top of the stairs, he nearly steps on a young child, curled up and fast asleep on the landing. Mohr stoops down for a closer look. The child springs suddenly to his feet and backs away. Mohr squats, and in the poor light of the stairwell recognizes the newspaper boy from earlier in the day. The boy presses himself against the wall, stammering, "No mama no papa no chow. No mama no papa no chow."

Mohr offers his hand, smiling at the boy. The child continues stammering, glancing into the corner where he has stuffed his unsold papers. Then he begins to cry. Mohr approaches cautiously, and again offers his hand. The boy recoils, passing a skinny forearm across his soot-smeared face.

"My pay chow," Mohr says, pointing down the staircase in the direction of the cafeteria. "Come."

The boy, very likely a regular caller at the hospital's kitchen door, stops crying and allows Mohr to lead him by the hand. They start down one step at a time, the boy slack-armed, yielding. His hand is hard and callused, but also delicate and failing substance. Halfway down, Mohr stops abruptly. The stairwell echoes with the noisy clanging and clattering of the kitchen. He and the boy regard each other. The child is staring at his camera, fascinated. Suddenly Mohr changes course and they are going back up, taking the steps two at a time.

It is a clear night outside, a damp November chill in the air. Wong is waiting just up the street. Still holding the boy by the hand, Mohr makes his way toward the parked car. Curfew started an hour earlier. Shantung Road is deserted. They pause to look at the bombed facades, the windows all boarded up. The crater in the road is cordoned off;

lying just beside it are the charred and gutted remains of two automobiles.

Wong steps from the car and opens the door. The boy stops short. Mohr nods toward the car. The boy tries to wriggle free but Mohr grips him tightly.

"Who have you got there?" Agnes asks from inside the car.

In his surprise, Mohr nearly lets go of the child. "A little friend," he answers. He glances into the rear seat, where she is sitting, He is pleased to see her, and pleased to see that she is smiling. "I found him hiding in a stairwell."

Agnes slides across the seat, steps out of the car. "Is he injured?" she asks, looking the child over. She says something Mohr is unable to understand, and with no further fuss, the child climbs obediently into the car.

Nobody speaks as Wong swings the car around and speeds up Shantung Road. The boy is sitting between Mohr and Agnes, rigid with excitement and mesmerized by the view out the front of the car. "His first motorcar ride," Agnes observes.

"I'm glad you're here. I was afraid you wouldn't come."

"How could I not?"

"Where were you all afternoon? I looked everywhere."

"I went with one of the ambulance drivers to look for Chen Siufang." She leans her head back on the seat. "We went everywhere. Even to her house."

"Did Timperly send you?"

She shakes her head. "I just went."

He is not sure he should press for details, but tells her it was crazy to leave the hospital without saying anything to anybody. She ignores the remark, closes her eyes. They drive for a while in silence. Mohr fidgets with the ashtray, opening and closing the slender receptacle recessed into the door panel, idly noting how well it slides on its polished hinge. The boy watches intently, is delighted by Mohr's invitation to try it himself.

"What are you going to do with him?" Agnes asks.

"I don't know. Feed him. Give him a bath."

He rolls down the window and takes out his cigarettes. Japan seems so distant now. Time had been so short, the nights so quiet. He would lie awake every night absorbing the peacefulness, listening to crickets chirping just outside the window, Agnes on the tatami beside him. Sleeping behind a paper screen was so much more intimate than behind a closed door. The corner where they slept was exposed, open to the whole cottage. At times, he was so overwhelmed by her presence that he was afraid to touch or be touched by her, for fear she might suddenly vanish, just disappear. He would then think of Käthe, and wonder if she and that other place, Wolfsgrub, were more real than the place where he now found himself. Where was his *real* life? Was it here or there? Could *real* life transpire someplace other than where one resided? It was the strangest form of guilt; absurd, of course. How could anything be more real than the moment? It is only the moment that is real. But it is also only the moment that passes.

They are on Thibet Road, approaching the checkpoint leading into the Settlement. Barbed-wire barricades stretch across the entire width of the street, but for a single lane for traffic to pass through. Sandbags at the curb are a curious foreground to the billboard advertisements for Benedictine and Vichy Salt Tablets.

Wong stops the car. A military policeman appears at the window. Mohr hands over his curfew pass. The soldier examines it, then points his flashlight into the car. "Who've you got there, Doctor?" he asks in a heavy Scottish accent. The boy turns away, buries his face in the upholstered car seat.

"My family," Mohr says, looking the soldier squarely in the eye.

The flashlight lingers, then snaps off. The soldier hands the document back and steps away from the car without another word. As the car passes through the checkpoint into the Settlement, he notices Agnes staring at him. Wong casts puzzled glances into the rearview mirror. By the time they pull in front of the Yates Apartments, he realizes some diplomacy is going to be necessary. "Come on in, everyone," he says cheerfully. "We have eggs and cod-liver oil!"

He leads the way upstairs, pausing on the landing at Granich's door. There is no reason to doubt what Timperly has told him, though he still can't quite understand how the actors and the scenes all link up. Delivering a letter? Basic decency seems to demand that he at least knock on the dead man's door.

"What are you doing?" Agnes asks.

He raps lightly, puts an ear to the door. "Nobody home." He leads the way up the last flight of steps. "I've gone into the hotel business since your last visit."

The boy causes a minor commotion as soon as they enter the apartment. Wong's wife objects politely but strenuously—objections that Mohr counters right away by rolling up his sleeves and marching the boy straight into the bathroom. The child resists at first, and refuses to undress, but when Mohr holds up one of his own freshly ironed shirts, and offers it to the boy as a gift, the boy strips off his filthy rags and climbs into the tub.

Agnes acts as emissary to Wong's family while Mohr tends to the boy, scrubs him down, delouses him with rubbing alcohol. Wong fusses in the background, looks in on the proceedings once or twice. At last the two emerge, the tails of Mohr's pressed shirt trailing behind the boy like an oversized gown. A compromise is reached. The boy will not take up any space in Wong's cramped family quarters, but will be allowed to sleep in the hallway by the front door. Bedding is produced. The boy is fed, packed off in the corner with stern instructions from Wong's wife, who seems to have softened at the sight of the little urchin wearing a shirt that she herself has washed and ironed. In turn, the boy seems willing to recognize her authority.

Well after midnight, Mohr and Agnes finally sit down to a cold supper of chopped carrots and sliced egg. Wong had prepared it for them before retiring for the night. As they eat, Agnes keeps glancing at the framed photograph of Eva on the desk.

"It came just the other day. A miracle that it got through." Mohr fetches the photograph, offers it to Agnes. "She'll be twelve next April."

"She looks just like you," Agnes remarks, and finishes eating. She puts her empty bowl down, pours out two cups of tea, then settles back on the sofa, blowing puffs of fragrant jasmine from her cup. "It's very generous of you, opening your home to all these people."

"Generous? As soon as this war is over I'll throw everybody back out in the street."

She sips her tea. "I wish I could joke about it."

The air in the room suddenly feels stale. He gets up to open a window, and feels immediate relief as fresh air rushes into the room. The November air is brisk, soothing. A ghostly quiet hangs over the city. Bubbling Well Road is empty but for a group of SMP volunteers manning a machine-gun emplacement in the middle of the intersection. There is a rumbling of artillery in the distance, a faintly acrid smell in the air, an ominous glow on the northern horizon. He feels a little stupid for consenting so readily to Timperly's request, but also pleased to have been asked. He smiles to himself. What will it be? Gaurisankar or *Klotz am Bein?* He didn't come halfway around the world to sit on his ass in the waiting room watching the express trains blow past.

He closes the window, steps over to Zappe's cage. "Still not speaking?" The bird cocks its head, bobs on its perch. He tries to coax it—*Brüderlein fein, Brüderlein fein*—then turns to Agnes. "The year I left, Käthe planted a field of flowers. Tall blue ones. *Rittersporn.* I don't know the English word."

"Delphinium," Agnes says.

"It was a very large field. She cleared it, planted it, and began selling bulbs to the local florists. I was mostly living in Berlin at the time.

Trying to earn money. I came back to Wolfsgrub as often as I could, but things everywhere were going from bad to worse. It wasn't only the Nazis. In some ways I wish it had been that simple. There were so many frustrations: personal ones, artistic ones. I couldn't support my family. Living in the countryside had become too confining, but spending half the year in the city wasn't working out, either. I made everyone miserable around me and knew the time had come for me to go."

He refills his teacup and begins to pace. "I was overjoyed by Käthe's flowers."

"You were proud of her success," Agnes ventures.

"No! That's just it. It had nothing to do with her. I was glad, yes, and happy. But mainly—mainly, I was relieved. It was completely self-ish. She had found a way to support herself. It meant I could go away and, whatever happened, she would be able to take care of herself." He stops here, jumbled and suddenly unsure why he's telling Agnes this.

"So it was a good thing?" she offers.

"No. It was all wrong." His voice quavers. "My guilt over leaving them behind was lessened by those flowers! It was so convenient."

"Why did you leave them behind?" Agnes asks, as if it were the simplest question in the world.

Mohr stops pacing. The simple why eludes him. It always will. He loves Käthe and Eva, loves them with all his heart. It is painful to think of them, all alone now in Wolfsgrub. How happy they'd *all* be to be together again. And yet, at the time, it seemed absolutely necessary for him to go away alone. He looks again at Eva's picture on the desk. A twelve-year-old looks back at him from the photograph, but she is fixed in his mind as a younger child—at eight, breaking an egg over his head for a shampoo, tugging at his arm to come outside and play. How old will she be when he next sees her? Will it be here? Or some-place else? Or never? He wasn't simply driven out of Germany but hounded out of existence. His existence and her existence. Who could

have anticipated how bad things would get back there? Or here, on the other side of the globe? Who could have foreseen any of it? Whatever the future holds, one day Eva will ask the same question, and, perhaps, she'll even have an answer for it. What will she say? That her father was a selfish man? Or just flawed and foolish? Will they all look back on this someday, and smile and stir their coffee, and say it was all for the best?

WHY DID YOU leave them behind?

"I DON'T KNOW," he says at last. It's true. There is no satisfying explanation. Any answer he gave now would be different from an answer given yesterday or one he might give tomorrow. The past changes each time you begin to explain it, like a telegram that rewrites itself each time you take it out of your pocket. "I used to think I knew. But I don't anymore."

Agnes is watching, hands wrapped around the cup in her lap. He begins straightening up the papers on his desk. Käthe's letter is among them. For a moment he considers showing it to Agnes, but is immediately disgusted with himself for the thought. The other night he had a vivid dream: Käthe and Eva arriving on the *Saarbrücken*. He was there and not there—watching them descend the gangway, and at the same time not there because he'd failed to come and meet the ship. His horror multiplied—at their surprise arrival, at his failure to meet them. Brehm was leaning over the top deck rail, waving his cap and laughing.

Agnes leaves the sofa, crosses the room. "It's all right," she says. "It's late."

He takes her in his arms. Confusion dissipates. Her uniform is flecked with bloodstains and smells of carbolic and rubbing alcohol.

She feels small, but also firm and contained within herself. He holds her tightly. No, they haven't merely blundered into each other. Not at all. She is integral and necessary, part of a vital circuit. They fall onto the narrow bed, embracing clumsily, and too tired, in the end, for anything but sleep.

He wakes up sometime later—hours or minutes, he can't tell—thinking about his last day at the Country Hospital, a talkative, fussily coiffed British woman whom he'd given a cholera injection. "We may have lived our lives to the full in this *burg,* Dr. Mohr." She pronounced the German word in a mordant contralto, as if pointing her finger. "But my friend Christabel says, if this conflict goes on much longer some of us will find ourselves in the predicament of *dying* beyond our means." The witticism came out as if rehearsed, which it probably was. He asked if she was leaving the city. Her reply had been as unrehearsed as it was muddled and disturbing. "My husband refuses to close down the office." She heaved a sigh and shrugged. "I suppose we'll stay here until the last bomb falls."

In a letter, Käthe had written, *There is nothing left in Germany that would interest you.* It was true. He was finished. *Quitt!* But it went so much deeper than skipping across borders and national boundaries. How to defend against something that must self-destruct? The entire German nation. Like an amputation on the battlefield, all one could do was get it over with as quickly as possible. But he has no place in this Anglo-Chinese colony, either. He told Timperly he'd chosen to remain here, but does he *really* have a choice? No. He was, finally, the outsider he'd always thought himself to be: stateless, without a passport. It irritated him to dwell on such a banal, bureaucratic detail, but he couldn't help it. The distinction had taken on an ontological significance and was now as emotionally rattling as the bombs falling all around.

He shifts to make room for Agnes in the narrow bed. Just before dawn the big naval guns begin firing from the Whangpoo. Zappe lets out a squawk, then falls silent. Mohr gets up and lights a cigarette. He sits on the windowsill, smoking, listening to the guns and sirens in the distance.

"You should try to sleep," Agnes says from the bed. She is awake, curled on her side with the sheet pulled up to her chin. In Japan she would watch him from bed the same way, as he sat writing in the morning.

"Sleep?" He smiles at the absurdity of the suggestion. A small convoy of trucks passes below, their roofs freshly painted with the Union Jack. They are driving in the direction of the Bund. Agnes joins him at the window, draped in the bedsheet. She helps herself to a cigarette. Mohr flicks his out the window, watches it fall into the street. *"So wirf auch noch den Kompass über Bord."*

"What's that?"

"Throw the compass overboard. From a poem I once wrote. *'Die Sonette vom Neuen Noah.'* Sonnet of the New Noah."

Side by side, backs to the window, leaning against the sill. Agnes pulls the sheet up around her shoulders, holds her cigarette just under her chin. "Do you feel like Noah?"

"I was thinking of this goddamn war."

Another big gun booms in the distance. Agnes glances over her shoulder. "And here we are, up here in your little ark."

He turns to look outside. "In my poem, Noah sees a whale and calls to it. He asks if it knows of any end in sight."

"What does the whale tell him?"

"Nothing. It just swims off."

She shrugs. "If you were a fish, the flood was not much of a problem."

Mohr laughs, gazes at her, silhouetted against the window. He plucks the cigarette from between her fingers, flicks it out the window, but when he tries to embrace her, she turns away, drawing the sheet around her and folding her arms. "My Chinese grandfather used to say that if you wanted to understand the English, you had to read the Bible. And then he would shake his head and say he could never read the Bible."

Mohr draws back, feeling a slight pang of rejection. It has grown light enough to see the plumes of smoke rising on the horizon to the north. "Timperly is sending a car for me today. I'm being taken to someone who can't come to hospital."

"Where?"

"I don't know." He regards the thick plumes rising up over the rooftops. "I just hope it's not in that direction."

"He wouldn't tell you where?"

"Someplace in Hungjao."

"Why didn't you tell me earlier?" Agnes shoots him an irritated look. She fetches her clothes from the back of the chair and starts for the bathroom.

"Wong will take you to work in my car."

She pauses at the door. "No. I'm going with you."

"I don't think Timperly would want that."

"I don't care. I'm going with you." She leaves the room.

"You can't. They need you at the hospital."

She closes the door without an answer.

"Von jedem Tier ein Paar!" he calls after her. "Two of every creature."

The great curtain of smoke rises up in the direction of Chapai. Mohr is secretly, selfishly pleased.

AT SEVEN O'CLOCK a large black Packard pulls up in front of 803 Bubbling Well Road. Mohr and Agnes have been waiting at the curb, watching a man in a quilted overcoat scrape up a handful of rice from the pavement into his ragged cap. He works diligently, keeping an eye on the rickshaw cart from which the rice has spilled. He is oblivious of the big black automobile until it is nearly on top of him, and struggles to collect the last scraps with glances over his shoulder as if fending off a territorial challenger. When the last grain has been gathered, he hurries to catch up to the rickshaw cart.

It is a bright November morning. Traffic is moving at the usual crawl. The main and side roads all throughout the Settlement are teeming with wandering humanity, fighting for space with sidewalk vendors, beggars, and rickshaw pullers. Mohr asks the driver where he is taking them.

"Hungjao," the man says.

"Where in Hungjao?"

The man doesn't answer, keeps his eyes fixed on the road ahead.

"I see," Mohr says, and settles back in the seat. He rolls down the window, lights a cigarette, thinking of the boy, his hardened little existence. Despite the thundering of guns and wailing sirens, the child slept soundly. Wong's wife gave him breakfast, which he ate sitting on his bedroll, just inside the front door. As Mohr and Agnes were leaving, the boy blocked the way and began talking rapidly, clutching his tattered cap in his hands.

"What's he saying?"

"He doesn't want any more castor oil, just egg," Agnes said. Wong's wife scowled as the boy pleaded his case. Mohr laughed and patted him on the shoulder. "No more castor oil, then." The essence of courage is not taking care of oneself, but proving how we need one another. The boy then tried to slip out with them, but Agnes put him firmly on notice.

"We can't keep him against his will," Mohr objected.

"A street orphan has no will," Agnes said.

"Oh? I would say the boy is pure will."

"I would call it luck."

"You call surviving on the street luck? He sells newspapers. That's not luck."

"And he hands over all the money to some gangster who has hundreds of little urchins just like him all over the city."

"You call that luck?"

"Certainly. And finding you. I call that purest luck."

Somebody had left a bicycle at the bottom of the staircase. It was English, the exact model Käthe had bought on their first anniversary.

"What are you doing?" Agnes asked.

Mohr put down his medical bag and mounted the familiar black contraption. It was identical, except for the fat silver bell, which he rang, then rang again. Eva would ride with him, sitting sideways on the crossbar. He had made a little seat for her with a towel and an old piece of saddle leather. They would ride together down to Rottach to swim or to buy fish or to watch the tourists getting on and off the boats that ferried them across the lake. What was it like there now? In March Käthe had written that Oscar Nathan had been forced out of his house on the lake by none other than Heinrich Himmler, who had simply appropriated the old villa as a vacation house for himself. "We used to talk about the coming of an age when money would be abolished," was Mohr's sardonic reply. "Who'd have thought it would happen so soon?"

How quickly everything had changed.

He turns to Agnes. *"Je n'ai pas oublié, voisine de la ville / Notre blanche maison, petite mais tranquille."*

"I don't understand French."

"I have not forgot our place not far from town / The peaceful white cottage where we lived alone. It's from Baudelaire."

Agnes smiles. "I have thought about it, too. The view was so beautiful." She reaches across the car seat to take his hand. They ride for a short time in silence, holding hands and looking out at the battered city through the windows. For some reason, the driver has taken them into the French Concession instead of following Bubbling Well Road out to Hungjao. He drives down a series of crowded side streets and, at one point, seems to be heading back in the direction of the Old Chinese City. Another series of left and right turns puts them on Avenue Foch, driving westward. Every intersection is barricaded with barbed wire and sandbags. Carts heaped with belongings fill the streets. Men, women, children—everybody carrying, pushing, or simply clutching

onto something. They pass a convoy of Japanese armored vehicles, evil-looking things with protruding guns and slits for windows. On top of each is a small turret with a soldier's head protruding like an open bud. The city is being smashed, picked apart, bit by bit, and Mohr begins to feel frightened. It is not a suspenseful fear, the fear of something immanent. He feels caught in a tremendous downward purling, turns to Agnes. "You need to call your mother. Let her know that you're okay."

Agnes lets go of his hand. "I spoke with her last night. Before we left the hospital, as a matter of fact."

They are entering one of the older suburban areas of houses and parks and gardens behind walls. "Is she okay? Does she have everything she needs?"

Agnes nods. "I wouldn't have left her alone if she didn't."

In Hungjao, the riding clubs and golf courses are not only open, but crowded. Every day, the newspapers publish letters from disgruntled suburbanites demanding an end to the inconvenient disruptions of the war. *Shanghai's Schemozzle*, a book by Sapajou, has just appeared on the newsstands. *An excellent souvenir. Shows no dead bodies, no burnt buildings, makes no attempt to impress one with the horror of war. The inimitable Sapajou captures the grave, the comic, the critical and the sympathetic aspects and spirit of this Shanghai war.*

IT IS HARD to know what to think.

"AND WHAT ABOUT your parents?" Agnes asks after a short pause. "You've never told me anything about your family. Do you have any brothers and sisters?"

"A sister," he says, and takes out another cigarette. He hadn't meant to begin a conversation about family, had asked about her mother because of the precarious state of things, the dangers all were facing. His sister? He has no idea, though he wonders from time to time how she is faring now in her beloved Deutschland. Hedwig was almost certainly still there. She'd worked too diligently scrubbing away her Jewishness to admit it now by committing so distasteful an act as— emigration.

"Were you close?" Agnes asks.

Mohr shakes his head. "Not at all."

Agnes is observing him closely. He turns to look out the window.

"What about your parents?"

"My father was a very gentle man," he says, aware of the arrogance in speaking of his own father with such distance. But distance is all he has ever been capable of in matters of the family. A peculiar by-product of assimilation. "Not a gentleman, but a gentle man," Mohr continues. "I was the difficult one. Always gave my parents a hard time. When I was seventeen, I went climbing in the mountains. Without asking permission. I just took my rucksack and left. My father took out an advertisement in the Würzburg newspaper." He chuckles and shakes his head, remembering. "I made it all the way to the Dolomites. When I finally came home, my father met me on the doorstep in his housecoat. He was furious. I wasn't sure he was going to let me in the house. Then he said, 'Who the devil is Peter Tambosi?' It was the name I signed to the telegram I'd sent home to say that all was well."

"Why that name; why not use your own?"

"To be funny. So they wouldn't take what I had done too seriously, and to signal that all was well. But partly because signing my name would have meant taking full responsibility. I was afraid to do that. So I made up a name—Peter Tambosi—and traveled under it incognito. It was fun. My first real adventure."

The driver has been listening with occasional glances into the backseat. "Are we getting close?" Mohr asks.

The driver nods.

"Is that why you volunteered for this?" Agnes asks. "For adventure?"

"I didn't really have a choice."

"You could have refused."

"On what grounds? I'm a doctor. I have professional responsibilities."

"On the grounds that you have no idea what you're getting yourself into."

He meets the driver's rearward glance, then turns to Agnes. "Better no compass than a false one," he says, smiling, and rolls down the window. The cold air is refreshing. Suburban houses flicker by in a hodgepodge of ever larger, ever grander European styles. Ragpickers and refugees are spilling over into the manicured parts of the Settlement, in spite of barbed wire and barricades being put up and manned by soldiers. Lawrence's comment about lost Eden comes back to him. Is war the first step in a return to wilderness? He turns to Agnes. "In any case, there's a big difference between lost and missing."

Agnes raises an eyebrow. "Oh? And which are you?"

Mohr laughs, realizing suddenly that he is happy, feels upbeat and cheerful. Also a little frightened; and without an answer to her question. Play like this always ends in the same place—tangled high up among the branches. If only she'd asked him that question earlier—as they were steaming eastward toward Japan. Or better, she should ask Käthe. Yes, Käthe would know the answer.

The driver hits the brakes, turns abruptly into a narrow driveway. He cuts the engine. "Wait here," he tells them.

It is an older house, packed onto a block of nearly identical houses with gabled, red-tiled roofs, arched front doorways, and servants' entrances at the back. The windows are all shuttered. At the end of the driveway is a trellised gate leading into a large garden. It could have been Dahlem, or Grünewald, any wealthy suburb. The driver returns minutes later and leads them inside. He has shed his chauffeur's cap, carries himself now as if vested with higher responsibilities. Inside, the house is cold and sparsely furnished, as if it will shortly be abandoned.

They are led up to the second floor. A Chinese man emerges from one of the rooms.

"Thank you for coming, Doctor." His English is unaccented. He is modestly dressed, a plain quilted jacket and loose-fitting trousers. He leads them into a darkened room, empty except for a narrow, military-style cot on which a man is lying under heavy blankets. Beside the cot is an upended wooden crate, next to which are two wooden camp chairs. On the crate are a canteen and a metal drinking cup.

Agnes draws open the curtains. Sunlight filters through the slats of the drawn exterior shutters. She opens them, flooding the room with light. Mohr kneels beside the cot. The man is Chinese, in his mid- to late forties. Mohr asks permission before pulling down the blankets. The man is disoriented, as if he's been sleeping. He doesn't answer. Mohr works quickly. When he presses the abdomen, the man lets out a howl of pain. Mohr stands, pulls the stethoscope from his ears. "How long have you had this pain?"

A familiar voice answers, "Five days."

Startled, Mohr turns. It is Vogel: gaunt, slightly hollow-cheeked. He comes into the room, acknowledging Agnes with a curt nod, and goes immediately to the sick man's side. Mohr is speechless, and stands aside as Vogel whispers to the patient in what sounds like fluent Mandarin. "Can you say what's wrong?" he asks, looking up.

"Acute appendicitis," Mohr answers, regaining composure. "But it's only a guess."

Vogel speaks again to the man, who responds in a weak voice. "Can you treat him here?" Vogel asks.

"Well, why not? Let's just cut him right open." Irritated, Mohr tugs the stethoscope from his neck and drops it into the bag. His sarcasm hangs in the air, and he is glad to let it linger, feeling betrayed and abused by all the secrecy and sudden surprises. Vogel stands aside to let Agnes adjust the man's blanket. She dampens a cloth with water from the canteen and presses it to the man's forehead. The young man who ushered them in and the driver are standing just inside the room. At Vogel's nod, they withdraw, closing the door behind them with a gentle click.

"Sit down, Max," Vogel says, gesturing to one of the folding chairs.

"There's no time to sit down." Mohr picks up his bag to leave. "This man needs to get to hospital immediately."

"Can you take him?"

Mohr regards his friend for a moment, then sits down, cradling his medical bag on his lap. Vogel sits across from him. Gesturing to the man on the cot, he says, "He is Liu Feng, a general of the Eighth Route Army."

Mohr is about to ask what the Eighth Route Army is, if it is the same army that is currently burning Chapai to the ground, but he suddenly feels too absurd and ignorant and, in the end, helpless. One war per lifetime is enough to teach a man all there is to know. "He needs a hospital," he says. "I can't do anything for him here."

"Will you bring him?"

Mohr stands, then sits down again, bewildered and suddenly unsure. He fumbles with the worn leather grip of his medical bag, looking Vogel squarely in the eye. His friend's face is tired, careworn, and yet—and this Mohr realizes for the very first time—without the slightest glimmer of skepticism. He is as tidy and crisply dressed as ever, with thinning hair combed straight back, suit newly pressed. To be so resolutely connected to a set of facts, and have one's days unfold according to them. Mohr used to think that the wear in a face such as Vogel's masked turmoil and inner conflicts. But maybe that's only the case with skeptical natures. For a man too firmly guided by commitments, and unhampered by doubts, maybe the lines and crags are simply lack of sleep, and sagging skin. "You called me naive the last time I saw you," he says at last. "So pardon me if I ask a naive question."

"Go ahead." Vogel clasps his hands on his knee.

"Why don't you take him there yourself?"

Vogel shifts in his chair. "Because the general and I can't be seen together."

It is quiet in the room. Mohr absorbs this piece of information the way he's always taken in Vogel's revelations: he laughs. "I'd never have taken you for a communist, Vogel. Not in a million years. That big house, the car and driver. The expensive suits."

Vogel shrugs.

"I suppose it's all just a cover. You'll give up all the luxury *after* the revolution, right? Were you a member of the Party back in Berlin, too?"

Vogel shrugs again. "It would be wrong to say that the Party in Berlin is the same Party as the one here in China. Comintern and the CCP are following a different course at present. The goal is the same. The paths are different."

This is all he cares to know. In a sense, he feels as if he's known this about Vogel all along. The city is full of people like him, like Timperly, and like poor young Granich. It is bursting apart because of men just like them, men of the world—presidents, secretaries, generals, bankers, revolutionaries, missionaries, priests. Yes, it is *power* that puts things into the world. But on the individual level, power doesn't seem much more than bullying. He can remember Lawrence once saying, "The tree that falls with a crash, grew without a sound." Could the world be improved by men who chose, simply, not to get involved?

"Was it you who asked me here?"

Vogel compresses his lips and nods. "I'm going away, Max, and don't know when—or if—I'll be back."

"You're leaving China?"

Vogel nods.

"Where are you going? To Palestine?"

"Eventually, probably, yes. You should go there yourself, Max. I can help you."

Mohr shakes his head. "And exchange one nationalism for another? You know my answer to that."

"You should reconsider, Max. This is no time for stupid platitudes."

"Stupid platitudes? You're one to talk. Out to build a socialist Zion in Palestine? Why not Uruguay? Or Tibet?"

Vogel cuts him off. "You don't know what you're talking about, Mohr."

"At least I can admit it. Anyway, I have everything I need right here."

Vogel seems surprised. "Oh? And what about your wife and daughter?"

Mohr glances over at Agnes, then gets up for another look at the general. "The man needs an appendectomy."

"You haven't answered my question. What are you going to do with Käthe and Eva? You're not still thinking of bringing them here, are you?"

Mohr feels the heat rising in his face, his pulse quickening. Just as he is about to tell Vogel it's none of his goddamn business, the two men who have been waiting in the corridor enter carrying a stretcher between them. Mohr beckons them over, steps away from the cot. "Be careful moving him," he tells them, gesturing for Agnes to follow him downstairs.

"Who is that man?" she asks as on the stairs.

"An old friend."

"I don't like him."

The living room is empty but for a few pieces of abandoned furniture, a stack of old newspapers. The floors are marked where carpets have been taken up. Mohr stands at a large bank of windows overlooking the rear garden. He puts an arm across Agnes's shoulder, draws her closer.

"For an old friend, you don't seem especially happy to see him," she says.

"He caught me off guard. It's true that we're old friends. But I had no idea he was a communist—if he really is a communist. I don't know the first thing about him, really."

A flock of birds flies from the hedge at the rear of the garden and disappears into the overgrown grass. Rooks. Refugees. They watch as the birds feed in the tall grass.

"I have my doubts, too." Agnes turns to him. "I don't know the first thing about you, either." She smiles. Upstairs a slight commotion is under way. Some magpies suddenly fly into the poplar tree at the corner of the yard, busily working on a nest. Rooks on the ground, magpies in the tree.

"Get the door, Max!" Vogel calls. They are carrying the general down the stairs. Vogel watches from the top of the steps as the two men struggle with the stretcher. Mohr holds the front door open and glances down as the general passes across the threshold. "Did you tell him I'm taking him to hospital?" Mohr asks, stepping outside. He stops short on the landing. The front fenders of the car have been fitted with Nazi flags. He turns to Vogel. "Is this some kind of joke?"

"Camouflage." Vogel hands him an envelope. "Use these papers if you're stopped."

Agnes appears in the doorway. "You forgot this," she says, holding up his medical bag.

"Why not a Red Cross flag?" Mohr asks.

"The Japanese have been attacking ambulances."

He watches as the general is lifted onto the backseat of the car, and gives the envelope back to Vogel. "Take them off."

"Don't be ridiculous, Max. It's for your own safety."

"I won't do it. Take them off."

Vogel heaves a sigh of exasperation. "You're being ridiculous. There's no saying what might happen if you're stopped. Those flags are your only protection."

"I don't want that kind of protection."

"I don't want it, either," Agnes says.

Mohr takes out his curfew pass and shows it to Vogel. "This is all I'll need." He takes Agnes's arm and walks down to the car. The general is stretched out on the backseat under thick blankets. "How do you feel?"

"*Ó bù shòu yùng,*" the general responds in a weak voice.

Mohr closes the door, then walks around to the front of the car and removes the flags. He marches back up the steps. "You use them," he says, handing them over to Vogel. "Or are you traveling under different protection this week? The Lion of Judah, perhaps?"

Vogel shakes his head in dismay. "You're making a stupid mistake, Max."

"Let's not argue about it," Mohr says, putting an end to the discussion. They stand for a moment together on the steps. "What are you going to do?"

"My car is on the way."

"Will I see you again?"

"I can't say." Vogel looks away for a moment. The face that betrays no skepticism suddenly shows a hint of existential dread. He offers his hand. "Thank you, Max. One day you'll appreciate everything you've done."

Mohr can only smile. The intoxicating quality of such presumption. The will and the shall and the future. Never-ending progress, a sequence of advancing and receding interests. The world as bottle factory. "I'll be happy if one day I can learn to live with all I *haven't* done," he says, and returns to the car.

Moments later the big black sedan backs down the driveway. They are in the frontseat, with Agnes in the middle, between Mohr and the driver. Tall hedges to the left and right create a narrow passage, a sluice down which the car slips like a new ship being launched into the sea. Mohr is facing forward, looking out the front window as the car backs away. Vogel waves, and Mohr waves back. As the car continues slowly down the drive, his thoughts drift briefly to those last few days in Wolfsgrub—his leap over the chair, the lifetime of possibilities closed and new ones opening up, the sense he has always had both of moving onward and backing away. He takes Agnes's hand, squeezes it in his lap as the car comes to the end of the driveway. With glances into the rearview and the side mirrors, the driver turns sharply, puts the car into gear, and speeds up the road in the direction of the city.

ONWARD AND AWAY you recede; you leave behind, and you are left behind; you look out from, and you look back at—moment upon moment upon moment—like the one when, chin on fist, your gaze was captured by a trick of light, a photograph.

Wolfsgrub

he first drops of rain begin to fall as she reaches the top of the meadow. Just a few hours ago, it was sunny, with hardly any wind. Then clouds from the east came rolling in, settled low over the valley. Now Käthe finds herself in a cold gray mist, and can't see more than a few meters in any direction. The early spring canopy provides some shelter from the rain, tender new leaves of oak and birch highlighting dark green patches of larch and spruce. She has counted her steps all the way up, every one. How pedantic. Like her brother, Otto, precise to the point of incoherence. She pulls back the hood of her loden cape. The cool air is refreshing. It is four hundred sixty-nine steps from the front door to the edge of the forest. It will be a different matter with snow on the ground, but next winter seems too far off to think about now. The last patches of snow in the upper meadow have already melted away. Spring came early this year. She wasn't waiting for it this year the way she usually looked forward to the changing seasons. It just happened—the way everything seems to be happening these days, suddenly coming upon and overwhelming her. A month ago the Wehrmacht marched into Austria. All the roads were clogged with columns

of marching soldiers, military vehicles, a steady stream of rattling machinery rolling toward Kreuth and the border.

Wolfsgrub is four hundred sixty-nine paces below. She can't see it though the mist, but can picture the smoke coiling up out of the chimney—not the long, thin stream of cold-weather smoke, but the thick, gathered smoke of low-pressure days, when the smell of creosote pervades the whole house and no matter how hot she stokes the stove, everything feels damp and pointless. She waxed the kitchen table earlier this morning. Eva helped drag it outside before going over to Berghammers', where she works every morning cleaning out the stalls. "You've never put wax on it before." She watched Käthe swipe the big block of sandpaper across the slightly warped surface of the table, digging into the grooves between the boards with the edge of the sanding block.

"Do you have your lesson ready? Fräulein Kraus is coming this afternoon."

Eva nodded, absorbed in what her mother was doing to the table. "Will it be all shiny afterward?"

"Not shiny, just smooth. And clean."

Eva watched, sucking the end of her pigtail. Käthe was bent over the table, leaning into the work with both hands, blowing away the dust and running her palm over the smooth, freshly revealed surface.

"Why not just leave it? Why put wax on it?"

"To protect the wood."

"You never worried about protecting the wood before."

Käthe stopped sanding, amused by Eva's concern, and tugged the pigtail out of her daughter's mouth. "Don't you worry, my dear. A little butcher wax is a good thing."

Eva left for Berghammers' without further comment. Käthe worked until her arms were sore and the sweat rolled, tickling down her sides. It felt good to be busy, out from under all the snow. She'd spent the whole winter reading, had poked her nose into every book in the house, lying beside the hot tiles of the stove. She'd never read so much or been so idle in all her life. If it hadn't been for the work at Berghammers', and Fräulein Kraus's afternoon lessons, Eva would have had nothing to do all winter long, either. She's been out of school for nearly a year, now. A whole year. Käthe liked to think that all her reading was compensation for Eva not being in school, but it also made her feel guilty; abstracted, negligent.

At Christmastime she'd roused herself, and managed to pull off what turned out to be a cozy little holiday. Otto came down from Göttingen—alone as ever, and loaded with wonderful gifts for Eva. But having him around had also been irritating. The perfect bourgeois in every way, right down to his stupid, fussy well-being. Professor Unrat, she called him, a joke he did not take too well. If he was overly tactful and reserved with his sister, it was because he claimed to understand her predicament. If she was taciturn, it was for precisely the opposite reason. She didn't pretend to understand anything—and especially not her brother's willful, obtuse blindness. Mohr used to say that Germany yielded more intellectual produce than it could use or pay for. Otto's Göttingen professorship was just one more overfertilized field. He'd joined the Party in order to remain on the faculty, and told Käthe that current politics didn't interest him in the least. "For God's sake!" she'd shot back. "What sort of utter nonsense is that?" But she didn't have the energy to fight him or argue any further, was grateful simply to have another presence in the house. They reverted to banalities. In compensation, she began reading everything that was left of Mohr's book collection—starting with Lawrence, and continuing with everything in the house. It seemed the only way left to protest.

Rain is falling heavily now, a thrumming of water high up in the canopy. All the counting has left her short of breath. Years ago, she and Mohr had built a little bench up here, a place to sit in the summer, or, in winter, to put on skis and set off along the woodcutter's trail that traverses in the direction of the Risserkogel and continues south in the direction of the border. In a fit of paranoia last autumn, she had chopped it up; decided she had to get rid of anything that might invite people to loiter. A clear view from above—straight down to the house. Mohr had written to her about it in a letter some time back, his dream of running down to the house in big, heavy boots. Suddenly she feels a tremor in the pit of her stomach. She struggles for a moment to fend it off, then, quietly, allows herself to cry.

THE TELEGRAM ARRIVED on November 17. An overcast, windy day. She and Eva had been sick with colds all week. That morning, Eva had decided she'd had enough of being inside, and had gone over to Lisa's to play. The details are confused, but vivid. She'd spilled coffee, a whole pot of it, in the kitchen. Scrubbed the floor. Taken a bath. She'd risen early, her back stiff from having spent the previous day in bed, and gone down to tend the animals. The lightbulb in the stall burned out as she was feeding Minna. There was no spare, so she went into the storage shed to look for the kerosene lamp, rarely used anymore. Luckily, there was still fuel in it. Carrying the lamp back to the stall, she recalled an image from an old film of just such a lamp falling into a pile of straw and burning down the barn. A vision of catastrophe, not a premonition. A catastrophe you can prepare for, but a premonition you're helpless against—and Käthe refuses to allow herself to become helpless. When, everywhere, things are growing dark, an old lamp becomes significant for the light it offers—and for the danger it illuminates.

Minna's nose was dry. Käthe wondered if the colds she and Eva had been suffering were drifting back here, making the animals sick. She gave the cow fresh hay, raked out the stall, and did the same for Ziggy, the goat. The hens had been busy. There were fresh eggs that morning. Going back into the house, she tested the rope Eva had talked Fräulein Kraus into tying to a rafter to swing on. It was now a permanent feature of the barn, and every morning Käthe tested it with a doubtful tug, smiling to herself at the thought of Fräulein Kraus tying the knot. There was nothing that woman wanted more.

Snow had fallen overnight. She put a fresh log into the stove, stoked the fire. The sound of crackling wood was different with new snow on the ground. The world was muffled. The room was warm. Käthe had finished her breakfast and was lingering over the slow beginning of another day, a third cup of coffee, when Eva came into the room. She crawled across the bench, took her place in front of the window, and sat for a bleary-eyed moment, staring at the egg in the cup before her. "Can I go to Lisa's today?"

Käthe glanced out the window at the fresh layer of snow on the ground, reached across the table and felt Eva's forehead. "How do you feel?"

"Fine!" Eva squirmed, then reached for her egg, began to tap it on the table. "I feel fine, Mama."

A day of play would be a good thing. In three days neither had left the house. It had started to snow again, big fluffy flakes, drifting. The windowpanes were frosted at the edges. It was quiet, inside and out. She considered going with Eva, walking her over to Lisa's, but was distracted by a sudden craving. She finished her coffee, cleared the table, and went to the cellar for some onions.

She wanted to make *Zwiebelkuchen* for supper. It was one of the things she could never make often enough. It wasn't just to please Eva that she enjoyed making it—though it was a favorite—or because she enjoyed it herself. It was the way the house smelled as it was being made—of butter and caramelizing onions. It always reminded her of her father, the way he used to rub his hands together and say, *"Ich habe gerochen alle Gerüche in dieser holden Erdenküche."* He said it with corny zestfulness, fully aware of the irritation his prim, old-fashioned humor caused around the table. She hadn't realized that the lines were from Heine until years later, and it had surprised her to discover that the poem was actually a dark lament, not the merry *Biedermeier* cliché that her father had made of it.

Eva finished her breakfast, cleared the rest of the table. Käthe was already busy in the kitchen, peeling and chopping onions. "Put on an extra sweater," she called. When, a few minutes later, she heard the front door slam shut, she went outside to watch as Eva set off up the road, pulling her battered old sled behind her.

The telephone rang. Käthe stamped her feet, stepped back inside. Hesitation had become her latest response to the ringing telephone. She hardly ever called out anymore, and so few calls came in that there seemed little point in keeping the thing. She'd heard from Jahn recently. He had called from Hamburg to say he was leaving for America, and promised to come and visit before leaving. She reached for the telephone, anticipating his cheerful "Hallo, Käthe!"—and was startled by an unfamiliar voice. "Frau Doktor Mohr?"

"Ja?"

"Telegram from China."

"Send it over. I'll be here."

There was a pause, then the line simply went dead.

She returned to the kitchen. The post office usually called ahead to make sure she was at home before sending someone out. She rolled out the crust. Telegrams were an old game of Mohr's. He loved to telegram, especially on the weekend, when rates were low. Nonsense kisses, he called them, and she always received them as such. *Black Schopenhauer wurst dadacrat reservation march I am so happy because of you.* Postcards to Eva were often nothing more than childish stick drawings with enigmatic little captions—completely impenetrable. The last cable had come in October. Just two words: *Alright Liebe.*

She pressed on the rolling pin with all her weight, leaned into it, then, abruptly, straightened up and left the kitchen. She went to the writing desk and took Mohr's latest letter from the drawer.

Shanghai
29 September 1937
It's so hard to know what to write from here. Thousands and thousands are dying all around. Gruesome sights and stories, but plenty of good-

ness as well. Air attacks on Nanking, Canton, etc. Horrible. Abandoned, orphaned children all over the place. Shanghai is quieter now due to cholera, mainly. Don't worry. I'm impossibly busy and will have to wait until things are calmer to describe it all to you and Eva. This is my second big war. I've seen it all—Germany, England, Japan, China—and now I've had enough. War is so vile and perverse. On top of fear for their livelihoods, some people here are so proud to be part of the experience. The biggest city siege in the history of the world! A tourist attraction. Their pride is so dreary and wretched and stupid. Don't worry about me. Trust in God as I have God's trust in you. Next spring I'll come and meet you over the border, at Achensee. I promise. We'll stay at the little Almhof, drink fresh milk and eat fresh cheese. Even if things here totally collapse, as the pessimists now believe (not me), I'll go third class on the Trans-Siberian. There and back. You write, "Everything is so distant, me and you in your letters." I don't know. I'm so worn out. War makes one so tired.

Third class across Siberia. He was only trying to prove his determination with a dash of cheer. But for some reason the letter had a bad effect on her, and it wasn't his dire circumstances, or the war. It was the train metaphor. He'd once told her he felt like a man standing on the tracks as the train pulled away, furious because his bags were too heavy. He said he felt weighted down with emptiness, with *Wichtigkeit und Nichtigkeit*. Now it was third class across Siberia, all raw need, like a child. He'd been like that always. When they'd first met, after the war, he'd told her all he wanted was to get a dog, and to wander the hills picking larkspur with a crust of bread and a piece of cheese in his pocket. The man she wanted to marry wanted to be a boy again! And, in her heart, all she wanted was to go along with him, to have a quiet life, to laugh and not care what other people thought. Even as she had joked about it, she could hear herself telling the story to her own children years hence, captivated by a sense only children fully grasp, of being in tow by wonderful enigmas: how the Westphals and the Kämmerers came together. How the Westphals and the Mohrs came together—exactly what was said and done, every joyful and terrible little family embarrassment right back to Adam and Eve.

She returned to the kitchen and finished rolling out the dough. As she put the pie in the oven to bake, she felt another twinge of foreboding. She couldn't define it precisely, except in the way that one can anticipate the very particular aroma of *Zwiebelkuchen* as it goes into the oven, the way everything seems foreordained and measured, a priori, down to the movements of one's own body. You mix onions, eggs, flour, milk, butter in a certain way, put them into the oven, until one certain day, when the result is: a telegram.

An Herzschlag verstorben. Vogel.

A HEART ATTACK.

THE GROUND BECOMES hard, the higher she climbs. Patches of snow here and there. She lost the trail some distance back, but rather than retrace her steps trying to find it, she alters course. The rain is falling steadily. Every few meters she pauses to catch her breath, the moist, sodden air condensing in thick clouds around her. She begins to sweat, opens the buttons of her cape. The path is overgrown and she is glad to have lost it, glad for the way the forest reclaims and covers everything so quickly. Some trees were taken down over the winter. The woodcutters brought the timbers down on an older, wider trail that runs about fifty meters above where she is, then descends in the direction of Sonnenmoos. Losing the lower path is a real comfort. *Auch bin ich dort, wo die Wege nicht gehn,* she says out loud. I am there also, where the paths lead not. The forest floor transforms itself so quickly, obliterates all traces of what once was. The old trail is gone, but overgrown, not fizzled out.

She remembers every detail of the telegram's arrival, down to the look of pained embarrassment on the delivery man's face as he passed the slip of blue paper across the threshold, cap tucked up tightly under his arm. She looked right at him, blank, her gaze locked. The man bowed his head and took a step backward. She could form no words, and turned back into the house. The man must have pulled the door shut before leaving. She doesn't remember. What she does remember is sitting beside the stove, holding the slip of paper in her lap, and trembling. Just sitting there and trembling. Eva was on her way to Lisa's with her sled. Suddenly Käthe realized that she needed to go get her; she must come home right away. She can't remember Fräulein Kraus arriving. Had she told her to go and fetch Eva? Or was it Marie Berghammer who'd told her? Or had Marie gone to get her herself? She remembers running next door, and she remembers coming back with Marie. But how much time elapsed between all these events? And who, in the end, had gone to fetch Eva? It was all a blur, right up to the moment Eva came into the house, with Marie and Fräulein Kraus right behind her. *"Papa ist gestorben,"* Käthe said, flat out. And then Eva was in her arms. Where had Marie and Fräulein Kraus gone? They were standing there one minute, then they were gone. Who had taken the *Zwiebelkuchen* out of the oven? She doesn't know. She doesn't know what else she said to Eva, or what Eva said to her—for days. All she can recall is a growing sense of panic; walking aimlessly around the house, room to room, chore to chore, meal to meal; and then one day waking up from her somnambulations and asking Eva, "What will we do now? What will we do?" suddenly and all at once, as if there had been no passing of days, no passage of time at all, no long resistance. And Eva turned to her with clear, dark eyes and in the calmest innocence said, "Don't worry, Mama. A widow with a child always gets by."

Telegrams arrived. Telephone calls from everyone and everywhere. Trauns, Kämmerers, Westphals; family she hadn't heard from in years. But no Mohrs. Where were the Mohrs? Was it possible they had all emigrated? Even Hedwig? Tante Elisabeth called, offered to give up the second floor of the Helwigstrasse house if Käthe wanted to come back to Hamburg. The rest she couldn't keep track of. She was too distracted by all the voids and absences. There was no body to bury, no service to plan. Neighbors dropped by with food and offers of help. But she didn't need help. The days passed into blankness. There was no further news. Nothing but silence. No how. No where. No when. No who. All attempts to contact Vogel were unsuccessful. Telegrams were returned as undeliverable. Had he left Shanghai? Was he dead now, too? Finally all she could think to do was cable 803 Bubbling Well Road. The servant Mohr had so often mentioned in his letters, Wong. And on the day she went to the post office, miraculously, a cable was waiting for her, had arrived just an hour earlier. *Have personal effects will deliver. Return Saarbrücken May. In deepest sorrow. Brehm.*

She sent an immediate reply confirming receipt of the cable, then rushed home and dashed off a letter to the captain care of Norddeutsche Lloyd. Over the next few days, she began to scan the newspapers, but news from China was sparse. Nanking fell to the Japanese in December. Only the barest outlines of the war made it into the newspapers. No news is good news, Mohr had liked to say; but no news, good news was now the motto of all Germany. She could feel herself being drawn into an enveloping ignorance, like a deep, snowy dream. It was almost comforting. But nightmares are also dreams, and with Mohr dead, waking up and dreaming on had become indistinguishable terrors.

Then, one week into the new year, an envelope arrived from Shanghai. It contained nothing but a single clipping from a newspaper called the *Ostasiatische Lloyd,* a Shanghai newspaper.

Jewish Comintern Agent Commits Suicide
Shanghai, 21 November
The Jew, Max Mohr, was found dead in his clinic at 803 Bubbling Well Road, of a self-inflicted gunshot wound to the head. The news came

as a surprise to the staff of the Country Hospital, where for the past three years Mohr had been posing as a medical doctor.

According to officials of the Shanghai Municipal Police, Special Branch, Mohr had been a member of a secret Comintern cell operating in the International Settlement. In August of this year, he traveled to Japan, where, posing as a tourist, he worked to gather information for Moscow on the Japanese war effort. Mohr arrived in Shanghai in 1934. After years of declining popularity, his literary career came to a final end when he was expelled as a member of the Reichsschrifttumskammer along with other Jewish writers whose work has been categorized by scholars as of no cultural or literary value. Posing as a medical doctor and a decorated war veteran, he set up a private clinic at 803 Bubbling Well Road, which became the center of an extensive espionage operation.

Referring to this incident, Ministerrat Adolph Fuchs said that the work of unmasking subversive elements in China continues, and is more important than ever, given the present crisis environment.

The rain slows to a drizzle. Half an hour after losing the trail, she is still struggling uphill; no sign anywhere of the little cabin. The forest seems unfamiliar now, and overgrown. She can't get her bearings, and because of the thick cloud cover, doesn't know how high she's climbed until, suddenly, she finds herself standing on the rim of the Kaltengruben, the deep gorge that runs like a gash down the southeastern slope of the Wallberg. She is just below the vertical cliff that forms the top of the gorge. The cabin is a good way back into the forest and slightly below where she is standing. Stepping back from the edge, she finds a dry patch of ground underneath a large spruce tree. She sits down, stretches her legs, and closes her eyes.

It has been years since she's been up in this part of the forest. Kaltengruben had once been a favorite destination, and before Eva was born, she and Mohr would often walk all the way up it to the base of the cliff. A flat outcropping of rock makes it a perfect place to picnic. It isn't the bare, blue vertical rock of the high Alps, but after the accident on the Gross-Venediger, Mohr had been happy for a nearby place to climb to. The entire Tegernsee comes into view up here, from Rottach all the way to Gmund.

The idea for the cabin had come to her in this very spot, on a midsummer outing with Eva. They'd brought food and water and thick woolen blankets, were embarked on the camping trip Mohr had often promised to take Eva on. Martin had been bragging all spring that *his* father was going to take him camping, and Eva, *a girl,* would not be allowed to come with them. When Mohr decided to remain in Berlin through mid-September, Eva begged her mother to take her. Käthe agreed, in part to compensate for her father's broken promise, but also because she thought of it as a little vacation they could take, just the two of them together.

He'd been so enthusiastic about her delphinium project. They'd cleared and turned the soil together. He was happier than she'd seen him in a long time; she only wanted to give him something to return to, not just family life and a sustainable livelihood, but a writerly keep as well. He didn't have to give up. It didn't have to be all or nothing. They would live apart from everything here, for themselves, the way they'd always done. Grow flowers.

The sky was bright with a full moon. Even wrapped in woolen blankets and with the embers of the fire throwing off a steady heat, they were cold. "I'm going to build Papa a little cabin," she said. The idea had simply popped into her head. Before Eva could respond, she was sitting up, drawing the blanket around her shoulders. "A place for him to write. Away from all the noise in the house."

Eva was curled on her side, bunched in her blanket like a cocoon. She'd brought the pillow from her bed with her, a smart detail that Käthe had overlooked for herself.

"A tree house?" Eva asked sleepily.

Käthe poked the embers with a stick. "I was thinking of something sturdier. A little house where he can go and work, even in winter."

"And sleep and cook?"

"Sleep and cook, too. Why not?" Her prodding kindled a little flame and their faces were illuminated in flickers of orange. A few moments passed, until Eva broke the silence. "Why doesn't Papa want to live with us?"

"He needs to go where there is work," was all she could think to answer.

Construction of the little cabin began right away. It was summer, 1934, and still hard times for many locals. Käthe was overwhelmed with helpers, several of whom were glad to work simply for a meal and something to do. The site was chosen and cleared. If it was a little more remote than seemed convenient or necessary, it had as much to do with the workers' wish to have the project drag on for as long as possible as it did with her feeling that the deeper into the forest he had to go, the happier Mohr would be to work there. For Eva it was a fantasy come to life. She was delighted to have a secret to keep, a surprise for Papa. She would return from school every day leading her gang of little friends. They would clamor to be allowed to go up and watch the men at work. It went far beyond what Käthe had originally planned, was bigger by half, and fitted with real amenities—a stone fireplace, shuttered windows, bookshelves, even a basin that drained through a pipe to the outside. On the day it was finished, Strohschneider and two other men hauled up the old sofa from Mohr's study. She followed with a supply of kitchen utensils, a pot for coffee, a kerosene lamp, and a stack of woolen blankets. The men drank schnaps and teased Eva and her gang about the little forest men who would make good use of the place when no people were about.

Mohr returned from Berlin in late September, having detoured on the way back through Prague. Looking back, it should have been obvious that he was preparing to leave. But things are always obvious looking back, including the fact that she was doing her best to ignore what was unfolding right under their noses. What was wrong with that? Why not ignore it? One doesn't dwell on every detail of an unfolding threat, but tries to escape from it—even if escape involves the self-deception of looking the other way. She liked to tell herself that ignoring politics was also a political act.

It was late afternoon when Mohr arrived back at Wolfsgrub. No sooner had he stepped from the taxi and swept Eva up in his arms than she began begging him to go on a walk. "In the woods, Papa. You and Mama and me!"

There was more hugging than was typical for Mohr. Käthe was surprised by his extravagant, passionate kiss. And the fashionable new suit. A jacket from Hurwitz & Sohn, and a pair of Scherer trousers. Normally, he would arrive as innocuously and unceremoniously as possible, drop his bags in the hallway, pull on his workboots. If work was under way, he would join in as if he'd been present all along, picking up the thread of conversation or interrupting it to relate some absurd incident he'd experienced on his way home.

They walked straight down to the field in the glow of sunset. The crop was just ready to be harvested, the flowers lush and heavy. Beautiful blue delphinium. They walked among the rows together, flushed with a rare pride and surging with happiness. She took scissors from the pocket of her apron, cut a large stalk, and offered it to him. Eva rolled her eyes and giggled with embarrassment as he drew her into his arms and, for the second time, kissed her extravagantly. "A field of flowers," he said, holding her around the waist. Then he threw up his arms. *"Lass die Winde los!"* Let loose the winds.

THE RAIN BEGINS to taper off. She opens her eyes, momentarily disoriented. Deep green moss grows in large patches on this slope, is particularly lush along the walls of the ravine. She stands up to orient herself, but the cloud cover makes it difficult. She decides to descend along the rim of the gorge, then turn back into the forest. If after a while she doesn't come across the cabin, she'll return to the ravine, descend again, and so on, traversing back and forth until she finds it.

She starts down, and after a short distance, just a few steps into the

forest, notices what looks like a fresh gash on the trunk of a big larch tree. It looks as if the bark has been slashed and peeled. As she draws nearer, she can see that the bark has not been stripped, but carved. Letters snap into focus: *Drecksau Hitler.* Filthy pig Hitler.

She approaches cautiously, glancing around, frightened but also slightly amused. She runs her fingers over each letter. They have been carved deeply, with patience and care. Recently. Sap still oozes from the exposed wood. She feels oddly vulnerable, as if she is being observed from a distance. If the message is heartening, there is also violence in it. She is wary, but curious, and tries to imagine who might have been driven to such a thing. It is juvenile in its rawness. And yet the way each letter has been carved—deeply and with care. It is not only an impulse but a marker, something to return to, and have others return to, and that implies a motive beyond the mere expression of forbidden speech. There is something odd about it. Some man—certainly it was a man—walked up here—most likely alone—and carved his message in the trunk of the biggest larch tree he could find. But he carved the letters on the side of the tree facing the gorge, not facing downhill. He hadn't intended the message to be visible to someone walking uphill, but to someone approaching from Kaltengruben, someone who knew to look for it.

She is suddenly anxious again. Is there some connection with her abandoned cabin? She scans the woods. The rain has stopped and the clouds are lifting. The light has shifted from lead to silver gray. She searches the ground and finds a large stick, snaps off the twigs, tests it with a few stabs into the soft ground. It feels good to hold on to something firmly. She is aware of the strength in her arms, the return of a physicality that, over the winter months, has been submerged and distorted. From above comes the sudden mooing of an elk. She stands still, listens. A few minutes later she hears it again, higher up. The animal is moving away. She feels a momentary connection, another solitary being moving through the forest.

Five minutes later she comes upon the cabin. The wooden shingles of the roof are green with moss. The stones of the chimney blend into the damp mist. The area that Strohschneider worked so hard to clear is now thick with undergrowth. The trailhead is still marked at the top by two small piles of stones that Eva had gathered and set into place one afternoon with Lisa and Rosi.

She doesn't go right down, but regards it for a time, leaning against her staff. How strange it looks. Solid, yet also grown over; abandoned, yet also settled in. She and Strohschneider had argued over the stone foundation. She wanted a simple little wooden cabin that blended into the forest, nothing more. But Strohschneider had been right. Imagine how sad it would be now to come upon a collapsed wooden shack.

On the morning after Mohr had returned home from Berlin, they had led him up here. It was September. The leaves had already turned and were falling, a thick carpet of red and orange and yellow. They had a clear view of it, perched at the edge of a small outcropping. Approaching from below, it almost seemed too grand. Freshly planed wooden planks and new shingles, with two sets of windows facing the valley. Mohr had been strangely quiet all the way up. Eva pranced ahead along the trail, bursting with excitement. Käthe became anxious. It hadn't felt extravagant as it was being built. The weeks and weeks of hard work annulled any thought of extravagance. In fact, she had felt that by building it, she was earning the right to have it, and on the day it had been declared finished, she'd told Strohschneider that it looked as if it had always been there, that it *belonged.*

At the first sight of it, Mohr stopped in his tracks. Eva had already reached the clearing and was calling to them to hurry up. Mohr's face remained blank, expressionless. He showed no sign of surprise, or even of curiosity. She took him by the hand and led him forward, her heart pounding now with excitement. He allowed himself to be led, but with the reluctance of someone being shown something that has been declared perfect in advance.

They came into the clearing, hand in hand, and stopped to take in the view. She resisted the urge to point out all the details. In the dappled light of morning, they struck her as all the more perfectly arranged. She withdrew the key from her pocket, was about to hand it over, but changed her mind and beckoned him to follow. An old brass padlock was fixed to the door, one final little touch. It sprang open easily. She pushed open the door and stood aside.

Mohr entered slowly, his face completely expressionless. He stood in the center of the cabin, taking it all in.

She felt the moment draining away. "Well?"

"Look, Papa!" Eva pointed to the kettle hanging from a hook in the fireplace. "You can cook and make coffee."

Mohr smiled. He crossed to the other end of the room, glanced out the windows into the autumn canopy. "You spent all the money, didn't you?" His voice was quiet. But the effect could not have been any worse if he'd shouted.

Humiliated and angry, she knelt on the hearth, pulled a handful of twigs from the kindling basket, snapping and breaking, piling them up to make a fire.

"Don't you like it, Papa?" Eva asked. The twist of uncertainty in her voice brought Käthe to tears. She averted her face, busied herself. "Now you don't have to go away to work anymore," Eva went on. "You can stay with us and work here." Mohr picked her up, kissed her on the cheek. He sat down on hearth beside Käthe, took off his glasses, rubbed his eyes, pressing hard with thumb and forefinger. There were deep black circles under his eyes. His fingers were stained yellow from his incessant smoking. He seemed more preoccupied and worn out than she'd ever seen him. She would later remember being conscious of having known exactly what was coming next.

"I thought you would be happy," she said.

"How can I be happy?"

Käthe stood up. "Yes, I spent the money. I spent all of it!" Her anger transformed into indignation. She took Eva by the hand, and stood over Mohr. "I did it so you would have a place to work."

Mohr stared into the empty hearth. "I have to leave," he said dryly.

The whole day lay ahead of them, and yet it was already over. She had planned it so differently. They would harvest the last flowers together, walk to Kaffee Angermaier afterward for tea with rum. If they weren't too tired, they'd hike back up to the cabin and have *Abendbrot* in front of the fire. If only she'd known then what she knew now, could have seen what was now so plain to see. Mohr never said, "I'm a Jew. I have to go." He never said, "I have no future here." Even with all the horrible new laws being passed, and violent Nazi propaganda, he never talked about being a Jew at all. Or having to flee because of it. It was almost as if he were denying that such a thing could happen, while submitting to it inwardly. Instead, he talked about a self that had been buried and grown over by years of pointless striving. He was through with all of it, with pretension and all things literary.

"We came here to get away from the city," he said on the way back down to the house. "But look at me. I've gone and become a city person! I have to find a new element. No more illusions. No self-deception."

And Käthe said, "Of course. But that doesn't mean you have to leave." She wanted him to find what he had to find, had always wanted that, had always told him so. "Maybe if you go back to doctoring, the poetry will improve," she said, trying humor.

He didn't laugh, but nodded, as if the same thought had occurred to him. "Why do I always go off on these wild tangents? Find the longest detours?"

They were back on the bridle path. She took his arm and for a little while they walked together the way they'd done in the early years: talking, gesticulating, so that from a distance they seemed to be arguing. Eva raced ahead. The little cabin up on the slope of the Wallberg had already become moot.

He never said, "Thank you for trying."

She never said, "I'll go with you, wherever you want to go."

Back at the house he showed her his ticket. To Shanghai. One way.

SHE DESCENDS THE muddy embankment, leaning on the stick for support, and approaches the front door. The padlock is missing. The evidence of tampering is alarming, even though she had anticipated it. Hunters, woodcutters, wanderers—any number of people could have made use of the place. She makes a quick circuit of the house, alarmed once again to find a small pile of wood stored under the eaves. The shutters are closed. Water drips from the roof in a steady flow, soaking the ground all along the stonework foundation, which has settled at an incline. From the side, the little cabin seems to lean into the hill.

The door swings open easily.

"Hello?" she calls into the darkened hut, then strides across the floor and quickly throws open the shutters. Light streams through the dirty panes. She is happy to see all the glass intact and breathes in the musty air, recalling smells from childhood, the shed at the back of the garden, hiding places, mouse droppings, spider webs. The old sofa is still right where she had set it in front of the fireplace. In the hearth, a pile of ash and a few charred pieces of wood. Anxiety gives way to cozy childhood memories: tucked away, she would imagine living hidden forever in some cranny like a mouse or a bird or a fox. She wishes she'd brought Eva along; she had considered it, but chose not to, uncertain of the effect upon Eva of seeing her mother brooding in the ruins. There has been enough weeping around the house. It seems right to protect her from the growing dread that things everywhere are in a very bad way and getting worse; that they are facing a gathering danger.

The newspaper clipping started it. It was a lie. Of course it was. A grave, evil lie. It shook her, but Käthe's instincts told her exactly what to make of it. The newspapers carried such pieces every day: stories of

Jews, communists, subversives, asocials, prostitutes, and common crim-
inals. The whole country is dripping with malice. Whoever had sent
the clipping had done her a favor—she isn't safely tucked away out in
the countryside. The machinery is grinding and grinding away. Her
only defense is to remain absolutely quiet. Invisible.

The day after the clipping arrived, she'd written a letter to Heinrich
George, who had recently been appointed director of the Volkstheater
in Berlin. At one time, they'd been good friends. Of all the friends
from Mohr's early theater days, Heinrich George was now the most
prominent. A careerist like Otto, but the film star version.

Dear Heinrich,
Six weeks ago I received a cable that Mohr died in Shanghai of a heart
attack. I am devastated. Please do me a favor. If it should ever come up
in your circles, or if anyone should ask, would you please put in a good
word for Mohr, his qualities as a human being, a person? And may I
use your name as a reference? I can't imagine it will come to that, but
wouldn't want to do it without your permission. Please do me the favor
of replying to this letter. Perhaps it's for the better that I feel I must write
to ask you for favors this way. Otherwise, I might not have been able to
bring myself to tell you that your old friend is no longer. As far as how
I am doing—surely that must be obvious. You must know all too well.

The answer she received—and it had come immediately—had been
more painful than no answer at all.

Dear Käthe,
Am at your service. Write when you want to come with your things to
Wannsee.

Go to Wannsee? With her things? Tent to tent like chattel? There
was no shelter anywhere; and especially not in the old friendships.

She inspects the cabin. Her footsteps fall on the wooden planks with a pleasant sound. She notices further signs that it is being used. The stone hearth has been swept with a broom. A rag hangs from a nail on the wall. In the basin she finds a tin can, fairly new. A row of candle stubs in hardened pools of wax stands on the wooden plank that she put up herself as a bookshelf. She takes off her wet cape, hangs it on a nail to drip. The crack of a branch outside.

A man appears in the doorway.

"Frau Mohr."

"*Oh Gott, oh Gott!*" she exhales, hand fluttering, and steps back. Seethaler stands in the door holding his armful of wood. "What are you doing here?"

He indicates the pile of wood under his arm. "I came to make a fire. I'll go if you like," he says.

"No, no. You startled me. Come in."

Seethaler enters, stepping gingerly over to the hearth. He puts down his load of wood, takes off his hat, and turns. "Shall I . . . ?"

"Please. Go ahead. Make a fire."

He puts his hat back on, squats, and sets to work.

"Do you come here often to make fires?"

"Not to make fires, Frau Mohr." He turns to her earnestly. "To get away from people." He pulls some scraps of newspaper from his coat pocket, wads and shoves them under the kindling pile.

"I never come up here," Käthe says.

Seethaler produces a packet of matches, lights the newspaper, watches the flames spread. "I was very sorry to hear about Dr. Mohr," he says without looking up. "It's so sad."

She is still uncomfortable accepting condolences, and watches Seethaler feed the growing fire, twig by twig, stick by stick. He is entirely absorbed. "You can't imagine how sad it is," she says at last. Seethaler breaks a large stick over his knee and lays it on the fire. Käthe goes to stand by the window. The rain has stopped. The green canopy is dense and seems impenetrable in the mist. "How long have you been coming up here?"

"Since you mentioned it to me last summer." He excuses himself and goes outside. A few moments later he returns with several split logs. "I keep a little supply around the side. It stays dry under the eaves." He stacks the wood on the floor beside the hearth, then selects a fresh log from the pile and carefully lays it on the bed of coals. The room is silent but for the crackling from the hearth. When the log has caught, he turns to her. "Why would you want to tear this place down, Frau Mohr? It would be a shame to demolish it."

"Do you come here often?"

Seethaler leans against the mantel. "Would you be angry if I said yes?"

"Why should I be angry?"

He shrugs, produces a pipe from the pocket of his coat, and fills it with tobacco. "May I speak personally?"

She turns to the window to look outside again.

Seethaler lights his pipe. "Did you want to tear it down because it reminds you of your husband?"

"Yes," she says flatly.

He shakes his head, puffing on his pipe. "I have very fond memories of Dr. Mohr." He picks up a stick from the hearth. "Remember the winter he taught us to ski? Me, Franz Schwartz, and Ali Limmer. Remember Ali?" He begins poking the fire. Käthe nods, watches the logs kindle. She's known Theo Seethaler since he was a boy, and has nothing to fear from him. Feeling suddenly exhausted, she sits down on the sofa.

"Do you still want to tear it down?" Seethaler asks.

"I don't know."

"I think it would be a big mistake, Frau Mohr. Especially now." He continues poking the fire with the stick, his back turned to her. "Jewish families are losing their shops, their homes, being pushed out into the street." He scrapes the glowing ember from the tip of the stick, then rekindles the smoking end in the fire, absorbed.

"What does that have to do with me?" Käthe says, flushing. She feels heat rising into her cheeks, her ears. Even as she forms the words, she feels a pang of complicity, of guilt. In adopting this strange new grammar of disassociation, she realizes she is implicated in a vast and virulent corruption. The look on Seethaler's face tells her that he understands this. He puts his pipe to his lips, begins to puff, eyes unfocused. "I know what you're thinking, Theo," she says, regaining her composure. "Don't worry; nobody is going to take Wolfsgrub from me. I am not a Jew."

In spite of the heat radiating into the room from the fire, she is suddenly chilled and begins to shiver. Sitting is uncomfortable. She gets up, fetches her cape. It is still waterlogged. She shivers again, feeling the full weight of the sentences she has just uttered. They have cost her something. She feels naked and vulnerable, wants only to be alone now, back inside her house.

"What about Eva?"

"What about her?" Tears begin to well as she looks squarely back at Seethaler. She brushes her cheek with the back of her hand.

Seethaler looks away, inspects the tip of the stick, then holds it in the fire. "Remember last summer? When I told you that I was also an outsider? You pretended not to know what I was talking about."

Käthe draws the rain-heavy loden over her shoulders.

"I am still an outsider, Frau Mohr. And this place you built up here—it's the one place that I can come and feel completely—myself."

"Yes. I've seen how you have marked it."

"I beg your pardon?"

"Your little bit of self-expression. I saw it coming up."

Seethaler shakes his head. "I don't know what you are talking about."

"On the tree."

"I don't know what you are talking about."

She pushes the door open to leave.

"Wait, Frau Mohr," Seethaler says. "If it ever becomes necessary . . ."

She turns, waits for him to finish.

"If you should ever need to send Eva up here, I will look after her
for you."

The rain has stopped but the forest is soaked and gray and dripping.
She has managed to outrun this particular thought until now. Over
weeks, months, years, she has driven it to the furthest corner of her
mind. But it has been there all along. Coming up through the forest,
she was glad to have lost the way. If she can get lost along so familiar a
path, so can anybody. There is a higher symbolism in the thought, one
that she has allowed herself to contemplate, while averting her attention from the basic truth; in this there is also a symbol and a warning.
There are warnings popping up everywhere and yet, today, if she has
purposefully lost her way—she is glad for the little self-deception.

A strange mix of fear and shame makes it impossible to look at him
now. She doesn't want to know the expression on his face. Standing
there on the threshold of the little cabin in her soaking loden, she feels
like some species of rodent scurrying along the forest floor searching
for places to bury her food and deposit her young. "Thank you, Theo,"
she says quietly, and steps out the door.

THE SPRING THAT began too early is now in peak bloom. The hills are
thick with new growth, the meadows covered in wildflowers. It is the
time of short nights and sweet grass. Minna has been out to pasture for
most of the week. This morning, Eva and Rosi went to the top of the
meadow to fetch her down. Her milk now has the flavor of the season.

Käthe pushes open the door of the barn and chases Ziggy, the goat,
out into the yard. She is still tired, drained of energy. Instead of washing out the stalls, which is what she'd planned for the morning, she
pulls up the dusty old armchair and sits down to rest. She'd been un-

able to sleep all night, thinking about Marie Berghammer's offer, and can't make up her mind. "She won't be the only young girl," Marie had said. "There are three families up there, two with girls Eva's age."

Send Eva up into the mountains for the entire summer? It sounded good as Marie had explained it. Anything to get her out of sight for a while. Hitler isn't going away. Neither is Frau von Stockhausen or Bund Deutscher Mädchen. A troop of girls in ugly brown jackets and black ties. Every Saturday they march up the footpath at the edge of the meadow and into the forest, singing and carrying on. Yesterday, Eva was out in the yard when they marched by. All waved, and Eva, who was feeding the chickens, waved back. Von Stockhausen called her over to the fence. Käthe watched from inside, wanting to let it pass, but then thought better and went out to join the little gathering at the fence. Von Stockhausen had been around for years. A big-bosomed Nazi, married to some baron who years back had run for local office and lost. They spent their summers on the lake near Weissach, had no children. "Why don't you let the child in BDM?" she wanted to know.

"No time," Käthe answered in her best Bavarian. "No money." She wiped her hands on her apron. Eva glanced over at her mother, unsure. Rarely did Käthe speak Bayrisch, and when she did it was usually to tell a funny story. A few more words were exchanged, then von Stockhausen commanded her troop to resume their walk. As they set off she turned back and said, "We'll speak about it later."

"Why can't I join?" Eva wanted to know when they'd returned inside the house.

"Because I don't want you to." She took her daughter into the kitchen, gave her a freshly baked biscuit. "All that marching around in those silly uniforms."

"I think they're nice."

She could think of no way to explain, so she simply dug in. "We in this family do not like marching or uniforms. Your father was in the

last war and when we were married we said that we were finished with uniforms and marching around."

Later that evening she went next door to talk to Marie.

"Send her up to the *Alm* for the summer," Marie suggested right away. "Stefan is going up to look at some new calves. Eva can go with him, and stay there for the summer."

"All summer? I can't send her away all summer."

Marie shrugged. "She'll have other children to play with. Fresh air, sunshine."

The idea made sense. Of course, she would prefer to take Eva up there herself, but it was a full day's walk, across the border into Austria. Two days there and back—and she couldn't leave just now. Not until the captain came.

The second telegram had arrived in mid-April.

Coming soon. Schedule uncertain. Brehm.

"Let's go swimming, Mama!" Eva races through the open doors of the barn, hops onto the arm of the chair. "Fräulein Kraus is sick again."

"Again? She must be in love."

"She said she would take me and Lisa and Ursula to Tölz to the cinema. Can I go, Mama? Please?"

"You just said she was sick."

"When she's better. She promised. Can I go? Please?"

Eva frees herself, jumps up. Light streams through the doors of the barn, sparkling clouds of dust and pollen. Käthe settles back into the bumpy armchair, lifts her face to the sun. She listens as Eva tells all about a balloon that has fallen into Daibler's outhouse toilet.

"Did it fall or was it put down there?"

Eva evades the question and prattles on about trying to fish it out of the pit. "It's still down there, Mama. Want to come and look?"

"I don't think so, no."

"But it's still got air in it! Come see! We can look at it and then go swimming!"

Käthe laughs, shakes her head. "It's too cold for swimming."

"No, it's not. It's hot!"

"How would you like to go up to the *Alm* with Berghammer?"

"What for?"

"An adventure. Up in the mountains."

"With you?"

"I can't."

"Why not?"

"Too much work to do."

Eva becomes serious, sits on the arm of the chair.

"It's lovely up there. Children to play with. Berghammer is going up to buy some calves. You can keep him company on the way. Then you can look after his calves for him. He'll need someone to look after them until it's time to bring them down."

"What about you, Mama?"

"I'll come up as soon as I'm done with all my work here."

Eva crams a pigtail in her mouth. "When?"

"Think of all the fun you'll have. You'll learn how to make cheese. *Kräuterkäse,*" she ventures, afraid she's taken the wrong tack, that Eva will begin to resist, stiffen and stiffen until she has no choice but to order her away. "Think it over." She tugs the pigtail from Eva's mouth. "Okay, let's go swimming."

They pedal down to the lake. The beach is empty except for an elderly couple walking their stiff little dog on a leash. Käthe spreads out the blanket and sits down. As Eva tempts herself into the icy water, she mends an old cotton blouse. Coming down to the lake feels less comfortable with each passing season. Rottach is more crowded than ever, with swastikas on every lamp post, in storefronts. *Juden sind hier nicht erwünscht.* The sign is posted everywhere, so many it almost seems normal.

She divides her attention between Eva and sewing. Another winter gone and she is just now beginning to shake off some of the grief that has blanketed her, a feeling of constant pressure at the temples and a constriction at the core of her heart. Her awareness of time seems altered, more connected to mood than to the progress of days or the changing seasons. She remembers being overcome by a similar feeling when her father, then again when her mother died: a feeling of being adrift. Their time on earth together had ended. It was over. She felt let loose in the world, flitting about, not bound by anything. Now, again, she is overcome. But her grief is different this time. It is extravagant and physical, connected with her limbs, her organs, her sex.

The church bell rings twelve o'clock. She stuffs her sewing back into the basket, stands, and calls to Eva, who takes her time coming out of the water. Käthe calls to her again, distracted by the growing numbers of *Kurgäste* and tourists out for their lunchtime stroll, the occasional familiar face—*Grüss Gott, Guten Tag, Servus.* Käthe feels a steadily growing and uncomfortable self-consciousness. What is causing it? Too much focus? Or disconnection. Is she merely floating? Aimless and adrift? No! She is facing life. All its hardness.

She towels off and helps Eva back into her clothes. Sensing her mother's sudden impatience, Eva asks, "What's the matter, Mama? Are we going someplace?"

"No. We're not going anyplace." She is about to add that they have no place to go, but manages to hold her tongue.

Shops and businesses are closed for the midday rest. Doors are locked, shutters rolled down. There is very little traffic on the main road. At Hotel Tegernsee the tables are out on the lawn and lunch is under way for the wander-jacketed, crisply clad tourists. Käthe pedals by all of it with her eyes fixed on the road straight ahead. At Saint Laurentius, she turns abruptly into the churchyard. Eva rolls up behind and they park their bicycles against the wall. They enter the church holding hands. It is empty inside. Narrow shafts of light stream in through old, heavily leaded glass. A renovation is under way, and both of the marble rococo side altars are covered by scaffolding.

"What are we doing, Mama?" Eva asks. Her voice echoes loudly, and Käthe presses a finger to her lips, then makes directly for the bank of votive candles set in an alcove to the left. Eva resists, tugs her mother's hand. Footsteps echo. They enter the small enclosure. Käthe points to the flickering banks of red glass. "We're going to light some candles."

"Why?"

Käthe takes two tapers from the dispenser, drops a few coins into the collection box.

"I thought we were Lutherans, Mama."

"It doesn't matter. We're doing it for our own reasons." She lights the tapers. "For Papa," she whispers, and begins to light candles, one after another, gesturing for Eva to do the same. When the entire bank of red glass is lit they stand back, smiling with pride at the beautiful spectacle. Mohr would have happily approved, as he approved of all the local idols set in shrines along highways, footpaths, in farmers' fields high up the mountains.

Back outside Eva says, "We're still Lutherans, right, Mama?"

"We're much more than that."

"What else are we?"

"A good question," Käthe says, standing astride her old bicycle. She pushes off, giddy from their little adventure. A small flock of pigeons is feeding on bread crumbs that have been scattered on the cobblestones in front of the church. "We're free-thinking pacifists," she calls to Eva over her shoulder, feeling a rush of pleasure as they ride directly through and scatter the birds. "What else are we?" Eva wants to know when they are back out on the road. Käthe glances over her shoulder as they approach the bend. "Frightened," she shouts, then signals for Eva to fall in behind her.

Eva follows close behind. A car honks its horn and speeds around. "Are you sad, Mama?" Eva calls.

Käthe tucks her elbows in and begins to pedal harder.

"I am, too," Eva shouts after her.

Rounding the last bend, Käthe slows, then pulls to the side of the road. A car is parked at the front gate. It is the same car that passed them minutes earlier.

Eva pulls up alongside. "What's the matter now, Mama?"

Käthe points to the car and Eva says, "Uncle Otto is back!"

"It isn't Uncle Otto."

"Who is it?"

Käthe takes a deep breath.

"Who is it, Mama?"

"Somebody from China." She puts her foot on the top pedal, but can't make herself press down or push forward.

Eva squints, then angles her bicycle so that their front wheels are exactly parallel. "Is it somebody who knew Papa?"

They are in the shade of a tall hedge. A feeling of shelter, something to lean against—or vanish into. Just across the road a wide field opens to a panoramic view of the valley and the mountains. All her waiting is concentrated now in the silhouette of that automobile parked at the front gate like some huge black bird, swooped down from on high.

"Is it somebody who knew Papa?"

Käthe's heart begins to pound. All she can think of now is Mohr's dream of landing high up on the meadow, running down to the house in those huge woodcutter's boots. Everything has come to pass, is now behind her, done with forever—the way she one day simply put aside the violin and never returned to it.

A figure appears at the gate. The trunk of the car is open and a man is fetching items from it. Suitcases and a trunk. They watch him make several trips. As he prepares to depart he tips his cap and waves.

"Who is he waving to?" Eva wants to know.

Käthe doesn't answer. The car backs up, turns around. Eva waves as it speeds by, leaves them in a wake of dust and fumes. Another image flares, the memory of a cold April day. Mohr is smiling, wearing a multipocketed English tweed coat, fedora cocked jauntily to the side. She is petting Wutzi, wearing city clothes. Eva is in her baby carriage. It is one of the few photographs that doesn't leave her feeling taunted by tricks of shadow and light, feeling that what has been captured is the illusion of a life she never really led.

A MAN IS sitting on the bench by the front door, dressed in a simple black coat and tie. Suitcases and a steamer trunk are stacked beside him. As they dismount and lean their bicycles against the fence, he stands up, drops his cigarette on the ground.

"Captain Brehm?"

"Käthe Mohr." He grips her hand warmly, and then turns to Eva. "And I know who you are, too," he says without the slightest trace of affectation. "You are Eva. I recognize you from the photos."

Emboldened by the kindliness in his voice, Eva says, "You're not Chinese."

The remark dissolves any vestiges of formality. "No." Brehm laughs. "Just an old *ostfriesischer* sea captain."

"The one who sent us all the packages from Papa?"

"The same." Brehm smiles. He isn't at all the typical naval type Käthe had been expecting, and is not, thank god, wearing a uniform or Party pins or insignia. He is tall and blond with light blue eyes, slightly stoop-shouldered and angular, but in a round, softened way; a man who enjoys and is comfortable with his position in life, but does not take it for granted. It's easy to imagine him sitting at a table on board his ship, reading cables, charting course, giving commands.

She glances at the pile of luggage, recognizes three of the cases. Her immediate sense is that they should not be opened but stored away. Upstairs, in the attic. It comes as a surprise that she should not want to open them. It isn't lack of curiosity, but their sudden presence leaves her feeling odd, uneasy, as if she should want to ask the captain: Where is he? Or

want to know which road they'd come by. The steamer trunk, with its locks and buckles, is pasted with foreign stickers and Chinese writing. But even as her curiosity is aroused, it is overshadowed by apprehension.

Brehm offers to bring the bags inside.

"Leave them," she says, and tells Eva to show the captain around while she prepares tea.

From the kitchen she can hear Eva's excited voice, first from the stalls, then over by the fence where Minna is grazing, then a little farther off, over by the woodshed. Through the sitting-room window, she watches Brehm, in shirtsleeves, allowing Eva to pull him along by the hand. The sight of it puts her at ease, conjures memories of her own childhood, where everything seemed light and bright and clear and happy. Fruit juice and glass dishes piled high with beautiful sandwiches and cakes. Nobody pinched with secrets, everything in order. No quarrels, antipathies, catastrophes. No rich or poor, no rumors of pitiful orphans.

She arranges the tray and carries it outside. This is not a time to be too careful, too remote, too private, too weary, too grief-stricken. It pains her to calculate, to be so precise about it. She gives Brehm's cargo a wide berth, and sets the tray down on the table. From May until September, she and Eva eat outside, under the eaves. The mountains are tinted with the scarlet and orange of sunset. The lower slopes of the Wallberg are unusually green this year, the result of a wet spring and the culling of blighted larches last autumn. She has been preparing herself for too long to dissolve now into mawkish grief. She wants the captain to feel easy, to answer her questions, and not feel he must spare her, or hold anything back. She doesn't want him to think of her as some gothic, National Socialist *Hausfrau*, stupidly proud of her sacrifices and her grief. She simply wants to trust him, and take him into her trust—not just as someone who had been a friend of Mohr's, but as her only link to an outside world she no longer recognizes, and which frightens her.

"Was it really a heart attack?"

All sit silently as she fills the teacups. Bread is sliced and butter and plates are passed. "I don't know where to begin," the captain says at last. "I wasn't there, so I can only tell you what Miss Simson told me."

"Who?"

"Agnes Simson, a nurse from the hospital. She was the one who packed his things for me to bring to you." Brehm breaks off and looks up. Eva is listening intently, her eyes going back and forth between her mother and the captain. "She was with him when he died."

"He died in the hospital?"

Brehm shakes his head. "No. He was at home."

"But the nurse was with him?"

The captain nods. "They were bringing a sick Chinese general into the hospital for treatment. There had been heavy fighting all over the city all day long. Wounded were pouring into the hospital. At some point during the afternoon, Mohr fainted and was taken into the super-intendent's office, where a bed was set up for him. Some time later he asked to be taken home. The nurse accompanied him."

Käthe is impatient now, and wants details. "They let him leave the hospital? Didn't anybody realize how ill he was?"

"It seems strange. But the place was in chaos." Brehm slides his hands between his knees, shrugs with a helpless look. "I can only tell you what Miss Simson told me." He continues with the story, lighting a cigarette. His tone is apologetic and he sticks to the barest essentials: how the nurse brought Mohr home. How she and Wong helped him to his bed and remained with him. How he drifted in and out of sleep. How everything in the apartment was very quiet and still—though in the rest of the city, war was raging. The captain repeats this last detail several times. "By evening they knew," Brehm says.

"Knew what?"

"There was nothing that could be done. He died that night."

A short silence, then Käthe stands up. "Excuse us," she tells the captain, and leads Eva away by the hand.

They walk down to the flower field, through the fence that has been knocked down in several places by cows scratching against the posts. She hasn't planted this year, and the field is overgrown with grass. The pond is swollen to full capacity. In the last rays of daylight, their shadows on the ground are like tall reeds growing at the edge of the water. She glances back at the house. There it is: part of the surrounding landscape, not merely an image or a shadow but something real, something whole. There is no filling the void in her heart. It is not loss, but a simple absence.

Mohr's death is stuck in an impossibly abstract realm, is too distant, not even a shadow on the ground. There are local legends of people who disappeared into the mountains; men and women swallowed by crevasses or buried in avalanches, who never came home. But disappearing into a landscape, and vanishing from it are two different things. There are no final proportions. Without a body to lower into the ground, there is nothing to prevent you from dreaming him running down to the house from high up in the meadow—forever.

"Are we going to China?" Eva asks.

Käthe puts a hand on the gate post and shakes it. It has become loose. "No." She opens the gate and waves for Eva to follow. They walk together down the overgrown beds.

"Are we going to stay here?"

"I think we have to."

"Can we keep bees?"

"Bees?" She can't help smiling at the child's surprising capacity for oddness. "Yes, of course. Anything you like." They continue through the fallow beds. When they return to the house, Brehm is still sitting at the table where they left him. He is now smoking a pipe. Before him is a large yellow envelope. Käthe glances at it, then goes inside to put more water on. Eva stays with the captain, eats bread and marmalade, asks questions about his ship.

Käthe refills the teapot and returns outside. The captain puts his pipe aside, reaches for the envelope. He clears a space at the end of the table, and spreads out a large nautical chart printed on thick muslin. Käthe and Eva examine the strange document. It is covered with lines and dotted with numbers. In the lower right corner is written *Deutsche Bucht.* The legend is decorated with the German eagle and the swastika.

"What is it?"

"The coast off Helgoland," the captain says, then points to a small X, next to which is written, "Max Mohr." Eva presses in for a closer look.

Käthe's heart pounds. "You . . . you buried him . . . at sea?"

"His ashes."

"Why?"

The captain steps to the table edge, traces his fingers on the chart, then looks at her. "I'm sorry. I had hoped not to upset you."

"But why?" she repeats.

"Because I had to."

"You *had* to?" Her temples begin to pulse. "I don't understand. Why didn't you bring him here? To me?"

"I intended to, Frau Mohr, believe me. But I couldn't. It's complicated. I was prevented."

"What prevented you?"

The captain clears his throat. "The law."

"What law?"

The captain clears his throat again. "Against importation of remains."

"A law against importing remains?"

"Jewish remains." His voice trails off in embarrassment, then he continues, "A customs inspector on board. Somehow he knew that I had the urn containing your husband's remains. Don't ask me how. He ordered an inspection. There was nothing I could do."

She stares down at the chart. This time she can see more than a confusing pattern of lines and numbers. Now she sees the North Sea coastline, the estuaries of the Weser, and the Elbe, and the familiar names of towns and cities, places she had been as a child: Cuxhaven, Scharhörn, Langeoog, Spiekeroog. She points to the black X and asks, "Where is that?"

Brehm is now standing directly beside her. He recites the exact location in degrees and minutes.

"Is it far?" Eva suddenly wants to know. She has been quietly following the conversation.

"Not as far as China."

"Is it deep?"

Käthe glances at her daughter, whose eyes are trained on the map. Twelve years wise, able to ask the perfect question.

The captain points to a figure. "Twenty-six meters."

Eva takes this in, then asks, "Are there mountains down there?"

Käthe is happy to yield all questions now, and sits down. The captain describes the coastal seabed, pointing with chewed fingernails, his bony wrist jutting from the sleeve of his jacket. Only half-listening, she holds her teacup, thinking of the early years: waiting for Mohr in a Kurfürstendamm café with no money in her purse but wearing a new hat. A man outside selling coal briquettes from a cart. The rush of pleasure she felt when he finally arrived, beaming, in his pocket, payment for his play. She sees him chopping wood, swinging the axe straight over his head, splitting logs with loud crack after crack; or sitting in the meadow wearing an old cap; or on skis, pointing the way with his pole, and telling some long-winded tale about the days long, long ago, when there were several moons circling the earth and people were forgetful and the climate was completely different from what it is today.

Now his ashes are sunk—beyond the reach of German laws—at the bottom of the North Sea. *Abgefahren, der schwarze Ritter.*

After Eva has been put to bed, Brehm helps Käthe drag the trunk and suitcases up to the attic. It is a dark night, with no moon. She lights a fire in the stove to take the chill out of the air, then fetches the newspaper clipping from the drawer in the writing table where she has been keeping it. The captain brings out a bottle of Irish whiskey. She allows him to pour her a small glass. He reads the clipping, then puts it aside in disgust. "Fuchs," he says.

"Who is that?"

"A minister at the embassy." He sips his whiskey. "It's his job to spread this kind of shit." Brehm shakes his head again, his face now slightly red and distorted. He reaches for his pipe. She can sense that there is more to the story, but isn't sure she wants to know it. Deep down, she already knows everything she cares to know. Without knowing, she knows. As he speaks, she feels as if she is shrinking, physically getting smaller, her arms, her legs, her head and torso becoming smaller and smaller while her clothes remain the same size. She leans forward, crosses her arms on the table to prop herself up. Is this what happens when there is nothing left? When everything is lost? You vanish into yourself?

"When did you last see my husband?"

"Just before he went to Japan."

"How was he? How did he look?"

"As good as ever."

"I mean, did he seem healthy?"

Brehm nods, slides his pipe to the corner of his mouth. "A little tired—which is why he went to Japan. He had a pet bird. A mynah."

She waits for him to say more, but he doesn't. He puffs on his pipe and sips his whiskey, gradually dissolving into alcoholic wistfulness. It is silent for a time. He pours himself another whiskey. "I can get you out of here," he says at last, looking directly at her.

"Excuse me?"

"I can take you with me. You and Eva."

"Take us? Where to?"

"I sail back to Shanghai in ten days. I can take you with me, if you like."

She searches the captain's face. His features have softened, seem sad now, no longer agitated. She stands up. "I am very tired, Captain."

Brehm stands. "Please pardon me. I didn't mean to upset you."

She pauses for a moment at the door.

"Good night, Captain. Thank you for all you have done."

She goes upstairs to her bedroom and closes the door. She can't fall asleep, and so she lies in the darkness listening to the captain rattling around downstairs. She can hear the steady uncorking of the bottle, the clink of his glass, his smoker's cough. The window is open. A slightly damp but refreshing breeze blows into the room, and she turns to it. How many nights has she lain here? In this one place? The presence of the captain downstairs isn't nearly as distracting as the thought that she has spent nearly half of her life in this house—alone. And, until now, unafraid. She has her memories. Upstairs, in the attic, are all that remain of Mohr's—so different from hers in the end, but rich and full and also wonderful. It occurs to her that she hadn't asked Brehm what he'd done with the ashes. Had they been scattered on the surface of the water? Or had they been sunk in the urn? Two conflicting images crowd her thoughts, of ashes dispersing on the surface of the ocean, and of remains plunging in a capsule to the bottom of it. Which was it? The difference seems crucial.

She wakes up just before dawn, gets dressed. Vivid dream fragments crowd her thoughts: A bare room. The old Hamburg stationer's shop in the Postgasse, Grandmother Kämmerer taking her by the hand and saying, *"Grüss immer recht freundlich wieder, wenn du nicht weisst wer Dich gegrüsst hat!"*—Be always right friendly, when you don't know the person who has greeted you.—And Mohr's accordion. She must remember to ask Brehm if it is among the things that were packed into the trunk.

"Are we going up to the *Alm* today?" Eva is standing in the kitchen doorway, rubbing her eyes.

"Up already?"

Eva nods sleepily.

"Maybe. Let's see first if Berghammer is going."

"You're coming with me, Mama. Aren't you?"

"I don't know. We'll see."

"But you said."

"Today is Saturday. You can go to Lisa's in the afternoon."

She finishes loading the tray, gestures for Eva to take the milk pitcher. They go into the next room, set the table for three. The room grows slowly brighter as the sun burns off the morning mist. She sets the captain's glass and whiskey bottle on a side table, empties the ashtray. His overcoat hangs on a hook by the door. The room feels altered by the stranger's presence, narrower, less cozy. Eva butters a slice of bread, pours herself a glass of milk. Through the window, Käthe can see Minna standing patiently by the fence. "Bring Minna in today," she tells Eva.

"I can milk her in the field."

Käthe shakes her head. "No, bring her in."

Eva shrugs, and turns to look out the window. "So, we're going then? Up to the *Alm?*"

"I don't know." She sips her coffee. When the captain's footsteps sound on the stairs, she sits up, reaches for and hastily begins to butter a slice of bread.

"Guten Morgen!" The captain is in a deliberately cheery mood. He is wearing a clean shirt and his hair is combed straight back.

"Did you sleep well?"

"Like a child."

Käthe fills his coffee cup.

"Do you like raspberries?" Eva wants to know.

The captain leans down to her, eyes glistening with hangover. "Do you have raspberries?"

"I know where to find them. Want me to show you?"

"First Minna," Käthe reminds her daughter.

"Then I'll show you afterward."

Brehm nods and Eva runs from the room. A few moments of silence follow. The captain sips his coffee. Käthe takes a nervous bite of bread. That she's lost some measure of composure is annoying. Finally she puts down the slice of bread, turns directly to Brehm. "I have been thinking all night about your offer, Captain."

Brehm puts his coffee cup down gently. "I didn't mean to upset you by it. Please, I hope you haven't taken offense."

Käthe pushes her chair back, drops her hands into her lap, and looks squarely at Brehm. "No, Captain. I didn't take offense. But even if it were possible, I couldn't imagine what I would do all alone in China. Thank you for your offer. It was very kind."

The captain looks down for a moment. "He always talked about bringing you. But the war . . ."

She cuts him off. "Yes. We had plans."

"What will you do now?"

She stands up.

"Now we will stay here," she tells him, and leaves the room.

Eva is just leading Minna into the stall as Käthe enters. She ties the cow to a post. "Is Captain Brehm going back to his ship today?"

Käthe strokes Minna. The warmth of the animal is reassuring. "Yes. The captain is leaving today." Then she gathers Eva into her arms, holds her tightly.

Eva squirms free and regards her mother curiously, then slaps Minna's hindquarter and says, "Don't worry. Minna will be fine without us for a few days."

The words hang for a moment. She watches Eva pull the stool up alongside the cow, set the milking bucket into place. She is smiling. "What's so funny?" Käthe asks.

"You're so funny," Eva says, and begins milking. "We shouldn't have guests anymore, Mama."

"Why do you say that?"

"Because every time a guest comes, you begin acting funny."

Brehm enters the barn, approaches slowly. "I have upset your mother," he says to Eva, then turns to Käthe. "I apologize."

She puts a hand on Eva's head. "Captain Brehm is just discovering how easily I cry these days."

She leaves Eva to finish milking, and beckons the captain to come outside. Pausing at the bottom of the earthen ramp that leads up to the doors of the barn, she says, "All night I've been wondering, what if we *had* gone to Shanghai? What would our situation be now? Would we be trying to come back here? Everything looks different, depending on where you are standing."

The captain says nothing.

"We live for ourselves here. It's the way we've always lived—even before Mohr left."

Brehm takes out a cigarette, lights it.

"Your children, Captain? If they were half-Jewish, as Eva is, would you take them away?"

Brehm puffs on his cigarette, contemplating for a moment. "The country has become stupid. If I could spare my children, yes, I would."

"It must be painful to be separated from them for so much of the year. But at least you'll see them again when you return."

Brehm shakes his head. "I won't be returning. I've taken a job with a Canadian shipping company. They're coming with me."

"You're going to Canada?"

"My wife is blind. I can't leave her and the children anymore." He is interrupted by the sound of a car pulling up at the front gate. "My taxi," he says, with some relief.

Käthe struggles to keep up with everything the captain has just told her. That he is emigrating—with his family—leaves her feeling even more desolate. Why hadn't he said anything about it last night? Should she reconsider? A sudden panic seizes her. She is cut off from the larger world, and also a hapless victim of it.

The driver honks the horn.

"I must get my things," Brehm says, stepping away.

"Wait!" Käthe calls him back, but can't formulate what is in her thoughts. Eva appears at the barn door. "Are you going now?" she asks. As Brehm ascends the ramp to bid her good-bye, a flood of images—of the ticking away of those last hours before Mohr's departure, down to the agonizing last few minutes at the train station. There had been no question then of going with him to Shanghai, only of joining him there at some later date, a resumption of things under different conditions. Still, there had been hope. A rearrangement of priorities, renewal. Those were Mohr's own words. How he had repeated them, in letter after letter. Let's put everything behind us. Everything. The good, the bad. To be forgotten. Start over. The world is big and life is long.

In the end, everything they did, they did together—even parting.

Brehm goes inside with Eva to fetch his bags. The taxi driver has opened the trunk of the car, is leaning against the rear fender. *"Grüss Gott,"* he says. Käthe returns the greeting; recognizes the man but can't remember his name. She hears Eva's voice inside the house, her footsteps on the stairs. When she and Brehm at last emerge, the driver hurries to help with his bag. Brehm is wearing his captain's hat and an overcoat with the insignia of the Norddeutsche Lloyd company. He seems already returned to a bigger, wider world.

"I was asked to give you this before leaving," he says, producing an envelope from the inside pocket of his overcoat.

She accepts the envelope, turns it over in her hands. It is thick and sealed on the back with red wax. "It's from a woman."

Brehm says nothing, and with a tip of his cap gets into the taxi and rolls down the window. "I have left my cable address on the table for you."

"Thank you, Captain." They step away from the car as the driver starts the motor. Käthe slips the envelope into the pocket of her apron, but continues to hold onto it, waving good-bye with her free hand. Eva holds her mother around the waist until the car disappears around the bend.

"He was nice," Eva says, returning to the house.

"Yes. He was nice."

THE SUN IS climbing toward its midday peak. Sitting on the bench at the side of the house, she closes her eyes, tilts her face to it. She holds the envelope in her lap. The captain has been gone just over an hour, but it already feels as though an age has passed. Immediately after he left, they cleared the breakfast table and cleaned the kitchen. Käthe kneaded dough to make bread, and is now waiting for it to rise. Eva has gone over to Berghammers'. Having swept and cleaned out the stalls, watered the flower pots hanging from the upstairs balcony and underneath the windowsills, Käthe can now sit down.

The envelope contains a long, handwritten letter. As she slides it out, she notices a small lump of tightly crumpled tissue paper at the bottom of the envelope. She shakes it out, unfolds it, and stares in astonishment at the familiar little gem in her palm. She holds it up to the sunlight, an utterly surprising little object, dropped from the sky.

She sets it on the bench beside her, closes her eyes, and turns again to face the sun.

She once thought that with memories, a person had everything; not a ruptured then and now, but a gift ready to be opened anytime. With memories, it is always today and yesterday at the same time. But how does memory speak to disappointment? To what you had hoped would be and never was? Now she realizes it doesn't. So much of who we are is also all that never was.

In another day, Eva will go up into the mountains with Berghammer and she will be alone for the rest of the summer. She is relieved and slightly fearful of this double life they are about to commence, another separation with no purpose other than to see themselves through these

uncertain and threatening times. The cows are grazing up in the meadow. She can almost hear their teeth ripping the grass, the grinding caverns of their mouths. She hears the stalls slamming at Berghammers', the scrape scrape scrape of Eva's shovel against the cement, the peck peck pecking in the henhouse, the tinkling of a single cowbell in the breeze. She opens her eyes, glances again at the diamond beside her on the bench.

YOU PICK UP the letter. It is long, many sheets of paper, neatly folded and written in English. You turn to the last page. *Tomorrow I will leave Shanghai for Hong Kong with my elderly mother. . . .*

Stop reading and return the letter to the envelope.

Pick up the diamond, hold it in your palm. It twinkles like a distant star. You put the tiny gem back into the envelope along with the letter, press the flap down, firmly, with the heel of your hand. You will put it back upstairs with the rest of Mohr's things.

I say *you,* but I also mean *me*—anyone who has imagined the receding past, or returned its passing glance in a photograph. An ambiguity exists between narrator and narrated, yes, but this matter of pronouns and subjects should not become too great a distraction. To appear in a photograph is to be depicted in relationship to what once was. To appear in a novel is to unfold in the mind of the reader.

To be *you* is to imagine points of contact between them.

SOMETIMES, LATE AT night, you like to go up into the attic and look at these old objects. You have looked at them many times, and can recall every image at will, but there is something especially satisfying in knowing which photograph you would like to see in advance, then going upstairs to look at it. Paradoxically, this makes it more spontaneous. Yes, you go upstairs to look, but what you *see* is different every time.

Hold a photograph up to the light.

Wong pouring Mohr a glass of water. There are several of these, taken in a series. Mohr and Wong standing in front of three silk scroll paintings. They look casual and comfortable in their light cotton clothes, a picture of easy colonial living. Mohr is holding a towel in one hand. It had been late November 1937 when Brehm arrived back in Shanghai. Cold weather. Wong would not have been dressed in that thin cotton tunic as he ushered the captain into Mohr's apartment. Trunks and cases had been packed by Agnes. Wong was downcast and sad. He spoke in a soft, mournful voice. He brought tea. Brehm made a quick inventory of everything. At one point a young boy poked his head into the room, eyed the captain curiously, and was called away by a woman's voice. . . .

Imagine what happened to all of them. You have formed your own mental images from scattered photographs of the setting: Chinese scroll paintings, medical cabinets, porcelain cups, a modern apartment with picture windows. An old farmhouse in upper Bavaria, a broad field, Käthe raking hay. She is alone now, truly alone.

The day after Brehm left, she took Eva up to the *Alm* with Berghammer. She will go with him again to fetch her when the cows are brought down from their summer pasture. It is beautiful up there this time of year, with the cows grazing on the mountainsides, puffs of breath condensing in the silvery morning light. But she is looking forward to winter snows, to being closed up quietly inside the house again with Eva. . . .

Late at night, with the full light of the risen moon shining through the window, you feel an intimate sense of company. The house is so familiar, its setting, its entire architecture—not just the beams and rafters and creaking floorboards, but the hidden architecture of the past that echoes within. How much night there is here. And life.

But as the hours pass, you grow tired of pictures.

Look out the window and see that the moon has already begun its descent.

An elk calls from high up on the mountain. A slight breeze begins to blow. The first birds have started to sing. As dawn begins to break, you turn off the lamp, gather up the photographs, and return them to their envelopes; the envelopes to their boxes; and the boxes to the trunk where they are stored. You are glad to know they are here—Max, Käthe, Eva—not locked away in a separate past, but real people in real places, joined again and again in future light, by a master-glance of seeing.

Acknowledgments

I inherited a photograph from my grandfather, a portrait of his favorite uncle, Max. It was taken in 1911 and shows, in three-quarter profile, a handsome young man in a cadet uniform, wearing a pince-nez and the stolidly neutral expression of that doomed epoch. My grandfather, a slightly younger member of that same generation of German Jews, would only say that his uncle Max had been a doctor and a writer, had fought in WWI, been decorated with the Iron Cross, and died in Shanghai in 1937. That was all he ever said. In my grandfather's house, all talk of the past was strictly on his terms, and because he had lost his entire family in the Holocaust, he was rarely criticized or challenged for his brevity.

Sometime in the late 1980s I found myself at the Library of Congress in Washington, DC, searching for what was there of the works of Max Mohr. It took every effort not to destroy the brittle Weimar-era texts as I photocopied them. Over the next few years I uncovered a diffuse trail of intriguing references and associations, but the trail became fainter and eventually stopped. Feeling that I had come to the end of the line, I named a character Mohr in my novel, *Horace Afoot,* as an homage to this vanished man from a vanished era. Then, in 1997, the very year the book was published, a novel of Max Mohr's appeared in Germany, *Das Einhorn (The Unicorn)*. It contained letters from Shanghai and an afterword by his grandson, Nicolas Humbert. I went to Munich to meet this unknown relative, and was immediately overwhelmed by the feeling of having stepped into Mohr's life. The search for Max Mohr, which over the years had become a diverting bibliographic treasure hunt, took a sudden, unexpected turn. It became a living encounter. By far, the greatest pleasure in writing this book has been this renewed family tie and the friendship of Nicolas Humbert. His sensibility and shared sense of purpose both inspired and sustained my effort.

Although the story presented here is a fiction, I have relied heavily on historical and documentary materials. In addition to photographs, I have had privileged access to letters, manuscripts and family oral history. I also took the liberty of fashioning parts of dialogue between Mohr and D. H. Lawrence directly from their correspondence.

My thanks are due to many people, without whose generous assistance, this book would have not been possible: To Monika Westphal, for her patient and painstaking efforts deciphering Mohr's script and making it accessible. To Fred Ramey, Joan Reuss, Werner Penzel, Christian Merillat, and Edward Weismiller for editorial and readerly insight. To Ursula Blömer of Universität Oldenburg for genealogical research, and Elisabeth Tworek of the Monacensia Archiv, München for archival resources. To Robert Leopold, Becky Malinsky, Ted Coyle, David Peterson, and Amy Marx for photographic assistance. To Robin Moody and Tamara Stock for a room with a view. And finally, to Gail and Sophie and Ava for everything else.